MAKING
OF A
GODDESS

Also by John Ricks

Freddy Anderson Chronicles
    Freddy Anderson's Home (Book 1)
    Protectress (Book 2)
    Colossus (Book 3)

Epic Adventures
    Making of a God (Book 1)

Sword and Sorcery (Short Stories, Book 1)

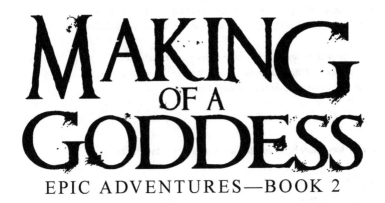

MAKING OF A GODDESS

EPIC ADVENTURES—BOOK 2

JOHN RICKS

iUniverse

MAKING OF A GODDESS
EPIC ADVENTURES—BOOK 2

iUniverse books may be ordered through booksellers or by contacting:

iUniverse
1663 Liberty Drive
Bloomington, IN 47403
www.iuniverse.com
1-800-Authors (1-800-288-4677)

Because of the dynamic nature of the Internet, any web addresses or links contained in this book may have changed since publication and may no longer be valid. The views expressed in this work are solely those of the author and do not necessarily reflect the views of the publisher, and the publisher hereby disclaims any responsibility for them.

Any people depicted in stock imagery provided by Getty Images are models, and such images are being used for illustrative purposes only. Certain stock imagery © Getty Images.

ISBN: 978-1-5320-7660-2 (sc)
ISBN: 978-1-5320-7661-9 (e)

Library of Congress Control Number: 2019909248

Print information available on the last page.

iUniverse rev. date: 07/19/2019

To the enjoyment of writing. To looking up from the keyboard at three in the morning and wondering why it's dark outside. To sitting down, starting from nothing, and creating your own passion.

This book was not written to have just one antagonist throughout the entire book, like most books; that is not life as I know it. No, life is a series of challenges, issues, enjoyments, and pains. This book is about Samantha and her life, and she has many challenges and many antagonists.

GODDESS

Map of the First Continent and Landtrap

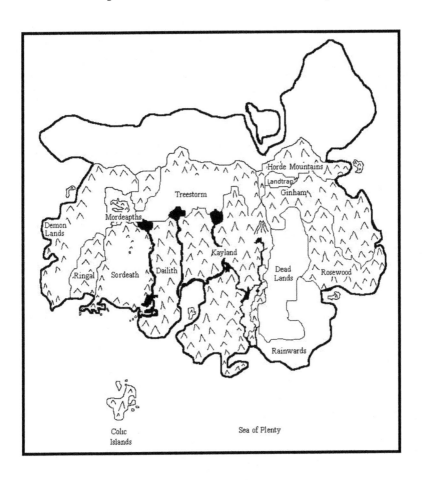

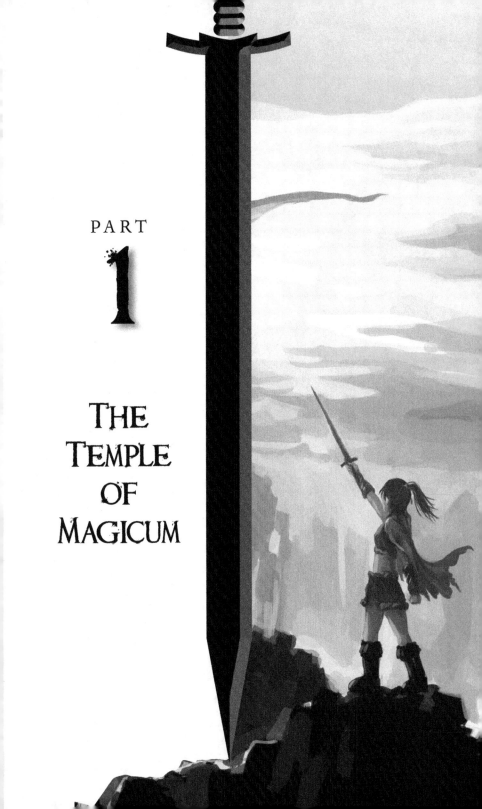

PART

1

THE
TEMPLE
OF
MAGICUM

PROLOGUE

I paused, looking out onto the farm that was nestled back into the forest, neatly hidden away. All that was left was smoke and a tiny stovepipe sticking up through a small rock chimney. The plowed ground was dark and burnt, and the strongest smells in the air were death and dragon. The charred remains of several bodies were visible—a man, a woman, and three tiny children. They were executed as if the one doing the deed had been set on tormenting its victims.

I pulled the hood of my long dark cloak tighter around my head and walked deliberately through the forest until I came out upon the northern cobblestone road to Farnorth. I turned north and joined the throng of people fleeing to the city for protection. Burning the farmlands was just the beginning. They would not find protection in the city of Farnorth. They would not find protection anywhere in the country of Landtrap.

CHAPTER 1

REVENGE

On the road to Farnorth, there were hundreds of people walking, riding, and in wagons. All were trying to keep pace with the rest, and all were working their way toward the city and the hoped-for protection that the walls provided. It was almost funny. *What protection will walls be against a dragon? Everyone knows it's a dragon that is burning the farmlands. They have seen it burn theirs or their neighbors' homes and lands. Even the caravan that I walked out and almost into knows. Thousands of acres destroyed in many separate places means only two things: war or dragons.*

A particularly large and wide wagon was directly behind me, and I was slowing it down. I could not get off to the side, as we were moving through a small section of the pass. The road was thin, the wagon took up most of the road, and there were mercenaries and guards riding back and forth trying to keep the caravan moving. Besides, I wasn't paying attention anyway. I was reading a particularly good book. With all these people moving in the same direction, you didn't need to watch very closely. Just move along with the rest.

"Hey, you! Get out of the way!"

I looked up and then back. Two horses were nearly breathing on my back. I started to move to the right, but several guards picked that time to ride by. I tried the left, and mercenaries were riding by on that side. One mercenary yelled, "Just run the runt over."

I flew up and kicked that mercenary hard in the face and out of his saddle and then flew over the wagon's horses and sat down next to the driver. I went back to reading and paid no attention to the jeers and jokes that mercenary was receiving for having a child kick him off his horse. The driver started to say something but thought better of it when he realized that to fly like that, I had to be an experienced magic user and therefore dangerous. Besides, I was out of the way and not likely to get into trouble again if I was riding.

The captain of the mercenary troop rode up. "You, in the robe!"

The driver saw I was paying no attention and nudged me.

I looked over at him. "Yes, sir?"

He motioned for me to look to my right, so I turned around. There was a mercenary captain riding next to us and looking at me. He rode an impressive black warhorse, and his steel-plate armor shone brightly in the evening sun. I marked my place in the book and put it down. "May I help you, sir?"

The captain was all business. "You, a tiny little kid, knocked down one of my men?"

"Your man suggested that this nice wagon driver should kill me."

The captain said, "That part was not mentioned. You are hitching a ride on one of my employer's wagons."

"It seemed the best way to rectify the issue until we leave this passageway and there is more walking room on the sides of the road."

"Very well. If you do not remove yourself from the wagon after the passage is over, then I will remove you."

I looked at him hard. My cloak was still pulled forward, covering my face, so it was difficult for him to see what I looked like. "Captain, I will remember to remove myself, but think on what you just said and consider that a sorceress may not like being threatened." I picked up my book and started reading again.

The captain did not like being dismissed in such a way, but the driver said, "Captain, I am authorizing this person to stay with me all the way into the city. If Master Ortherntus has a problem with that, then he can take it up with me."

I looked up and said, "Why, thank you, sir. That is exceptionally kind."

The wagon driver said, "Don't thank me, my lady. If you're a sorceress, then you will protect yourself from the dragon. As you are riding my wagon, I am hoping you will protect us as well."

I smiled and tilted my face so the smile showed in my eyes. "Your wagon will not come to harm as long as I am riding." Then I turned back to my book. I wasn't really reading as much as I was watching. Seeing all the devastation the red dragon had created led me to believe that this dragon had been terrorizing the land for a long time or it was an elder dragon. One could not tell from the stories that the farmers and outer villagers were telling. Stories raged throughout the ranks and ranged from "It was so immense it blocked out the sun" to "It blocked out the entire sky." When people are scared witless, their eyes and ears play tricks and add to the fear.

When I was very young, I used to think there were monsters under my bed. I was in total fear. Father and Mother tried to comfort me and tell me that there were no monsters under my bed. My brother told me they couldn't be under my bed, as he kept them out in the shed. Still, I swore I heard them nearly every night and even saw them on several occasions. We found out later they were real, but they were tiny and not harmful. My imagination made them much bigger and deadly.

However, I knew the size of this monster. I had known it since the day he flew over my home and destroyed my house and killed my family. To him and the flock of dragons that followed him around, we were just an after-dinner snack, following their gorging at the war fields between Ginham and Kayland. When I found his cave, I thought I had found him. He had not been there for weeks, but he had guards. Two eye sundries—evil, smelly little floating eyeballs on ten-foot-long tentacles that fire intense light that burns through your skin if you're not quick enough to dodge it. I killed both and searched for clues. The tracks told me that a man had visited and the dragon flew off with him. I cleaned out his treasure, every last copper, and waited for him to return. I waited a month, and he did not return. I tracked his devastation to this small country at the top of Ginham on the Horde border.

We were out of the pass now, and the guards came by saying, "Keep an eye out. Keep watch."

I could see the city from there. It was a long way off, but the spires of the castle and one taller, dark tower stood out in the distance. This large valley would have been lovely and green if not for the fires and overwhelming smell of burning vegetation. The driver said, "The master cannot push the horses any farther tonight. We'll camp here—no lights, no fires. It's cold food tonight."

I marked my spot and then closed the book and placed it in my haversack. I looked around as if it was the first time. "The dragon will not be around tonight."

The driver looked shocked. "How can you know this?"

I looked out across the valley. New fires were everywhere. "He was here today and will need to rest."

The driver passed that to the guards, and they told Master Ortherntus. It wasn't long before a little fat man with black beard and bald head made his way to our wagon. "You! You're telling people that the great red will be sleeping tonight?"

"I did, sir."

"And you know this for a fact? No you don't. Keep your mouth shut. I am having a hard enough time trying to get the caravan organized without input from fools like you." His face turned dark, and he looked like he did not trust me. "Why are you so covered? It was a nice day. There is no reason to be so covered. Guards!"

I looked directly at him and asked, "What are you afraid of? I am causing no trouble."

Several guards rode up, and Master Ortherntus smiled for the first time. "I like to know who is traveling with me. I will see your face. Remove your hood."

"No."

A guard started toward me, and instantly a ball of light crackling with lightning stood in my hands. The guard backed up.

Master Ortherntus ordered, "If that creature does not show its face this minute, then kill it."

Swords were drawn and bows mocked. More guards started showing up, and the driver was getting anxious. I could smell his fear. The mercenaries started showing up, and the captain said, "What is this! People are supposed to be getting into a circle and setting up for the night. They are not supposed to be holding up the entire road."

Master Ortherntus said, "I want to know who I am traveling with. I want to see its face."

The captain said, "She is a girl, and I would bet that she does not like being called an *it*." The captain turned to me and asked, "Why do you not wish to show your face, child?"

"My face gets me into trouble."

"Why?"

I said sadly, "That is my business, and I wish to keep it to myself."

The captain gently said, "Like Master Ortherntus, I do not like traveling with someone whom I cannot see or do not know enough about. Please show your face."

I turned to the driver. "Thank you for allowing me to travel with you; however, Master Ortherntus and this captain insist that I leave. Therefore, I will not be able to protect your wagon. My apologies."

Master Ortherntus said, "It matters not if you stay or leave. I will not have an unknown at my back. I will see your face and know who you are."

I let the glow in my hand disperse. I created an illusion of my staff. An illusion has no powers, as it's an illusion, but it glows, sputters with lightning all around, and has the wickedest-looking, fire-engulfed red crystal ball on the top. I pull out the real one only during extreme battle. I turned toward him and floated in the air so that I was directly in front of him and said, "Is it so important to you, Master Ortherntus, that you and all your guards would be willing to die to see my face? I assure you that I can and will protect myself."

The captain slowly drew his sword and asked, "Is not showing your face worth killing all the guards, mercenaries, and Master Ortherntus?"

I thought for a moment and said, "No, it is not. Then again, neither is staying around here." I teleported to the front of the caravan and started walking. It had been nice riding for a while. When I was clear of the circle the caravan was making, with a quick hand movement and a few choice words of power, I made my own place to stay, called a protection hut, and walked in. I was getting much better at making the hut-like shelter. The hut is always magically made of materials close at hand. This one was made of rock with a stone door. There was a fire in the fireplace and food on the table. The bed was stone, but it had a stack of freshly brushed bear pelts for cushion and comfort. All in all, it was a nice place to stay for the night. I could hear the mercenary captain outside, and he was not happy.

The captain said, "I know she is in there. Leave her alone, but set a watch. I don't want her coming out before morning."

As if they could keep me in if I wanted to leave. Fools! They should have known better. I couldn't have cared less. I ate dinner, magically removed the leftovers, and went to bed.

I awoke an hour before sunup. I needed to prepare for battle, and that meant preparing spells. Normally, I didn't have to prepare, but today I would need some "fast" spells, and I couldn't create them on the fly. Fast spells are created ahead of time and leave the last word hanging, to be said at the time of need. However, you need to be careful and not say the final word accidentally at the wrong time. When you're a master mage, it takes even longer because you know so many spells to use that it's difficult to pick them out ahead of time. In addition, there are other particulars to take into consideration—shaping, lengthening, and stuffing to name a few. Being a sorceress makes it impossible to do fast spells, spells that take almost no time, but my ancestry gives me the supernatural ability. I only have to take time to think it out first and ensure none of the other planned spells have that final word in them. After preparing, I left the hut.

The guard said, "Good morning, my lady. Have a nice sleep?"

I answered, "Yes, thank you. I hope your night was good."

"The first half was. I had the Lady Watch for the last two hours."

"Tell the captain that I said thank you for the protection, but I did not really need it. I can easily protect myself." I raised a hand and said a word, and the hut disappeared. I started walking toward the city, and the guard ran to the captain to report.

It wasn't long before the captain rode up. "Hello, little lady. I see you have decided to come out of hiding but are still wearing the cloak."

I said, "Captain, I am not anywhere near your caravan. Why are you hounding me?"

"Curiosity."

"People die of curiosity, Captain. That is not a good trait."

"Curiosity has gotten me through life so far. You will be walking toward the city for most of the day. You could be riding."

I looked up at the captain riding his big warhorse and said, "I am not wanted near the caravan. I do not go where I am not wanted."

"My wizard has heard about the spell you used to make that hut last night. It is beyond him to do such a spell."

I chuckled. "Then I truly hope you are not planning to use him to tackle the dragon. If he can't do a simple Protective Hut, then he is no match for an ancient red dragon."

"My thoughts exactly. We were told it was a young adult dragon."

I nearly choked on that bit of information. "Someone lied to you, Captain. I would have his hide on a pole. If you prepared for a young adult, then you are way underprepared."

The captain laughed. "Going by the looks of the devastation, I would have to agree. You do not seem to be worried."

I smiled. "I am not worried. If the dragon is foolish enough to attack me, then it will die."

The captain let his horse slow, and I walked past. He continued to watch me for some time, allowing the caravan to catch up with him, and I listened and watched him magically. Master Ortherntus met up with him and asked, "Learn anything?"

The captain said, "That child is more than she looks. I found out this much. She is not afraid of the dragon, but the dragon should be afraid of her. In her voice, I heard a near challenge when we talked about the dragon. It was as if she welcomes it. The problem is I don't think she cares if a battle between her and the dragon destroys everyone and everything around her."

Master Ortherntus said, "You think I should order the wagons to stay behind her?"

"It matters not. A fight between those two will destroy leagues of land. We are too slow to pull ahead that far, and she is too slow to allow us to create a gap that large. Our best hope is that the dragon does not show up two days in a row or that she meets him out in the fields."

"And if that does not happen?"

The captain earnestly answered, "Run for your life."

"Can't we talk her into being a little friendlier toward us?"

"After your threats last night?" The captain turned to give orders to his men while thinking, *Fool!*

When the road widened at the bottom turn, one wagon turned out and sped up, passing all the others. Master Ortherntus yelled out for the driver to stop, but the driver sent him a dirty look and continued. He pulled up next to me and asked, "Want a ride, my lady?"

I looked up and smiled. "Sure." I floated up and sat on the seat next to him. "Thank you."

He smiled. "No thanks necessary. I'm still hopping for that protection."

I laughed. "You shall have it."

We drove on for some time. The caravan pulled up directly behind us. Master Ortherntus took the time to apologize to me and try to make me more aware of the need to protect his goods.

"My lady, I am sorry about last night. It's just that I am very nervous about getting this order to the queen safely. The city needs this food badly, and I am trying my best to ensure that they get all they need. This may be the last caravan through here for months. Many will starve if we do not make it intact."

I turned to him in such a way that he could see part of my face and said, "I know."

His eyes widened, and he quickly sped his horse back to his caravan. The captain, who I was still magically watching, came up to him. "Find out anything?"

"I think I know why she is hiding."

"Do tell."

"She is the most beautiful female I have ever seen. I think she is a princess or something. She is wearing a diadem. And ..."

The captain took this in. "And?"

Master Ortherntus looked at the captain. "*Power*. I felt such power in her eyes. Both eyes glowed blue. They glowed!"

The captain laughed. "Don't worry, my friend. I have seen that before. Higher-level magi use that spell to permanently see magic. She seems prepared for something. I hope it's to fight."

It was near high noon when things became interesting. Over the city was a dark speck, and from it came fire. The dragon was there. It started a pass over the road and used its breath up the line of the road until it came to my wagon. Its breath did nothing to the driver or the wagon, though he cringed and tried to drive out of the way. I was free to act.

I could see that the dragon was looking back, and he appeared to be upset that his breath did nothing to the entire caravan. It saw me rise from the wagon, and it turned.

Once attacked, I knew I could get his attention. I flew up so quick that he and the man on his back had a difficult time keeping an eye on me. I continued up and sent several lightning bolts changed to acid at him. I knew lightning would not harm a red dragon, so he would not move out of the way, but acid does a lot of harm, and he had no idea it was coming. They hit, and the dragon screamed in pain and then looked at me with hatred. I flew up and up. He started the chase. The man on his back was casting spell after spell, trying to hit me with fire, lightning, anything he could from that range. Several wicked red arrows of Acid Shafts stuck in me, and I quickly pulled them out and cast them aside. I turned at one point and sent a weakened fireball at them. The grin on the man's face was expected, and I tried to show fear even though I was laughing inside.

They were catching up, and I was letting them. I flew in circles and upside down, did wingovers and loops, everything to make them think I was trying to run for my life. Then I went straight up as fast as I could for as long as possible without running out of air. They followed me up and caught me in several fireballs and his breath at the top. I created an illusion to look like I was smoldering and near death. At the top, I dove down, picking up as much speed as possible. When we were going as fast as we could, I tossed several minor spells of Dismiss Magic at them, and the man laughed a wicked laugh. I tossed an Enhanced Dismiss Magic, and they lost all their special magical protections.

Then, nearly at the bottom where I would need to pull up or smack into the ground, I did a Force Confinement directly in front of them and Faster Shift to above them. A Force Confinement spell produces a cube of immovable force, like an invisible prison cell but made of light condensed so much that it becomes solid. Shift teleports me a short distance, in this case up, so I was behind them. They hit the cube of immovable force just enough to throw the man off the dragon's back and mess up the dragon's flight. As the man was not flying, his momentum took him to the ground and splattered him into mush. The dragon landed directly on top of him and broke its neck. The fight was over. My revenge was over.

I was suddenly very tired. I healed myself with healing wands I keep in my quick-draw bandoleer and repaired my clothing with simple repair spells. Then I floated down to the dragon and started taking parts I would need for spells and potions. A little nose hair for a wand of fire protection, some liquid from the chemical sack that produces the dragon fire for a wand of fireballs, and most important were the four fangs for strength bows with maximized fire damage.

As I was cutting away, the caravan continued to move toward the city. Most people were turning around, heading home to see what they could save of their farms and villages. A mass exodus from the city had started out slowly and was building. It was now pouring out the gate, and when the caravan reached the city, it had a difficult time entering. A line of soldiers came out and headed my way. A large, flat wagon followed them. I watched out of the corner of my eye as they came closer. They were dressed raggedly, with burnt holes in their pants and shirts as if they had been fighting the fires or the dragon. Their leather armor looked burnt as well, and some were missing their hair and eyebrows. The front person was of high rank and looked both worried and pleased.

He stopped directly behind me as I was removing the last fang. Difficult to do when the fang is nearly three times your length.

"Hello."

I looked up at him and said, "Hello, General. Having a bad day?"

His smile was radiant. "I was until you came along. The day is looking up now."

"I am glad that I could be a bit of help. Perhaps you can return the favor."

"I would be glad to. What do you need?"

I flipped back my hood and allowed him to see my head. The intake of breath from his soldiers was loud. I cannot help it if I am beautiful. It runs in the family. My mother was a platinum dragon, and my father was a male succubus. He was so good at his task that he seduced my mother, and she was so good he fell in love. They married and raised a family. I got the charisma, wisdom, and intelligence, and so did my sisters and brother.

I said, "I could use some local knowledge. Where is a good place to spend the winter? It's coming quickly, and I do not like the cold."

"There are many places to stay in the city. If you can afford it, the best place is the Road Head Inn. The food is good, and the beds fresh. There should be plenty of rooms now that the dragon is not a threat. It is a good, safe place to stay."

"Sounds good, General. I will search for it when I enter. *There.*" The fang popped out of the socket. I placed it in my pile and then magically moved my pile into an extradimensional place I accidently created during a bad spell gone bad. It's a nice place to keep things. Food does not spoil, treasure is there when you need it, and I am the only one who knows how to get in. Staying there would not be good, as it has no air. I must hold my breath or take a bottle of everlasting air with me to suck on.

I turned to the general and did a few cleansing spells, as my clothes were covered in blood. Now I looked, smelled, and felt clean. "That's better. As I was saying, I will look for the Road Head Inn when I enter the city. Thank you."

The general looked at me and asked, "Should I be off this horse and kneeling, my lady?"

I reached up and touched the diadem. "No, General. This is not a crown. It is a circlet of Correct Vision. I wear it because I don't like to be surprised. As far as I know, I am not royalty and hope to never be."

The general said, "It looks more expensive than the crown my queen wears."

The wizard next to him, an old man with long white hair and a funny little pointed cap, said, "A circlet of Correct Vision is considerably more expensive." He turned to me. "I am Formack. I am the queen's wizard."

I purposefully changed my attitude to full acceptance and said, "Hello, Master Formack. Did you not attend the University at Sordeath that King Charles set up? I seem to remember your name on the rolls."

He beamed. "I did. Are you a graduate of the Sordeath University?"

"Yes."

Formack asked, "How is old Nester?"

My eyes turned sad. "He is no longer with us, Master Formack. He died during a lesson with a particularly foolish student. The student died also when his spell went bad. I am surprised you do not know."

Formack turned to the general. "She is telling the truth. She went to the university and probably graduated. The incident was kept quiet. If she knows and is sad, then she knew old Nester the janitor."

Another man rode up a few feet. "She is of goodly nature—however, just barely." His eyebrows went up disapprovingly. The insignia on his burnt armor showed he was a cleric of Solbelli.

I said, "Thank you, Cleric of Solbelli. I was not sure if I was good anymore or not. It is nice to know that I am."

The general said, "The queen would like to meet you tomorrow after breakfast. Please be prompt. What name shall I give her?"

"Samantha Altera Woodcutter."

Now the general's eyebrows went up. "You're the demon Sam's daughter? Your mother was called Nim and was a platinum dragon?"

I answered with a little worry, "Yes, sir."

The general smiled. "I fought alongside Sam during the Pirate wars. Good man, Sam. Nice to have at your back in a fight. Totally lost in that wife of his. How is the old demon?"

"Both my parents are dead, sir."

His face turned upset with wrinkled brows and sad eyes, and he leaned forward in his saddle. "What happened?"

"During the Ginham/Kayland wars, the dragons returned to the mountains; however, they stopped off long enough to eat my family. I was hidden in a deep hole." I kicked the red dragon. "Cleric of Solbelli, I appear only barely good because I have spent most of my life planning or taking revenge on the dragons that ate my family. This was the last one. I spent years looking for him."

The general dismounted and walked up to me. He gave me a hug and said, "Then it's all over, and you can rest now."

"Rest sounds good, sir."

He stood back and pronounced, "I am General Simon Jarrett. General to the queen and head of the Landtrap army. Welcome, daughter of my friend." He turned and in a single leap was in his saddle. "Want a ride?"

I smiled. "No, sir. I have a bit to do before I leave this site."

"Very well. See you tomorrow morning."

They left, and the wagon pulled up. On the breast of the shirts of the driver and workers was the insignia "Road Head Inn." A man came up to me. "Hello, my Lady. I am from the Road Head Inn. I was wondering what you plan on doing with all that fresh meat."

I looked him over. He was an average man with a good smile and a nice face—young, but the look and stance bespoke that he was in charge in some way. I said, "I was planning on disintegrating the creature so I can get to the human underneath. I want to see who it was."

He smiled. "I hear you need a place to stay the winter."

"Yes, I do."

"I am Mark Simpelton. I am the owner of the Road Head Inn. I will trade you a single with bath for the entire winter for the meat on this dragon." He pointed to the back of the wagon. "Conall can preserve the meat. He knows a few spells. You will not find a better offer. When we cut down to the man, we will strip him and return all the stuff to you, what's not smashed. I hear he took an awful fall because of you." He was smiling.

I was not looking forward to cutting the dragon up any more, and I had all the parts I needed, so I said, "Look for correspondences. I believe he was here for a purpose, and I would like to know what that was."

"As you wish, my lady."

CHAPTER 2

A HOME AT LAST

I started the walk into Landtrap's only city, Farnorth. I entered the end of the line about two hundred feet back. The captain of the guard sent two soldiers out to give me a message. "My lady, our captain wishes you to know you have earned the right to come to the front."

I smiled at them. "Please let your captain know that I said thank you, but I will stay in line. I am no better than anyone else in line and do not wish to upset the balance."

They both bowed. "Yes, my lady." They turned and headed back to the gate.

It took only a few minutes for the line to reach my point. I was still the last in line, and that would give me time to ask directions while the captain wasn't busy. There were cheers from the guards when I reached the front of the line.

The captain was off to the side, leaning against a column, looking amused. The gate clerk, sitting behind a heavy wooden table, said the same to me as he did all the others. "My lady, I need to ask you three questions." I had heard the questions several times but allowed him to do his job. "Who are you?"

"Samantha Altera Woodcutter of the Green Mountain Forest."

He wrote that down. "What is your purpose here?"

"I have finished taking my revenge on that dragon and now wish to rest for the winter."

He wrote that down also. "Do you plan on doing any harm while you are here?"

"I do not plan on harming anyone or anything."

He looked over at the cleric, and the cleric nodded. He smiled brightly and said, "Welcome to Farnorth. Do you have any weapons on you? It is a silver piece for each weapon."

I took my money pouch out and asked, "Does that include natural weapons?"

"No, my lady."

I pretended to think for a few seconds. I handed him two gold and eight silver, which is the same as twenty-eight silvers. His face turned white. I asked, "Is something wrong?"

The captain stepped up. "My lady, do you have twenty-eight weapons on your person at this time?"

"I did not count the arrows. There are two bows and three staffs in my deep-pocket quiver of Natura, I have one dagger on my leg, eight wands that are specifically used as weapons in my belt, and a dirk in my belt. In my haversack, I have a sword, several rods and wands, and two weapons I took off bandits that I do not recognize. Oh, just a second." I opened my haversack and pulled out the two weapons. "Captain, both are low-level magic in that they are magically easier to handle, hit a little harder, and slightly more accurate, but I am not sure what they are called."

The captain reached out and then pulled his hand back a little and looked at me.

"Go ahead, Captain. It's just normal enhancements, so they're safe to handle."

He smiled and picked up a long barbed chain. On each end were heavy metal spikes. He turned to his men. "This is a nasty fighting device." He moved it around his head and body so fast it was difficult to follow, and then he let go. The head of the chain crashed into a barrel and smashed it. It went all the way through and stuck deep into the post behind it. The men cheered. "It is called a two-headed, spiked chain. It has a ten-foot reach, and in the hands of an expert, it is a devastating weapon." He pulled it back with a yank and caught it expertly. He sat it down and picked up the other weapon. "This is a rare weapon, my lady. One of the bandits must have been a Blood Assassin. See these holes?" He showed the weapon to all his men. "Those are for poison. This is a duel-bladed, punching dagger. It is designed for one thing and one thing only. Sneaking up on someone and stabbing them in the back. It is designed to cut the spine in two, and if that does not work, the poison will normally kill the victim." He turned to me but said to his men, "You see anyone with one of these, expect the worse." He put it down with the chain.

I smiled and said, "You are very good with the chain. It is yours if you want it, Captain."

With a surprised look, he said, "Thank you, my lady. And the dagger?"

I picked up the dagger and tossed it into the air. A beam shot out from my other hand, and the dagger dripped to the ground as melted steel. "Target practice. I will not sell an evil weapon like that to anyone. You owe me two silvers."

The guard handed back two of my silvers.

I asked, "Captain, where is the Road Head Inn? The general told me it was a good place to stay, and they have offered me room and board."

He smiled while hefting the chain in a pleased way. "The Road Head Inn is straight up through the market district, and just when the road ends at the castle, turn right. The front door is the first door on the right."

"Thank you." I started off in that direction. The captain was already showing his men how to hold the spiked chain and telling them how to defend against it.

As I was leaving, I heard one man ask, "Captain, you think she can help us?"

The captain answered, "I don't know, but I don't think she will harm, and that's all I am concerned about at this post."

Another said, "She seems more powerful than our wizard."

The cleric answered, "She is."

The city was mostly housing and shops made with stone foundations, brick going up ten or so feet, and logs on top for second stories and roofs. Windows were mostly just shutters, though a few had thick, opaque glass. There was an overhang on the main street where most of the shops were, so that water dumped from the second stories would not hit the shoppers. The walkway on both sides of the main street looked like an afterthought, as there was a small gap between the shops and walkway. This was a lovely country city, well maintained and clean. Well, except for the fire damage.

I walked up the street to the cheers of the people. I had not planned this. I had been expecting to be kicked out of this town like every other town I had been in. Being half-demon is looked upon with hatred, and being half-dragon is seldom looked at as a good thing. Their general was a friend of my father. That was a big surprise and a pleasant one. A considerable number of buildings had burned down, and some major fires were still raging. I did a minor detour to help put out a fire that had spread to another building.

A fire brigade captain, according to the fancy outfit and the title on his wide helmet, was yelling out orders. "Protect the good building! Forget the other. It's lost. All brigades, save the Lapsons' house."

"Excuse me, sir."

"Grab a bucket and—" He turned enough to see me. "My lady, get out of the way please. We are busy trying to save as much of the city as possible."

"Good sir, I can put that fire out completely if you will tell your people to get out of the way of my spell."

He immediately turned toward the fire and screamed, "Pull back! Pull back! Get out of the way of the wizard's spell!" People scattered. When the area was clear, I flew up and did an Expanded Ball of Freeze that covered the two buildings. The fire was extinguished. I flew over to several others and did the same thing. As soon as I showed up, people scattered. I exhausted myself doing high-level spells like Ball of Freeze and summoning water elementals. All the fires were out except some small smoldering areas that they now concentrated on. I flew back to the road and continued up to the castle.

Meanwhile, up in the castle, Queen Iseaia Danberry watched from the throne room balcony. Her thoughts were mostly on her evil brother, but they were also on the wizard flying above her city. When the fires were out, she said, "Master Formack, please tell me how good a wizard has to be to do seventeen cold spells and summon over twenty large water elementals after battling an evil dragon and wizard."

"I would have to say higher than my instructors, my queen, and far higher than this old wizard. She is young. She can't be more than twenty. She must have started early, but I think some of it is her blood."

"Her blood? Explain."

The wizard said, "First, let me tell you—I knew both her parents, and they were both good. Not an evil bone in their bodies. She has been checked, and the cleric pronounced her as being good."

The queen looked hard at the wizard. "I have already heard this, Formack. What is wrong with her blood?"

Formack said, "It is not something wrong, my queen. It is something different. She is half–platinum dragon and half-demon. The general fought with her father, and he saved the general's life several times—as did the general his. They were a team during the war. The general told me that Sam was a good demon. He said the dragon turned him good with her love. I would bet that the child has been asked to leave anyplace she has ever tried to stay. The moment people find out she is half-demon, they would tend to kick her out."

The queen sat in thought. "I am told she was taking revenge, but I don't care. She saved my kingdom from that monster. And now, purely out of the kindness of her heart, she helped put out the fires. Tomorrow, the wizards and clerics could have done the same, but the losses between then and now would have been horrible. She did not know others would be watching. She did this to be kind. I think she is more good aligned than the cleric gives her credit for."

The old wizard said, "You're not thinking of asking her to do it, are you?"

"She is powerful. You said so yourself."

"She is young and inexperienced, my queen. The chances are very slim, and we need her for the coming battle. We need to talk her into staying."

The queen said, "She will set roots here in my city. Here, she will be welcome. Here, she will have her own tower if she can tame it."

The old wizard nearly cried, "My queen!"

"No! I will hear no more. We must remove that evil, or the

battle is lost before it starts. She will remove the evil or die trying. Of this I have no doubt. Leave me. I have much to think on."

"What of your brother?"

"Malicetric! He is with the Horde. He has chosen his side. Now leave me."

I made it to the castle and turned right. Something felt wrong. There was an evil someplace close by. I could feel it crawl up my spine, and the hairs on my arms were standing up. There was a sign on one of the buildings that read Road Head Inn. There was a little carving of the castle, with the road going up to the gates directly below the letters. I walked into the inn to cheers from many soldiers.

One soldier said, "Took your bloody time. I'm almost done celebrating." He hiccupped and sat down in a controlled fall.

The general stood up, raised his glass, and said, "Three cheers for the lady."

They all joined in with, "Hazar! Hazar! Hazar!"

He walked over to me. He did not look drunk and did not slur his speech like so many others. He said quietly, "The boys are in a great mood. Many would like to ask you a question or two. I have no idea what they want to know, but it's important to them."

I said, "Thank you for the warning. There is evil someplace near. I can feel it, General. It is coming from the castle area."

The general said, "You will be informed about that tomorrow."

"Thank you." I turned to the owner behind the large, simple but highly polished bar. "I see you've returned. Did you find anything for me?"

He was very happy that people were drinking up his beer, but I could see the worry in his sad face over his furniture. Things were getting a little rowdy. "Yes, my lady. We found a pouch but decided not to open it, as it belonged to a wizard. His things are up in your room."

"Thank you. I will have anything for dinner except dragon. I do not eat my own kind." I turned to the men and asked, "You have a question?"

It became somewhat quiet, but it's hard to shut off the singing when you're drunk. An old soldier came up, took off his hat, and bowed. "We are told you are a half demon whose demon father, the general pointed out, saved his life several times. We have also been informed that you are half-dragon. Is this true?"

"Yes. My father was a good-aligned demon. They are very few, and I doubt you will find many others. My mother was a platinum dragon, and she was good aligned. Together they did many good things."

"Why have we never heard of the good things they've done?"

I frowned. "Because, like me, humans didn't care to affiliate with us. They had to live way out in the forest and work with elves and others of nature's creatures. Only the elves know what good they have done."

The old soldier, who seemed to be the voice of all the officers in the inn, said, "You are a good person. This we have seen. You destroyed the evil dragon and then helped with putting out fires. We know the first was for your own reasons, but the last was purely out of kindness. Why did you say, 'like me'?"

I looked at him kindly. "Like me, because every place I have been, I have done good, yet every place I have been, I have been asked or told to leave. Interesting—people seem to love me and want my help until they find out my father was a demon. Then they turn angry and blame me for everything under the sun. I have been blamed for stealing husbands I have never met, a dog that was born missing one leg, crops that failed due to a drought that I was told I caused, milk going bad, wine going sour, too much rain, not enough rain, hair that was not manageable, and a thousand other things that happen to people, including me, every day. The university was more open-minded and judged me on my own merits. I did well there and made many good-aligned friends and a few enemies that I believe are evil. The short of it is I am good, and I hope to always be good. If I turn bad, somebody kill me quickly. I don't want to live with the shame and pain of harming others."

Cheers rang out. The old soldier said, "You are not alone, you know. Misschance and Deepsting, come on over here."

Two demons stood up and walked over. Both were humanoid. One was very small, in fact shorter than I, with deep purple skin and a long tail with what looked like a sharp, scorpion-like, curved barb at the end. The other was at least eight feet tall, a normal human color, dark brown eyes overly large and perfectly round, muscles bulging, with razor-sharp teeth made for meat in two nice rows. The old soldier said, "My lady, these are two of the best soldiers in the queen's army, Captain Misschance and Sergeant Deepsting. Both are full-blooded demons, both have families, and both are welcome anywhere in Landtrap. Here in Landtrap, with Ginham on one side and the Horde on the other, we cannot afford to be prejudiced. If someone proves to be good with deeds and the clerics say they're good, that's good enough for us. In your case, the cleric said you're good, and your deeds so far say your good, and that's good enough for everyone in this land. You are a welcome resource here. Yes, we look at you as a resource, someone to be used, but we look at everyone that way. I am a resource, the general is a resource, the queen—may she live for a long, long time—is a resource."

I had tears in my eyes. I could not help myself. In two hundred years, this was the first place to accept me as I was. This could be home. I said nothing. I couldn't think of anything to say. I wanted to hug them all.

Captain Misschance said, "He is telling the truth, my lady. My wife is half-demon, and she works in one of the stores. She gets paid the same as those working with her, and she spends the money wherever she wants without worry of people thinking badly about her. She is a good person, and the people here know it. We sometimes have problems with foreigners, but that is taken care of quickly when they find out that everyone sticks up for everyone here.

Sergeant Deepsting added, "I apologize, but if you stay, and we hope you will, they may ask you to be part of the women's circle." One of the maids smacked his arm, and the men started laughing. I did hug most everyone there. I could not remember ever feeling genuinely welcome before. I stayed down with them, talking most of the night. The bath and bed felt very good.

The next morning, I got up, and after eating a nice breakfast with raw bacon—my favorite—I had some time left, so I went through the papers and junk in the wizard's pouch. There was one note of some interest:

Joffre:

I need you to weaken the pass into Landtrap. We are planning our advance this spring and want them easy to run over. Ask Red Tail for help; he owes me a favor.

Red Tail:

Do this for me, and you will be free of all debts.

Malicetric

I wondered who this Malicetric was who would be advancing, and from which direction? I looked at the sky, and it was about time to see the queen.

I placed the note in my pouch to give to the general and then headed out the door. The walk wasn't long, as the gate to the castle was only a hundred paces from the door to the inn. The gate guards were expecting me and let me in, saying, "Stay away from the grassy areas." I felt sadness about them. Probably hangovers from last night. I didn't ask why. The castle stood tall and large, light brown stone mostly, lots of arrow slits and shuttered windows. All the first-level window shutters were tightly closed, as was the big, heavy main double doors. There were guards stationed everywhere, as if waiting for something. In the center was a large grass garden with several massive trees. As I was walking up to the main double doors, I had to pass in front of the Dark Tower. Evil radiated from it and the surrounding grounds. I wondered who lived there.

I entered the double doors and was met by an elderly serving woman, straight, proud, and professional, who showed me through the castle to the throne room. The throne was back to the far end and on a raised dais almost like a short stage. The room was big and tall. There were pillars, six to a side, which helped hold up the massive ceiling and chandeliers. Wall rugs adorned the sides, and a fifteen-foot-wide rug sat in the center, leading to the throne a good fifty paces to the back. Several balconies adorned one side and looked out to the black tower and the courtyard. The queen was just entering the throne room when I entered and was announced. "Samantha Altera Woodcutter—heroine of Landtrap."

The queen turned and smiled. "Come forward, child."

I walked up to the queen and curtsied as low as was proper and stayed down.

"Rise, child. Thank you for the show of respect, but here in Landtrap, we never curtsy or bow so low that our hand cannot easily reach our weapons. Nor do we remove our eyes from those around us."

I looked at her but not at the creature walking across the top of the sixty-foot vaulted ceiling. I whispered, "I am sorry for being blunt, but do you employ magical assassins?"

She looked hard at me and returned the whisper. "No, but I have had two deaths lately, and we cannot find the murderer."

Whispering back, I said, "There is a creature walking across your ceiling and dripping a liquid onto your food at this moment. Do you want me to dispatch him?"

"Can you catch him without killing him?"

"Easily done." I stepped back and, turning quickly twice, I said, "Habitum Creatura," which temporarily paralyzed him. Them I did a simple levitate spell on him and a dispel that removed the walk-on-walls magic on his boots. I did a telekinesis to draw him down to our level and turn him right-side up. Then I dispelled the telekinesis. He was standing on the floor in front of me.

The queen said, "Tie him up and ensure he cannot harm himself." She pulled her sword and sat it in her lap. The way she handled it told me she was used to using the blade. The calluses on her fingers and the palm of her right hand told me she spent a lot of time in practice. I noticed she looked at my hands. "Where is your staff?"

"I put it away, Queen Danberry."

The queen said, "In most countries, it is forbidden to have a weapon in front of or near royalty without direct permission. Here it is considered a sign of stupidity to not have your weapon at hand. Keep it with you. In this land, everyone carries a weapon at all times. There is no time for running back home if we are attacked."

I held out my hand, and in it was my favorite staff. It changed to another, then a long sword, then a dagger, then a mace, then a bow with arrows, and then something I doubt she had ever seen—a small whip made of feathers.

She smiled. "Are you planning to tickle someone to death, child?"

"Queen Danberry. This is probably the most dangerous single item I have as a weapon. It is a whip of cockatrice feathers. With one touch, it can turn most creatures to stone. It will not work on someone with great resilience or undead, but I assure you, the fool you have tied up would not go far if struck."

The queen looked most interested in weapons like my whip, and we discussed other weapons and substances, totally ignoring the soldiers, who were beating the crap out of the assassin they had nearly stripped while he was helpless. Finally, he became unparalyzed, and the queen decided to pay him some attention.

"Bring him before me." The soldiers dragged him to the throne. "I will ask this just once. If you answer, you die quickly. If you do not answer, or I think you are lying, you die very slowly. Who sent or hired you?"

He looked stubborn and said nothing.

The queen said, "Take him away and play with him. I don't care to see him again."

The general said, "Take him to the dungeons. I will be down shortly."

I said, "I may be able to shed some light on what is going on, though the information means little to me." They were both looking at me now.

The queen said, "Continue."

I pulled out the note and handed it to the general. "This was found in the pouch of the wizard that was riding the dragon." The general took it to the queen, and she read it out loud.

The queen spat out the name, "Malicetric, my bastard brother. One day he is signing a treaty, and the next he is planning to destroy us."

The general asked, "You are surprised, my queen?"

"Not really. We knew they were going to attack sometime, and now we know when. Set special watches and start preparations for war. At least this time we have notice and time to ready. Now, if we could just find funding." She turned to me. "Thank you. We were fairly sure Malicetric was behind the little nuisances like the assassins, but we were not sure he had the guts to actually join the Horde in an attack. However, I bore you with the problems of being queen. I want to thank you for killing the dragon, for putting out the fires, and now for saving my life. In return, I would give to you your own land. She pointed out one of the balconies to the dark tower. That tower is no longer occupied. You may have it."

My eyes must have given me away, as she added, "You know, don't you!" She looked at the general. "Who told!"

I thought, *Business, how fun. Let's see how badly she wants me in the place.* I said, "No one told me a thing about the tower, Majesty. It is not hard to feel the evil radiating from that place. What was it you did not want me to know?"

The queen looked at me as a cat playing with a rat. "The tower use to be owned by a wizard that was evil to the core. He was very skilled in the art of summoning creatures that most wizards would never think of summoning. Every few hours, one finds its way out of the tower, but normally the trees in the court kill it. Sometimes they make it all the way to the gate or castle. We have to stop everything we are doing and run for our lives. Fighting them is stupid, as they don't last long. Just long enough to smash down the door or gate and terrorize the city or castle. They make it impossible to get anything done. The wizard has been dead since before my grandfather was king. Many have tried, but only one ever made it past the trees. He died trying to open the door." She moved to the balcony.

Now it made sense why the throne room was in the back and difficult to get to. I looked out at the tower, and a small devil jumped out and was instantly smashed to pieces by the closest tree. Apparently, the trees were live creatures. I had never seen their like. I said, "Interesting challenge. If you make my dealings and belongings tax-free for as long as I stay in this land, you have a deal."

"Done!" She turned to the others and said, "Write the deed up." She turned back to me. "The key to the front door is still stuck in the door. Good luck, but if you cannot do this, come to me and say so. We will find you another place."

I smiled. "I hope there is no hurry. I will take my time and study the place. I will figure out this puzzle and clear it of all evil."

The queen said, "No hurry. Take all the time you need."

An old man who was sitting in the corner stood up and lightly brushed the sand off the parchment he was writing on. "My queen. I filled in her name and added the line about everything she does in this land being tax-free. It just needs your signature."

I said, "That was fast. Don't want me to back out of this?"

While scribing her name and adding the seal, the queen said, "I need the tower issue corrected so I can properly protect this land. I lose a hundred men to that tower every year, and that has weakened us considerably."

I raised my hand, and in the center of the room stood a large chest. "I will be busy working on the tower issue, so I will not be able to help in preparations for the war. Here is my monetary contribution."

One of her men opened the chest. It was filled with gold bars.

The queen stood between the chest and me, with hand on hilt. "You did not have to do this."

I said, "You made this land mine. I will make that tower my home. I will not lose it due to some fool trying to mess with who is now my queen!"

She smiled. "I will leave you to your task them." She placed a hand on my shoulder. "Good luck, Lady Samantha."

CHAPTER 3

THE TOWER

I headed out to view my tower. It was funny-looking: cone shaped, smooth skin, black marble with red veins. It looked almost like a volcano overflowing with red-hot lava. I flew around the tower several times, checking for ways to get in, and when I checked for magical gaps, I fainted. I drifted down to the ground just short 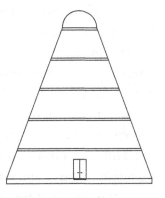 of the trees. When I came to, the guards were watching me. They never left their posts, but I think they thought me dead. When I awoke, they cheered. I flew back up and started my check again, but this time I was prepared for the overwhelming magical aura of a grand artifact. The tower was an artifact, so high in magical artifact level I had a difficult time looking at it, even while prepared. From a rogue's perspective, I would say it was well guarded. There was only one way in, the front doors. No other doors, no windows, and no gaps in the protection spells built into the tower.

I sat down on a bench just beyond the reach of the tower grounds, which were clearly marked as the grassy areas. My staff of power was in my hands. I checked for magic on the grounds and found many permanent spells in place. The entire area was protected from magical travel, a common thing to do for a castle or tower. I could identify all the spells except one. That one was the spell holding the magical trees on the property. Several times, I witnessed devils or demons or creatures I had never heard of come out and get attacked by the trees. One made it through, and I destroyed it instantly. One devil came out, stood on the doorstep, and looked around at the trees. He saw me, and in my mind I heard, "Nice trap."

"Yes, it is. Any idea how I can get around it?"

He looked disappointed. "I was hoping you would tell me." He went back inside.

On the third day, I noticed that one tree was not moving around. All the others moved when a creature tried to cross any part of the tower grounds. A bird flew in, and the nearest tree smashed it. A demon came out, and the nearest tree ran over and smashed it. These tree creatures could not only move, they were fast. However, one tree was not moving. I watched as a bird flew right past that tree and was destroyed by the next tree. I walked up to the border of the grounds and asked in the language of plants, "Why is it you are not protecting the grounds?"

In a low and long voice, with a magical mouth and eyes about ten feet up the tree, it answered. "I have been assigned to watch you. The others think you will be sneaky."

I looked up to the tree and asked, "Who is your master?"

"My master is Reginald Slinger. He is a great wizard of the dark arts."

"How long has it been since you have seen him?"

"One hundred and five seasons of snow."

"Where is he?"

"In his tower."

"How do you know?"

"He is still summoning creatures."

"What is your purpose? Why did he place you here?"

"To keep others out of his tower."

"Then why do you destroy those coming out?"

"They hurt other creatures. We have seen this and decided that he meant to keep others from getting out."

"Then why are you keeping others from getting in?"

"We are not sure if we are correct, so we are doing both."

"Why don't you ask?"

"He does not come out, and we cannot go in. We cannot trust the creatures that come out to ask. The only one we allowed to enter died at the door when a creature came out at the same time he was going in."

"Bad luck that."

"No one else has cared to talk with us until now. Do you wish to try?"

I took a step back. "Not if you are trying to trick me into coming on the grounds so you can smash me. No thank you."

"You will not be harmed by us if you do us this favor."

"I believe you, but I am not as powerful as your master. If—he is in there?"

In an angry tone, he said, "What do you mean *if*!"

I took another step back, acting frightened, and he changed his tone. "I am sorry, little creature. It is just that we have been guarding for such a long time. We would be very upset if he was not there."

"I understand, but he must be very powerful, nearly Godlike, to be able to summon creatures like I have seen all day and all night for a hundred years without rest. The queen says he died a long time ago. She gave me what she believes is a tower with no owner. I need to do one of two things. Prove the master is still alive or shut down that summoning porthole. If he is still alive, I would ask him your question."

"Wait here, little creature." He moved over to several other trees. I went back to my bench. They were still talking when night came, so I left and went to the inn.

The next day, I went back and sat on my bench. It was near lunchtime when they separated. Two walked toward me. I got up and met them at the edge of the grounds. One said, "Thank you for waiting."

"I did not wait. I went to the inn, had dinner, and then went to bed. I came back this morning."

The taller tree said, "She is honest. Very well, she can pass as we agreed."

The other tree said, "We have talked about what you said. It is possible that the old wizard died and left a summoning portal open. Sad that would be. We have been guarding him a long time."

I said, "Still, you have been grand guards. If I were running the place, I would be very happy with your abilities and your honor."

If a tree could smile, I think this one did. Hard to tell. It said, "I am glad you think that. If the wizard is alive, please have him come out and talk to us. If he is not there and it is a summoning portal, please close it if you can. If he is not there and you can close the summoning portal, then you are the new owner. We have all agreed on this. We are hoping that you are the new owner, as we do not like staying here without any sign of our master."

The other one said, "We are hopeful you do not die before completing our request."

I chuckled. "I can do this, but it will take time, and I may have to leave the tower very quickly. If there are creatures finding their way out every hour or so, then there are many more that have not found their way out. I will need to destroy these in order to reach the place they are coming from. That could take me a lot of time and energy, as they are replaced continuously. Please don't smash me if I run out screaming or just run out, as I am probably being chased."

He laughed a booming laugh that nearly shook the ground. "We will watch for you, little creature, and for any chasing you. If you can lure them out, we will destroy them. Save your spells for the ones you must fight."

I said, "Very well. I will enter tomorrow morning after preparing for the day."

"We will be ready." He stood taller and stiffened. If I hadn't been talking to him, I would have sworn he was just a tree. I went to the general and warned him that traffic coming out of the tower might increase for a few days, starting tomorrow. He stationed an entire garrison around the tower.

The next morning, I came back in full battle gear with my staff of power at the ready. No one there had seen me in full battle gear before. I don't wear them very often as they are covered in gold trim and that attracts thieves. The clothes were especially designed to look impressive and warn that this tiny little girl is dangerous. The armor was highly decorated with magi symbols and was extraordinarily magical, with flickers of light dancing here and there as if the whole outfit were made of suppressed sunlight trying to escape. I had a dozen wands and rods in their quick-release holders, potions of all colors were in a bandolier and easily accessible, and I had eight weapons with me. My staff of power was in my left hand and could instantly disappear into my Gauntlet of Holding. My other hand was free for casting spells, but that Gauntlet of Holding carried a staff that would create an impenetrable, immovable force sphere of protection that could lock me away from harm for a few minutes. That would be enough time to heal myself and prepare. I could also put a Force Confinement around me, allowing me protection and rest until I dispelled it. On my head was a Circlet of Annihilation, and on my feet were Boots of Exceptional Speed. They provided me with extraordinary speed when fleeing or flying. I wore a Belt of Godly Might, and on my right hand was a Ring of Mental Protection. My left hand had a mixed ring of maximum custodia, arcane armor, and essentia. I always wear that ring. On the finger hanging around my neck was a mixed ring of toughness and shielding. My cloak would help me with absorbing magical effects, my vest could help me escape something's grasp, and I had protection spells on me that would last all day. In my Natura's Deep-Pocket Haversack were more potions and scrolls. I also had twelve magical stationary hooks. As I passed the guards at the gate, they stared. One whispered to his friend, "War sorceress." The children on the street stood back with everyone else. One woman went to her knees and started praying for my success.

I stopped and stood before the grounds to the tower. No tree moved toward me. I waited until a creature tried to leave. Two trees destroyed it before it left the step, and it disappeared. I took a step onto the grounds, and nothing happened. I walked cautiously toward the door. One tree turned a little, following my movement, but I was not attacked.

I opened the door in such a way as to not be in front of it. Good thing too. There was a creature standing there trying to figure out how to get through. It stood about ten feet high and five wide, with six massively muscled arms. It looked like a dire great ape with extra arms. Those arms could easily tear a young lady apart, and the strong-looking hands had talons that dripped with poison. It jumped out, and the trees smashed it to a stain on the ground before it disappeared.

I cautiously looked around the door. No other live creatures were in the foyer. There was plenty of dust, and remains of shattered furniture were scattered across the floor. If that was the norm, then walking or running would be difficult. I cast Terrain Flight on myself and flew up one foot in the air. I took out a stationary hook and placed it in front of the right-side front door, saying the activation words. Now the front door could not close unless someone could deactivate and remove that hook.

My plan was simple. Open the doors leading to the outside and let the trees do the rest. At this time, I could not make more plans, as that was all the information I had to work with. The night before, I did some research but could not find anything at the university research library about the mage that created the tower. In addition, local knowledge turned out to be worthless, as it was filled with too much distortion.

I entered to the cheers of the men standing ready to fire on anything getting past the trees. The room was a simple foyer and nothing else. Any furniture that may have been there had long ago been picked up, shattered, or burnt to ash. I did protection spells from fire, cold, sound, acid, and shock. There was a feeling of great evil in this place. There were four doors in the foyer. I had come from the west, and there were doors east, south, and north. I listened at the south door. No sound. I listened at the east door. No sound. I listened at the north door, and something was banging around. I stepped to the side and opened the door. It ran out so fast I hardly saw it. It stopped in the middle of the room and looked around. The thing was dripping wet and looked more otter with demon horns than anything else I could describe. Seeing the front door open, it ran in that direction and was instantly smashed when it reached the grounds. It was very fast and almost got past the trees before one caught it and grappled. That stopped it long enough for the trees to break it in two and toss the parts around for a few seconds before they disappeared. Those trees were playing with their kill.

I placed a stationary hook in front of that door and activated it. This small room led to stairs. I could go up or down. I stepped back out and checked the east door again. It was locked. I checked the south door. It opened into a professionally appointed waiting room with comfy chairs, tables, and bookshelves adorned with books and figurines of varying size and shape. Other than being dusty, everything in this room looked intact. I closed the door and magically locked it. The creatures had never come this way, and I wanted to ensure that they never did.

I went back to the stairs and listened. Noises were coming from both directions. I headed up. At the second level, I activated a stationary hook to keep those doors closed, and then I headed back down. At the first floor of the basement, I listened. There was talking. It sounded like devils, but it was too low for me to hear clearly. I did an invisibility spell on myself and slowly opened the door. Two devils were looking in my direction. I waved, and one waved back. Darn, they could see invisibility.

They stayed where they were, and one asked in standard, "Are you the owner of this place?"

I answered, "Sort of."

He looked troubled by my answer. "Explain."

I told them what was going on and what I was trying to do.

One looked at the other. "It's just as we thought. We are not here permanently. Soon we will be going back."

The other said, "Then let's create as much havoc as we can while we're here." They turned in my direction and started toward me. I flew as fast as I could up and out the two doors and on to the grounds. They followed and were instantly smashed. I thanked the trees and went back in. I slowly traveled down to the door I had just opened and looked inside. The room was smashed and burnt with bits and pieces everywhere. I had been hoping that this was the norm, as it would identify where the monsters and creatures had a chance to set off traps and where there might still be issues. Besides, it left a devastated trail to the summoning portal.

I entered that room. There was a door directly to my right and another door on the far side, and it was open. I went in that direction. I didn't hear it as much as I felt it. A small creature poked its tiny puppy-dog face with the biggest sad eyes around the corner. It saw me and tried to mentally grab my mind. There was great evil in that mind touch. I quickly hit it with a lightning strike that had no effect. It stepped out of the other room and tried harder to take my mind. I fought back and used a shaped acid ball. The creature screamed and ran out of the ball fast enough that it did little damage. It sent a spell my way, and I felt dizzy for a second, but I fought it and recovered quickly enough to send a quickened Force Barrier behind it, blocking off the door it came through and the door to my right, and then an acid cloud where it was. I moved out of the room.

It could not see the exit through the thick cloud, but it moved in my general direction. I closed the door and barred it with two stationary hooks. It found the door and tried to get out. The screams were deafening even through the thick door. It tried to grab my mind, but without eye contact, it had no chance. It was in too much pain being stuck in an acid cloud to concentrate its mental grabbing. It tried to go the other way to get into the room it had come out of but smacked into the Force Confinement. It screamed louder.

I waited a couple of minutes before removing the hooks and entering. The acid cloud was gone, the confinement was gone, and the creature was gone. That's the thing about summoning. The summoned creature dies and goes back to its home plane fully alive. It will remember what happened, and some creatures who can plane travel will try to take revenge if they gathered enough information while there to be able to find the place. That's why there were no remains of long-dead creatures in the tower. They died, or their time ran out and they returned to their own homes. Time was on my side and against me. I had no idea how powerful the portal was, so I did not know how long the summoned creatures would last. I also did not know how often they were summoned. More than once an hour, I was sure, but how much more?

I placed a hook holding the door open and went across to the next door. I cautiously looked around the corner into the next room. This room was another central room. Four doors leading off north, south, west, and the east one I was standing in. Just like the room above. I checked the north door, and it was unlocked. I listened: no sound. I placed a hook holding that door shut. I checked the south door and did the same. I checked the west door, and there was fighting going on.

I heard grunts and pain, hits and slams, and ripping. I waited until the sounds stopped and then turned invisible. I turned the handle. It was bent from use. I opened the door a crack and looked in. I slammed the door closed and hid in the corner.

A creature slammed open the thick, iron-bound door and slithered out, squeezing its immense body through the opening. It looked around and did not see me. It was damaged badly and left a long train of green ichor. It slithered out the open door and headed up. It took several minutes to cross out of the way. It had to be at least fifty feet long. I heard the fight outside. It lasted a long while. I went back up. Two trees were turned to stone, and so were several men. The creature was dead, as its head had been smashed. I pulled out a wand and turned the men and trees back to flesh and wood. *Good wand. Note to self: only twenty-three charges left. Make another soon.*

The men and trees were thinking that I had done all the damage that the creature sustained before coming out and it did nothing to me. They were impressed. I was not going to tell them otherwise. I said, "Sorry I let that one get away." They thanked me, and I went back in.

CHAPTER 4

CORRECTING AN OLD ISSUE

I slowly traveled back down and checked the room it had come out of. This room was big, at least one hundred feet across and two hundred feet wide, and in the center was a raised dais. Near the top of the thirty-foot ceiling were ever-burning torches that lit the room. On the dais, a staff

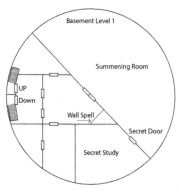

was sticking out of a book. The staff radiated four continually changing rainbow glows that formed four circles about ten feet from the dais on each side. The circle in front had an intricate diagram of holding drawn on the floor. While I was looking, creatures—one demon, one devil, one looking like a large bear with no fur, and one tiny one that resembled a wolf with fire eyes and dripping fangs—formed in separate circles. They saw me and attacked. Only the three that did not have the diagram of holding could leave the circles. I flew out and hid behind a thick stone barrier that I created with a spell. They shot past and headed up and out. I disintegrated the wall and went back into the room. I didn't have much time. I needed to stop what was going on before more creatures came through. I flew around the room and saw the bones of a man scattered around the floor. There were clothes and a pouch. I went down and found a book and some notes with a rod. I grabbed them, went to a corner in the previous room, and created another stone barrier. I did a light spell so I could see colors and started deciphering the script. I was glad to be out of the big room because I did not see any pillars. A tower was above me, with no pillars holding it up. Not good. It was a miracle the tower was still standing.

I continually heard creatures summoned, fighting, and running out. Several times the creatures tried to tear through my wall, but they never made it before some other creature attacked them. I continued to read and was surprised with what I found.

Day 627: I have finally deciphered the text of the Death Nell Summoning Book. According to the book, if I open it to the beginning and touch it with the Great Staff of the Planes, in the circle at the top right, I can create a summoning circle that will summon any creature from anywhere I wish. I will try it after I paint a holding circle where the summoning circle will be placed.

Day 629: It worked! The circle showed up exactly where it said it would. I summoned several creatures, and they lasted about an hour each.

This is far better than the few seconds I achieved in the past. Interesting point: all creatures summoned are evil. The staff stands up and stays in the air until you take it down. I have read that if I turn to the back of the book and touch it with the Great Staff of the Planes in the circle at the top left, I can summon different creatures. I will try that tomorrow.

Day 630: It worked! I summoned demons using the back top left of the book. The circle and holding spells worked great. There are three other places in the book with marks for touching the staff. I must try them all.

Day 633: I tried the circle on the bottom left, two pages past the beginning, and the circle on the bottom right, three pages from the back. Some of the creatures are fantastic and very dangerous. Tomorrow I will try the spot in the center of the book. There are warnings that I cannot decipher, but the holding pattern is working perfectly.

That was the last entry. The fool tried the mark in the center of the book, and that apparently opened all four circles with random summoning at the same time. I would bet the warnings were for you to make four holding patterns at specific spots. He opened four circles, and three were without holding patterns. Summoned creatures poured out and attacked him, and he died leaving the circles open and working correctly. Normally, summoned creatures could be controlled, but if the creature you summoned was far superior to you? Well, only a fool thinks he can control everything. There was also a statement, "All summoned creatures will match the alignment of the wizard doing the summoning." No wonder they were all evil.

Apparently, all I had to do to stop the summoning was to remove the staff. I don't trust *apparently*. I sat down and started studying. It took a long time. The text was old and faded. I was running out of air in the little corner I made, so I used Stone Configure to create a couple of small holes on each side. "Much better." I sat back down.

About two hours into my reading, a tentacle poked its way into one of the holes. I cut it off with my knife, and the creature pulled the rest back, screaming in pain. The cut-off piece of tentacle started growing and changing. Darn. I annihilated it and accidently a small portion of the back wall as well. Surprise, there was another room—a study of sorts, with a big desk, a large, padded chair, and bookshelves lining the walls, filling the chamber with more books and golden figurines, extremely fancy painted plates, and carvings of all kinds of creatures. I went in, and after doing a few cleaning spells, I sat down. The room was lit with ever-burning candles, so I had plenty of light. I studied until I was sure that I could remove the staff and the circles would close. I found the trick. To take the staff, I needed to say the trigger words. I did not know the trigger words, and they were not in the man's notes. If I had the staff in hand, I could figure out the trigger words, but I didn't.

The secret door into the room was easy to find. From this side, it looked just like a door. I went over and listened. I timed the summoning. New creatures were summoned every 240 count. So, every four minutes new creatures appeared. As soon as the next creatures entered, I waited two minutes and opened the door. They were fighting each other on the other side of the chamber. I shot an Annihilate spell at the floor below the dais, but nothing happened. The tower had been built with too many protections. The dais looked newer, so I shot an Annihilate spell at the dais. The book and staff dropped to the floor. I closed the door and waited. A few minutes passed, and I heard one creature leave. I waited for several more minutes, and nothing happened. I opened the door, and there were no creatures. I walked over to the center. The book had closed, and the staff was on the floor. I picked up both, opened my special place, and gently placed them inside. Then I went up and out.

I stood in the center of the front doors for several minutes. Nothing happened. No creatures came out, and none went in. The soldiers and trees were watching and quiet. I went back in and deactivated my hooks, closed the doors, and returned outside. I deactivated the hook to the front door and closed and locked it, virtually trapping any creature still inside until its time ran out and it returned to its own plane.

I turned around and said to the trees. "I was wrong. It was not one summoning portal. It was four summoning circles. Your old master's bones are scattered on the basement floor. He has been dead a long time. I will have them removed at a later date. Right now, I need some rest. Please don't let anyone in. There are probably traps and other issues I need to clean up. Do you have a home you want me to send you back to?"

"This is our home, and you are our mistress. We will obey."

I said, "I keep no slaves. You are welcome to stay and guard my place for as long as you wish, but that is up to you. If there is anything you need, please let me know."

"We will be staying."

"Thank you. I would ask that, unless I say otherwise, no one comes in or out except me. They can come to the door and knock, but if they try to force their way in without my permission, they die."

They bowed to me, and I walked off the grounds to the cheers of the men. I said to the men, "After that, I need a bath and a good meal. The place is filthy, and now that I have the rodents removed, it's time to clean up. Please tell the queen the four summoning circles are deactivated and destroyed. Tomorrow I will start the removal of traps and other nasty issues. Any volunteers for trap removal? I would expect that 5 or maybe 10 percent of you will live through the first day."

They laughed, but none came forward. I left to their happy cheers and laughter. I entered the inn and said, "Bath, please, and then food."

The innkeeper said, "Nice to have you back. You were gone six days. We were worried."

I stopped dead in my tracks. "Six days?"

"Yes. Is something wrong?"

I ran out of the inn and back to the tower. I asked the first tree, "How long was I in the tower?"

"Six suns. We started to think you were dead."

I looked at the tree and said, "I was in there only one day. Something is wrong." I went back inside to the study. I pulled out the book from my private area and started studying.

I came out three days later knowing what had happened. That fool wizard set up a time distortion using the staff and book. I was lucky that it was only six days and not six centuries. The book said that the time distortions could change, dependent on when you entered. The issue was gone now. I was worried that the entire tower would be displaced in time. I had just won the tower and was not about to allow it to leave without me.

As I left the tower, one of the guards ran into the castle, and shortly after, the general came out. I had stopped at the trees to ask a few questions and explain my concern. "By my calculations, I was in there three days. Is this correct?"

The tree bent down a little. "Yes, little sorceress. Three suns ago, you entered, and you just came out."

"Good. The time distortions stopped the moment I disabled the summoning circle. I was worried."

The tree said, "Time distortions, little one? It is never good to mess with time."

I looked up. "I know, my friend. I wish your old master had realized what he was doing. He did not take the time to study the warnings clearly written in the book."

The tree said in a growl, "If that book can mess with time, then it is too dangerous for humans or any other creature to have." His voice was a warning to me.

I said, "I agree, and I would give it to you to rip apart, but it is an artifact. Destroying it will cause other problems."

The tree said, "What god allowed the book into the hands of my old master? A foolish god or an Evil God he would be."

I smiled. "I have no idea."

The tree smiled and said, "Oh." It turned stiff, as if the conversation was over.

I turned and left the grounds. The general was right on the edge, waiting for me. He took my arm and gently led me back into the castle. "The queen wants to have a talk with you."

"But I—"

"She does not care if you haven't had a bath—and you do need one. She cares that the tower does not need watching anymore. She would like to know what happened, why, and is there any chance of it happening again."

I did two quick cleaning spells before he could drag me in. I also materialized my Staff of Power. In front of the doors, I yanked my arm free and said, "Do that again, General, and I will bite you." I pulled myself together and walked in standing straight and proud. However, I wasn't fooling anyone.

The queen said, "There you are. I was wondering why you came out wanting a bath and dinner and then ran back in. I am told the crisis is over?"

I told her everything I found out and what I did. I did not tell her it wasn't me who battled the great snake that came out. Apparently, they thought it was running from me, and that was putting a little care in their voices. You'd think that destroying that dragon and then cleansing the tower would do the same, but I am so tiny and charismatic that everyone sees me as a child. It takes constant reminding and lots of patience to get it through their heads that I am not.

The queen summoned up everything I said. "So, the four circles for summoning are closed, and that stopped the time distortions. All creatures should be back in their own plane, and we should never have that problem again, as soon as you get rid of that book. Is that correct?"

"Yes, Majesty."

She smiled. "We owe you our highest commendations. How will you get rid of the book?"

"I will go talk to my mentor."

Instantly there was a Caelum, a type of war angel, in the room with us. All, including the queen, went to one knee with their heads up and hands on swords, except me. I took a stance of attack and did not leave it even when he said, "I am from Solbelli. I have come for the book."

I said, "Three things. First, how do I know you are from Solbelli? I would bet others would love to have the book. Second, why would I just hand it over?" The queen's eyes went wide, but I knew she could not feel the evil radiating from this creature like I could. "Third, why are you here, devil?"

He looked directly at me and said, "I was summoned several times by that book, and I want it. I want the staff also. You will give them to me, or I will destroy this land."

I attacked with the Staff of Power using the lightning ability. The power I could wield when using the Staff of Power was great, but it did not affect him much. Smoldered his clothes a little, but that was all. He turned into the fifteen-foot, overly muscled, red fire devil he was and attacked back with domination. It slipped off my mind doing nothing. After all, I was wearing an artifact ring of Mental Protection. I now knew exactly what kind of devil it was, so my next attack took greater effect. A tiny little green-black dragon acid ball formed in my left hand, and I threw it at him. Tilting my head back, I followed up with a targeted banshee wail. The surprised look on his face and the amount of bleeding from his ears, nose, and eyes told me he was not prepared for my getting past his spell resistance. He now took the fight more seriously. I did a Shift Lock on him so he could not depart magically and then a quickened Force Confinement I had prepared earlier that day, my last quickened spell. He was now trapped inside the confinement with me; therefore, what we did would not destroy the throne room.

He went directly to spells that would affect my life essence, ripping part of my soul with each spell; however, they did not work, as I also had resistance to spells. I hit him with an acid shaft. He tried the same on me, and it burned badly and started my robe on fire. I did a Resistance to Acid spell. He did the same and added a surprise for me, a supernatural spit with poison. It hit exactly on my right cheek. There are some good things about being a demon. I am immune to most poisons, and fortunately, this one did not affect me. I instantly changed into a demon and bit him. While in my jaw, he became easy to hit, so I used my claws to rend. His eyes went wide, and he pulled out a potion and started to drink. I slapped it away and then bit him harder, used both claws to rend his chest, snapped him with the razor-sharp points of my two wings, and stabbed him with the spear shape of my long tail. He was easy to hit, and my rend is really a wonderful weapon, and it feels good doing it. He tried to use a Butcher Living spell, high-level spell that would have chopped me into little pieces, but it took too long to verbalize in a close-quarter fight. I slammed him against the wall of the cage, and he choked on it. Take my advice: never get stuck in a small space with a mad demon. It took a while with his fast healing, but I killed him when I finally tore his head off.

I cleaned myself up by licking my wounds. My fast healing had kicked in, and I was in perfect condition. My clothes were torn and had holes, but my body was still fully scaled and spotless. I stayed in the confinement, ignoring the two outside trying to get my attention. I searched through his clothes and found nothing of interest. The two rings were magical, and so was his necklace, but I needed some spell components to identify them. This was a major devil, and now he was permanently dead. I needed to get rid of that book, but I am not the kind to just give it away. What to do, what to do. I dismissed the confinement.

The queen was faster than the general. "Servants! Clean up that mess. Lady Samantha, find out a way to get rid of that book and then ensure everyone knows it's gone."

"As you wish." I teleported to the university.

CHAPTER 5

UNIVERSITY OF MAGICUM

I walked up the last few yards and entered through the massive quadruple doors. Magical guards were standing watch, and if the spell that identified an intruder wishing to do harm had gone off, I assure you I would have been dead. However, I was a graduate and welcome. There, in that fantastical university that so long ago had me in awe, was where I had grown up. The buildings spread out for miles, and all were more carved and magical the farther back you went. As I was watching, one big building got up and disappeared, only to reappear in another place. That only happened when the grand master wanted someone to hurry. I was protected by spells that King Charles, the creator and head of the university, had put in place himself. No devil was going to attack me there. I saw one of my professors and headed that way. When I drew close, he saw me and opened his arms. "My child, this is a wonderful surprise." He hugged me and then held me out at arm's length. This old elf had white hair with a little tint of yellow. His tiny frame nearly matched mine, and there was strength in his embrace. His brows furrowed. "You look rather beat up. How is your revenge going?"

I smiled. "I am finished with revenge." Then I did several spells that cleaned me up and repaired my clothing.

He smiled. "I am so glad. Revenge was holding you back, you know. Magi and cleric or not, you could have done better."

In this master's opinion, everyone could have done better. I said, "I need to summon King Charles."

Now he was worried, as both eyebrows raised. He said, "I will not ask you why, but I will point out that the last time someone rang that bell three times, Charles came instantly. The mage's emergency was not an emergency in Charles's eyes, and the mage is still in a bottle floating in the ocean somewhere. Charles took care of the issue for the mage. However, the mage paid and is *still* paying very dearly, for all we know."

I nodded. "I know, sir. I will ring only twice."

He said, "It could be a long wait."

I said, "Then I will bring reading material and a chair."

He smiled, turned, and took me to the special room. He unlocked it and let me in. There was only one thing in the room. A bell with a sign.

Ring once to drop off mail.
Ring twice and wait if you want to talk with the king.
Don't ring three times. Your emergency
is not necessarily mine!

I summoned a chair from my special place and several books. Then I rang the bell twice and sat down and waited. I waited eight days before King Charles showed up. He was covered with tiny little, slimy, cold, blue, water snakelike creatures trying to bite and sting him. There had to be thousands of them, but he stood there as if it were nothing.

King Charles said, "I ran out of convenient spells for handling this. You have any fireballs?"

I did a Sustained Explosive Fireball stuffed and shaped so that it took him and the creatures in only. When he was clear, I went to one knee.

"Oh, get up, child. I don't need that crap. Thanks for the fireball. You did that very well, Samantha."

"You, you know my name?"

"Of course I know your name. The moment you entered my university, I started receiving reports about you. Sorry about the Tenamites. I'm working on a water planet, and those things are all over. I am attempting to get rid of them. So far, nothing has worked. Still, I have a few more ideas. I think I will try importing a load of giant fire salamanders next. They won't remove the problem, but they might make it manageable so that I can. What did you want to talk about?"

I reached out, and the book and staff were instantly in my hands.

He took them and read the book like it was a child's story. He took the staff, turned it over, and pronounced, "As you know, this is the Great Staff of the Planes. It derived its beginnings from Commeatus. In fact, he would love to have it back. He loaned it to some minor mage a long time ago, and the fool died and left it in some time issue. The Death Nell Summoning Book should not be here. Where did you find it?"

I started to tell him of my adventure, but he stopped me right away, saying, "Start from the beginning and don't leave out any detail."

I started with my family's death, and two days later, I ended with ringing the bell twice. He looked at me for a while and then said. "The book belongs to the Over Gods. I will buy it off of you. I will raise all of your abilities up three times and give you a set of books on first through fourteenth circle spells. You do read draconic?"

"Of course I do. You have a deal."

He took the book and opened it again, and, to my astonishment, he absorbed it. It became part of him. He raised a hand, and I felt my body change, and instantly there was a set of books at his side. He gave them to me, saying, "Put these away and do not let others have them. It is the only copy from the originals other than the one I gave the university, and their set only goes to major wish spells. You have been doing three levels higher already with those magical enhancements, so you should be able to learn. I warn you. Be good, child, or we will meet in ways you do not want."

I put the books in my special place.

He took the staff and said, "I will be right back." He left. About an hour later, he came back. Now he was smiling. He said, "You don't worship a god, do you?"

"I have never picked one, sir. My mother's god would not have me, and I would not have my father's god."

He laughed. "Several are interested in you. Commeatus is especially interested, but he is not for you. Your alignment is firming at naturally good, though it fluctuates a little. You are good, and I foresee you will do good things." He handed me a nut and said, "Chew this and swallow."

I took it and popped it in my mouth. I chewed it and swallowed. It tasted bitter but not too bad. Then my entire body moved and changed a little. I asked, "What just happened?"

He said, "That was Commeatus's payment for returning his staff. You are now immune to any type of mind control by anything short of a full god. He foresees you needing this gift."

"I will thank him in prayer."

"You do that, child. It will amuse the old man." He left.

He called a major god an old man. I hope I never reach that level. It's scary. I went to my knees and prayed while thanking Commeatus for the gift.

I heard in my head, *Old Man! I need to teach that boy a lesson.* As an afterthought, he added, *Oh, yes—yes, you're welcome.* Then he was gone.

I thought to myself as I stood up. *So, it is true. The gods do know what's in your heart.*

I walked out into the hall. The far window showed it was night. There were two first-year students waiting. One said nervously, "Please wait, great mage. The master wants to talk with you."

I thought to myself, *Was I ever that nervous around the masters and magi?* I knew the answer. Probably more so.

I waited for only a few minutes before Master Ohm, a clean-shaven, tall, old human with a bald head, came into view. He walked up to me and said, "Let's walk."

We started down the corridor leading to the great hall and the way out. "Child, it has come to our attention that you are a free agent. No god, no responsibilities, no home, nothing to do. Is this correct?"

"No, Master."

He looked at me a little shocked. "Then may I ask what your agenda is at this time?"

"I have found a place that accepts me as I am. The queen gave me land and a tower for my services, so I have a home. She is in trouble, as there is a war coming."

He looked concerned. "I am not aware of any wars going on or about to go on."

I too was concerned. He should have known about this long before I did. "The northeastern horde is planning to attack the Landtrap in the spring."

He stopped for only a second, nearly cussing when he said, "Not again!"

"I am afraid so, Master, and this time they have the brother of Queen Iseaia Danberry to guide them. He is evil and is willing to trash everything."

"I am glad you have finally found a home. Formack still there?"

"Yes, Master."

"You tell him I said hello. You are in the right place. Please take care of this issue. I will talk to the counsel and see if we can send help. Until then, you are on your own."

"Thank you, Master."

He walked off, mumbling to himself.

Just before I left the university, a wizard that I did not recognize ran up to me. "Are you Mage Samantha Altera Woodcutter?"

"Yes."

He handed me a note and left.

I opened it and read.

> Samantha Altera Woodcutter:
> It is with great pride that we promote you to mage general in charge of the Landtrap area.
> Good luck.
> Counsel of Mages

I wrote on the back: "I will do what I can, but I will not accept any assigned position that gives you power over me or can make me obligated to follow your orders. Nice try, gentlemen. At this time, I will remain free and help Landtrap and her queen where I can without interference or the chance of being recalled in the middle of battle like Joey was." I handed it to a student and said, "Counsel chambers immediately."

He took off, and another came running up to me and handed me a message before the other was out of sight. I opened it and read.

> We thought you would say that. You can't blame
> us for trying.
> Counsel of Mages

I laughed and stepped outside. Several yards away, I teleported back to the city and walked to the inn. I finally got my bath and dinner. Sleep that night was grand.

CHAPTER 6

DRAGON PEPPER

The next morning, I awoke to a knock on my door. "Package for Lady Samantha."

"Leave it by the door."

"Too big. It's piled up in front of your tower. Nice stuff. I would take it inside right away, or it may not be there long."

I got up immediately and dressed for trap finding. I did take the time to have a magical feast. As I walked through the castle gates, I could see the package. In front of my tower was furniture and lots of it. There was everything needed to furnish a tower, including stacks and stacks of books for a library, kitchen equipment, hangings, pictures, linens, desks, chairs, tables, flower vases, and beds. It was enough to furnish a castle. I checked for magic and found everything was magically preserved. This furniture would last forever. A book was of a higher magic, so I picked it up and opened it. There was a note inside.

> I knew you'd search for magic right away. After
> hearing your story and all the broken furniture,
> I decided to clean out some of my storage space.

This is extra junk I had sitting around. Thought I'd palm it off on you. If you don't need it, give it away to somebody you like. I checked out the tower properties, and you are correct, it is an artifact. Made so long ago that Magicum nearly forgot that he made it. The transportation key word is "Nanmal." Magicum, you, and I are the only ones alive who know it. Leave it that way. Don't tell anyone else, even if you think they are your best friends. The tower is called the Tower of Sight. Magicum considers it a temple of his, and now that his mind has been pointed that direction, he is probably paying attention. That can be good or bad. One more thing. There is great evil in that tower. Be careful.

King Charles

The message flashed into fire and burnt to dust.

Now that was a very nice thing to do. I didn't really know if I needed all that stuff, but it appeared to be top quality and better than anything I had seen in the castle. I realized I had better move it inside before the queen got her hands on it. I checked in with the trees and walked into my tower. I used the magical hooks to keep both doors open and then the same with the doors going into the stairs and down to the first basement level. I opened all the doors on that level. There was enough space in the room where the summoning was going on for storing all the extra furniture. After removing the bones of the old master, I went back up and outside. At the pile of stuff, I started doing levitation spells and movement spells. Slowly, each item carefully lifted off the ground and moved into my tower in a line until it found a good spot to rest in the summoning room. It took hours, and I had to concentrate the entire time. When the last piece sat down, I went inside and sat down also. Concentrating for hours was difficult.

After sitting and resting for several minutes, I removed the hooks and started mapping the place. I decided to start with the first floor and work my way up and then tackle the bottom layers after I had a place to stay.

Also, I was doing dismissal spells on all the spells that were present. Someone had consecrated the place to an Evil God, and I was not going to allow that to stay in position. When I had first come in several before, I checked the door to the south and found a waiting room. Now I was checking for traps and secrets.

The waiting room was clear. I returned to the foyer. The east side had a set of double doors that were both five feet wide. They were carved dark wood with raised murals. On the left side was a mural of a man reading a book, and on the right was a man eating a nice meal. I checked the door, and it was still locked but not trapped. I took the time to unlock it gently.

There are many ways to unlock and open a door. With a key is preferred. But if you don't have the key, then you can try lock picks, magic, bashing, or blasting. Bashing, or a good annihilation spell, will permanently open the door, but then I would have to replace what's left of it. Picking the lock takes a skill I don't have. I trained under a thief for a few years and became very good at finding traps, but I never did well at picking locks or disabling traps. Well, that's not true. I am very good at disabling traps. The thing I am not good at is disabling without setting them off. I have fried myself many times.

However, there were no traps on this set of ten-foot doors, so I did a simple Open spell, and both doors opened. I looked in. The doors led to a fifteen-foot-wide passage going about ninety feet to a dead end. To the south and north were double doors about midway down the hall. I walked up the passage to the double doors and checked the northern side for traps. None detected, so I opened the doors. Everything in the room had been smashed. Books were torn to pieces, and paper was everywhere. Interesting. If the foyer doors were locked, how did they get into this room? I walked the room, looking for traps and secrets. The entire room was totally destroyed, yet there were no marks on the floor or walls. *It seems that you can destroy anything you want in this artifact, but you can't harm*

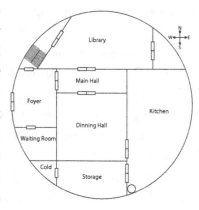

the tower. There were double doors to the east leading to a large room with no other exit, and there were double doors to the west that led to what used to be storage under the stairs. Both rooms were trashed. After removing the spells and evil consecration in those rooms, I returned to the hall and opened the south double doors. There were several long tables with cuts and burns and the remains of destroyed chairs and cupboards. So this was a dining facility for a large number of people. I checked for traps and secrets and found none. There were double doors to the east, and I opened them. They led into a large kitchen. This had, at one time, been a very nice kitchen. It was big enough to feed a small army. I checked everything, and there were no traps or secrets. In several places, there were ropes and some four-inch holes in the floors and the bottoms of several very nice sinks, but other than that, the place was trashed.

In the kitchen, there were two sets of double doors on the west wall, the one I had just come through from the dining room and another set next to spiral stairs going up. While keeping an eye on the stairs, I checked the double doors. They were locked. I did an Open spell and found a large storage area that was packed with enough food to feed an army. I checked it out, and it was all bad. The spells to keep out bugs had long expired. This area had a large metal door on the far western side. I checked that door and found cold storage. This artifact came with cold storage to keep things frozen. My professors would be jealous. The room was packed with meat and other items. All over, there was ice in small cubes and large cubes.

I had now checked the first floor. I checked for traps on the spiral stairs and headed up. It took me to a small room with a door to the north.

I checked the door and found it half-open. It led to a very large room with no pillars. I understood now that Magicum made it this way. I was not so afraid the thing would collapse. The tower had probably been around for thousands of years, or he would have never forgotten about it. It was difficult to make out what the room was used for until I spotted one bunk that was still partially intact. It was open barracks for about two hundred men. There were doors all over the room, and I checked out each one, starting on my right. The first door led to privies.

Surprisingly, the privies looked and smelled clean. I walked over to them, and there was a hole in the bottom of each potty. There was a rope hanging to the side of each potty with a handle on the end. I pulled on one to see what it would do. A spell went off. I did it again and this time watched to see if I could detect what spell. It was a cleansing spell. Nice. I sat down and did

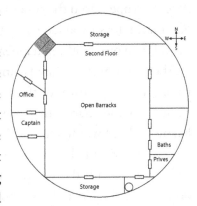

my duty, and pulled the handle, and the potty and I were cleaned instantly. Nice idea. I was going to have to have Master Mage Orale up for dinner someday. He had been working on a way to do just that for several years.

The next room was some sort of wet room. There were three handles on ropes for each little stall, and there were thirty stalls. There were also fifty porcelain reverse saddle-style sinks on pedestals with the same three ropes. I gently pulled one rope, and water started to pour. It was cold and refreshing. I washed my face. I then pulled the other, figuring it would dry my face. Wrong! Hot water came out and mixed with the cold water. The two mixed together above the saddle and floated gently down. It started to fill the saddle, so I tried to shut it off. I made it run faster instead. I tried again and made things worse. Finally, I pulled the center rope, and they stopped. I was curious and pulled one rope only. In a short amount of time, the rope returned to its resting position. Though the sink was full about halfway through the pouring, it never overflowed. I was so interested in this I spent hours in that room playing with the ropes. The stalls were a kind of water-cleansing station. You could stand in them, and water poured over your body, and the water would drain down more of those three-inch holes. You could soap up and rinse off. A center rope raised the other two up and turned off the water. Fascinating! As I walked out, I felt another spell. I walked back in and then out. Nothing happened. I walked back in and turned on the water, wet my hands, and turned off the water. I left the room, and a spell went off, and my hands were dry. I decided right then and there—that was my room. It may have been a barracks, but I wanted to use those two rooms.

I checked out the third room, and it was just a busted-up room. Same with the fourth and fifth rooms. The next sets of doors were double and just about where the stairs should be. I opened them, and that's what they were. Now I knew how they reached the library. They came up, entered the barracks, found the spiral stairs, and went down. Darn, if just one of those doors had been locked, my kitchen and library would still be intact. Then it hit me. I saw those ropes and drain holes in the kitchen. There was flowing hot and cold water in the kitchen. Nice.

Only two doors left. I checked the one on the west side. It was trapped. I went back over to the stairs and checked the door there. It looked like it was going into the same room. This door was trapped also. I got out my equipment and said every protection spell I knew. I tried to pick the lock, and a face appeared in the door, and the door talked. Apparently, the door had a trapped sprit.

"Who are you and what do you want?"

I jumped back, startled. It took a moment to catch my breath. "I am the new owner of this tower, and I want to know what I own."

"Where is the captain? This is his office and rooms."

"What captain?"

"Captain Jack Blackard, the Scourge of the Ice Mountains, the Blasphemous Bloody Blade. Where is Captain Blackard?"

I thought to myself, *Nice names. I wonder who occupied this place and how long ago.* I wrote down the information on my map. "Excuse me. Can you tell me anymore about this place? Who lived here before me, what year that was, and what they were like?"

"I would be delighted."

"We exchanged information for hours. I brought her up to date, and she told me as much as she knew of the old residents. I released her sprit from her entrapment. Then I talked to her sister at the other door and released her sprit from the magical entrapment. I escorted their sprits outside and past the trees, and they drifted away. They were heading to a place where their bodies had been entombed long ago in another land. As they were not part of the tower, I did not need them there.

I went back in and up to the second floor. I opened the door to the captain's room from the stair side and entered a nicely furnished office area. There were hundreds of books and records and a magical portal that looked like a window. I had previously checked the outside, and there were no real windows, but this portal showed the outside looking directly at the front of the castle, as if there were a window. I could see people entering and leaving the gate. This was another grand aspect of the tower.

There was one extra door in the south, so I checked it for traps. I did not detect any traps, so I opened the door and was engulfed in deadly cold. Ball of Freeze trap! After I stopped shivering, I reestablished my protection from cold spells and looked for the trap. It took several minutes, but I found it. I did not see any way to disable it without setting it off, so I set it off by cutting the cable that triggered it. Sure enough, another Ball of Freeze engulfed me. I opened the door and entered. This was a military-style bedroom with bed and locker, two nightstands, a small table and chair for study, and a washbasin. There were old uniforms that were crumbly to the touch. I was beginning to think that the mage who had this place last did not understand half of what was here and checked out even less.

There was a door at the south end of the bedroom, so I checked it for traps. I found none, so I carefully tried to open it. It was locked. I stood back and used an Open spell, and—click—it opened. I entered and nearly dropped my chin to the floor. This room was filed with battle dragon gear. These men were dragon riders. The saddles, harnesses, tack and gear, and lances were all there. There was dragon armor for both man and dragon, and weapons with the dragon on the hilt. There was enough to outfit twenty dragons and their riders. I picked up a breast plate big enough to fit an enormous dragon, and it instantly changed to a breast plate about my size. I set it back down. I was already wealthy. In my revenge, I had collected eighteen dragon hordes. But each one of these sets was worth a thousand times more than all my wealth put together. These artifacts were something to tell King Charles about but not the queen. She would sell them. If it got out that I owned even one piece, the entire realm would be looking for ways to remove it from my hands, even if it meant my hands had to be cold and lifeless. Yes, I would tell Charles. He would be glad to know of these. He always took time out for artifacts, and those were major artifacts.

I checked the room for traps and secrets and found none. That was it for the second floor. I went back out and up the regular stairs. At the top, there were double doors to the immediate south. I checked for traps, and there were none, I hoped. I checked for secrets and found none. I checked the doors, and they were locked, so I did another Open spell. Click—open. I pulled the door the rest of the way open and found a fifteen-foot-wide passageway running the entire northern center length of the tower. Across from me was another set of double doors, and down the passageway were two other doors, one north and one to the south. I checked the doors in front of me, and they were locked. Teach me for not looking for traps first. The entire floor shot up and slammed me against the thirty-foot-high ceiling. When it came back down, it did so fast, and I fell the entire way. This caused me to bounce and hit the door, and the stupid floor slammed me against the ceiling again. This time as I fell, I rolled away from the door. I shakily pulled out a wand and worked on healing myself. Difficult to do with both hands broken, trying to protect my head. After healing myself and resting for a few minutes, I buffed up my protection spells, including my reflexes, and tried to find that trap. Slam—drop. It took eight times before I found and disabled the trap. I nearly used up a fully charged wand of Heal Major Injury.

I checked for more traps and secrets. Darn, there was an invisible secret lever on the wall. I pulled it to the center, and the trap snapped back into place. I pulled it all the way down, and the trap snapped out of the way. What—an—idiot. I opened the doors and was standing in a laboratory for making potions, scrolls, wands, rods, staves, and any number of magical devices. There was a good wand charging station and books and records at almost every table. The lab was meant to be used by several wizards or clerics at the same time. It was open space and had parts and ingredients in shelves and chests all over. There was an entire wall of potions and wands. One section held rods, and one small section had staves. There were magical swords and bows. I had everything there to outfit an army if the items were still good. I did a magic check, and most were still magical. I concentrated and found that the potions were in stabilizing fields created to keep them fresh. Most of the ingredients were also in magical fields. This was going to be fun. I checked them a little closer, and each had a tag written in draconic, telling everything about them. These weren't artifacts or anything like that. It appeared that it had been created for a war that never happened.

My best guess was the dragons had departed for the undead lands to fight in the dragon pepper wars. This had been left behind, and so were the riders and their equipment. All this time, the great mages believed that none of the dragon riders' equipment remained. It was generally thought that all twenty sets had been destroyed in the dragon pepper wars.

Something else was in a glass box on the counter. It was in status and protected from time. One plant, and it was easy to determine what it was without reading the sign, Dragon Pepper.

It had long been thought that dragon pepper was extinct. There, in my tower, was the rarest of all plants, and this one was not cursed. All dragon pepper had been cursed before the dragon pepper wars, making it impossible to grow any plants on any plane that the gods had access to. I placed my own protections on the place, the room, and the tower and teleported to the university.

I ran to the room of the bell and slammed the door. I rang twice and waited. Charles showed up nearly immediately. He had a leg of some small animal in his hand, and it was still hot from the cook fire. "What? I was just enjoying a meal."

I did not go to a knee. Instead, I said, "Protect this place so no one can hear what we say, not even the gods."

He looked at me with curiosity. The leg disappeared, and so did we. We were in a druid grove looking out into the stars. We were on the edge of the plane, and looking down was the same as looking up. I quickly stepped back. I'm not afraid of heights, but this was insane. Charles said, "No Worldly God can hear us in this place. What is so important?"

"I am sorry for disturbing you again, King Charles. Can you reach into my mind and see what I just saw?"

His hand came up, and his eyes widened, and as he put out his other hand, in it appeared the glass box. Around us were the twenty sets of dragon rider equipment. He looked at the box with great interest, and a staff was instantly in his hand. I recognized the staff. It was part of his hand, as if the two were one and melded together. He waved the Great Staff of Nature over the box, and the plant came alive. He said, "You know not what you have here, child."

I said, "Dragon pepper, my lord god."

He smiled. "Not just dragon pepper, child. The last and only plant. There is none in the Druid trap where we are at this time and none in any other plane except this one plant. I know, as I have looked long and hard. The Staff of Nature cannot create it, and neither can any of the Worldly Gods. If any god knew you had this, he would take it instantly. With this, a god can command all dragons. They would worship him and no other. It is a dragon's only weakness."

"What should we do with it?"

"I would destroy it instantly, but the dragons need it badly. Do you know why the dragons fought to the death over this spice?"

"No, not exactly, sir. I think it has something to do with reproduction."

He looked at me with curiosity. "What gave you that idea? The university does not preach that." He walked back to the edge and sat on a mossy rock, so I sat across from him.

I answered, "When I was going through the classes on history, we discussed this very issue." I put my hand to a thinking position, resting on chin. "I thought to myself at the time, *What would drive a dragon to kill others of its own color as well as many other colors?* As a woman, only one thing came to mind." My eyes widened, showing my excitement at my discovery. "The right to have a child." I grew serious again. "I told that to the professor, and the entire class laughed."

Charles shook his head with half a smile. "Closed-minded fools. Reproduction is exactly why dragon pepper is so important. The dragon population has been dwindling because eggs are created thin shelled and often unfertilized. You see, the male takes about half an ounce of dragon pepper the night before fertilizing the female. Without it, the fertilizing takes place but is not very potent. The female takes one ounce about six days before prepping the egg for birth. This hardens the shell, which allows it to remain intact during the birthing. Without dragon pepper, only one in a hundred baby dragons are strong enough to live through the first year. With dragon pepper, they reproduce normally. They still lose a few, but losing one in a hundred is far better than only one living."

"I did not know."

"No one knows. The dragons keep it a secret in the hopes that some fool will find some old dried pepper and sell it to them cheap. A dragon would part with his entire treasure for just one and a half ounces."

My eyes went to the path under my feet, and I thought on this for a moment. I finally lifted my head and said, "Sir, we cannot just give them the plant. Whoever we gave it to would keep it for themselves."

"Very good, child. No, we cannot give them the plant. Besides, it can only grow in one place. Somewhere the foolish gods did not curse." He gestured with his hands. "This place right here. The Northern Druid Suppository for Knowledge and Magic. It's a good place to keep your toys also. I think I can trade them for you in such a way that you will gain in all your abilities." He laughed, paused, and then sat down laughing so hard he could not sit. I looked on, wondering what was so funny. This was a serious problem. He sat back up and waved a hand. The plant disappeared. "Right here in the Druid Trap, where Worldly Gods cannot enter, I will grow that plant and multiply it until I have a good-size garden of dragon pepper. Then I will start the drying process. In about thirty days of earthly time, I will have one hundred pounds of dried dragon pepper."

"That would help the dragons greatly."

"Oh, child, we are not just going to give it to them. Oh no. You are going to use it to buy their help. They are going to go insane having to deal with a half-dragon, half-demon, blood exile. I will love watching this, and so will the gods. This will be fun and a big surprise. Did you know that your mother was a princess?"

"Um, no. I'm in exile?"

"Well, sort of. I knew your mother and your father. Your father was a demon lord and prince. The oldest son of King Deathdealler and Queen Laughatyou. Your mother was the youngest daughter of King Split Tail and Queen Long Tongue. I can understand why they didn't tell you. You can imagine the scandal when they married. Both were cast out. Both sides tried several times to kill your parents but gave up when the losses became far too heavy. Your mother and father, what a pair. Good friends. I was there for your hatching."

"I did not know that."

"Why would you? Your father and mother seldom talked about your heritage or their relatives, as they were trying to protect you."

I had to ask, "Do my grandparents know about me?"

He laughed. "You should have seen their faces when I told them the good news."

"You told them? Why?"

"Sam insisted that someone tell his father. Nim decided that if one father knew, then the other should."

"Why did my father want to inform my grandfather?"

"To rub it in of course."

We talked for another hour or so, firming up his plan, at least as far as we could go with the information we had so far. I was not too keen on playing this kind of trick, but he said it would be great and would be talked about for thousands of years up in Caelum. He wrote something on a piece of parchment, used his ring to seal it, and teleported it away.

King Charles said, "This tower holds many surprises. Find any more artifacts, let me know first." With a touch, he sent me directly back to the university. Not because I could not go home but because I shut and locked the door to the bell. I opened it and left the university, then teleported directly into the laboratory at my tower.

CHAPTER 7

NEVER ANGER A GOD

Unknown to me, the parchment ended up in the castle of Queen Iseaia Danberry on the desk of Wizard Formack. Formack picked up the parchment and recognized the seal of King Charles. He broke the seal immediately and read the message.

> To whom it may concern:
>
> It has just been announced to Princess Samantha Altera Woodcutter that her ancestry has been affirmed as the following:
>
> Father: Prince Sam, legitimate oldest son of King Deathdealler and Queen Laughatyou on the 457th plane of the Abyss. Father exiled for turning good and marrying a good-aligned dragon. Father deceased.
>
> Mother: Princess Nim, legitimate youngest daughter of King Split Tail and Queen Long Tongue of the platinum dragons on the Prime

Material Plane. Mother exiled for marrying a demon. Mother deceased.

Status: Princess Samantha Altera Woodcutter, after graduating as a mage from the University of Magic in Sordeath, traveled for 120 years gaining experience and knowledge. She now resides in the Tower of Sight, Temple of Magicum, in the city of Farnorth, in the country of Landtrap, the world of Wellic in the second hub of the Milky Way Galaxy, in the Prime Material Plane.

Affirmed and sealed this day by King Charles.

Pinned on the third day of Rest during the Moon of Storms in the year of the Horned Kitten.

Formack immediately took the letter to Queen Iseaia Danberry. "My queen, my queen. I have irrefutable news about Samantha."

The queen looked up from the table strewn with papers regarding supplies and possible help from different interested countries. So far, every country had promised help with the upcoming war. Though, how much help and when was still to be determined. "Come in, my friend. So, what is this news? I hope it is good. I could use some good news."

"King Charles the Honest and head of my university sent this message." He handed her the letter.

As she read it, her worry lines began to relax a bit. "So, the young lady was telling the truth. Everything she said is confirmed in this letter. Are you sure it came from King Charles?"

"It was his seal and his touch of magic enclosing it, my queen."

"Then, that is one worry off my mind. Now how can we use this?" Their talk went on for hours.

Back at the tower, I had entered the third floor and disabled the trap again. I entered the southern double doors and triple-checked the large laboratory. There was only one other door in the room, and I checked it out. No trap found, no secrets, and no magic other than the normal on the rest of the tower. I opened the door, cringing. It hurts to be smashed against the ceiling and then dropped thirty feet to the floor. I did not want more of the punishment. The door opened, so I walked through and—slam, drop. The trap was on the other side of the door. After healing myself, I looked for secrets and disabled the trap.

This large room had been smashed, so the summoned creatures made it this far. The door to the south was open, so I checked it out. It was the top of the servants' spiral staircase. "That's how they got up here." I checked the northern door, and it was locked. I checked for traps and 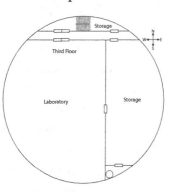 secrets. None found, so I opened the door and checked for traps and secrets before walking through. Same type of trap. I disabled it and walked through. I was back in the passageway. I checked the north door for traps and secrets and found nothing. I tried the door, and it was locked, so I stepped back, and a fireball went off about forty feet down the passageway, directly in front of the two sets of double doors. Nasty trap. If a party of adventurers tried to get in, the rogue checking the door would be safe. However, just after telling everyone else it was safe and stepping back so a fighter could open the door, the trap would go off. It would catch all the rest of the party that had stayed back in case of a trap, now stepping forward because they had been told it was safe. Ta-da, fried adventurers. I stepped up and found the trap. I disabled it and then had to unlock the doors with an Open spell. This magical storage room was intact and filled to the brim with wands and potions. These people were prepared for a big war. There had to be millions of gold pieces worth of magic in the room. All preserved for a time of need. There were also about a hundred artifact lances with different shaped blades. I picked one up and read the attached tag. The trigger was marked on the tag, along with the following information:

> This Shock Lance creates a stuffed lightning bolt with a reach of one thousand feet. Warning: Except when in the hands of a dragon rider, if removed from tower and taken more than one league away, it will return automatically to the tower.

Nice, and I have a hundred of these.

I walked out into the passageway, and the fireball went off again. *Darn. I thought I disabled that.* I shut the door and went to the stairs. "Let's try the fourth floor." I headed up. The stairs ended at the fourth floor, but to my calculations, there had to be at least two or three more floors. I checked the door for traps and found one. I checked for secrets and did not find any. I redid my protections and tried to disable the trap. I did it. I disabled the trap. I check the door to see if it was locked, and I would have dropped a long ways, as a pit to nowhere opened up below me. Luckily, I was using terrain flight and staying a foot off the ground. A second trap. I yelled out, "Nice trick, Magicum."

I checked the door again, and this time I took my time and checked really well. I found three traps. The next one was a dismiss magic. It went off as I was disabling it, and I dropped straight down the hole and continued to fall until my emergency spell went off. It's a simple emergency spell. If I start panicking, I teleport to the university. I was definitely panicking. I teleported back to my tower from the university and walked up to the fourth floor. I realized that I had to wait until I had enough power to cast more spells. I had used most of my middle spells and some of my top. So I returned to the second floor, took a shower, had a magical dinner, and slept in the captain's bed. It wasn't very comfortable, but I was so tired that I slept well.

The next morning, I had a magical Protection Banquet and set my contingency so that I would have Soar (Fly) if my terrain flight ended.

I walked to the fourth floor and worked on disabling the traps. Six attempts before I finally had it. I unlocked the door and checked for more traps. None found, so I walked in. Here was a fantastic sitting room and office area. Someone had a lot of money and used it in there. The problem was evil dungeon décor was not my taste. There were fabric hangings depicting different types of torture, with annotations in demonic on how to lengthen the life of the agonizing subject. Several pictures showed demons with different good-aligned animals being tied and tormented. I was fascinated, but I pulled them all down and did an annihilate spell. Expensive or not, my blood is too close to being evil to have that kind of temptation hanging around. The desk, chairs, and lamps had to go as well. I cleared out all the paperwork and scrolls and then checked for secrets. In the desk was a little compartment. I checked it for traps, and there was a poison needle trap that I disabled after being stuck three times. I opened the compartment and found a tiny ornamental pin in the shape and look of the tower. I did a Find Magic spell, and it was major artifact level. I put it on.

Instantly, I had free access to all areas and knew how to use all items, including the showers. I could control the strength and shape of the water flow. I'd try that tonight. The tower's traps and monsters would obey me and let me through. However, many of the traps were set by others over the centuries, and I had no knowledge of them, except the ones I set off that were not part of the tower defenses. In addition, I had no knowledge of any secrets, yet I already found a couple, so I

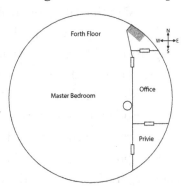

knew they were there. Best bet, continue with what I was doing. I rechecked the desk for secrets and then destroyed the furniture. I could pick up the paper later.

There were three doors in that room, the one in the north I came through, one in the west, and one in the south. The east had a magic window looking out over the east side of the city. I tried the door to the west, and it opened for me as I walked up to it. Nice. I stepped in, and the door closed. Inside, I found the most hideous bedroom I had ever seen. There were skeletons hanging from the walls in various forms of torment, braziers for branding, along with branding irons, and everything needed to cause pain. This bedroom was a perfect chamber for screaming victims. The acoustics would allow the screams to echo off the walls for minutes. The bed was centrally located so that the sleeping demon would have full view and sound of his victims.

I checked everything for anything important and moved the papers, journals, and other writings into the office area. I checked everything for secrets and found several. I opened them and removed the contents. When I was sure I had everything of importance removed, I started doing spells to cleanse the room. I melted all the instruments of torment, cleansed the stains of spilled blood, and removed and melted the manacles, chains, and all that hung from wall and ceiling. When I was done, there was no sign that the room had been anything other than empty with a lot of melted metal bars on the floor. The tower was magnificent. No matter what I did to get rid of the junk, the walls, floors, and ceilings remained clean and free of marks. Nothing damaged the tower. Magicum would hear a few prayers of gratitude for such a tower.

There were three ways into the room: one from the office in the upper east wall, one in the lower east wall, and a spiral staircase in the center of the east wall. I checked the one at the lower end of the east wall. It opened into a nice shower and privy, the automatic type that I found downstairs. Only this one was a private one. It was a mess with bones and dust from dried-up and turned-to-dust bodies. Two simple cleansing spells took care of the whole room. It was now spotless.

I looked at the stairs and started to climb.

"Who is it? What are you doing here? Help me! Oh please help me."

I checked my protection spells, redid a few, and then started up very slowly. Near the top, I could see into the room. It was circular and had magical windows in all directions. Near the north window was a young female. She was in some kind of cage. I came up the rest of the way and started checking the room. I looked out each window except the one behind her. I paid her no attention, though she begged me constantly. My checking allowed me to find

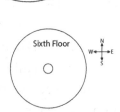

what was radiating the evil. The room was cluttered with more tormenting junk, but the evil came from her.

The spiral staircase went up one more level, so I took it and checked out a small, round room that had a continuous view. It was like I was standing on top of the tower and there were no walls or roof. The wind did not reach me, but when I went over to the side, I saw the guards talking and could hear them as if they were next to me. I looked out over the mountains, and they became closer. I picked out a spot, and it became closer still. I could see anything within my view as if it were next to me. I picked out a vendor in the city, and he became close, and I could hear his conversation with the maid. They were arguing over the price of carrots.

I went down on one knee and said, "Magicum, this is the most wonderful tower I have ever seen or heard of. Thank you."

Instantly I was taken over. I felt the god inside me, and he was angry. I walked against my will down to the floor below and turned to the female in the cage. She hissed.

I asked, "What are you doing in my tower, pretending to be a prisoner, and a female one at that, Selob? So, this is where you've been hiding. Your old owner, Advorsa, has been looking for you."

As soon as I heard Selob, the demigod of torment, and Advorsa, the god of slaughter, I tried with all my abilities to cast spells at it. I had no chance. Magicum said inside me, "Stop, child. This is beyond you."

The cage and the female disappeared, and an ugly, bent little man was in her place. "I am here because I want this tower and all that is in it for my servant. It has been consecrated to me. It no longer belongs to you."

Magicum was getting mad, and he was showing it in a thunderstorm that was building inside the temple. "This is my artifact. My temple. No minor consecration spell can change that.

My champion has dispelled almost all of them and will finish dispelling the rest when we are finished. It will be reconsecrated to me. This is my tower temple and has always been my tower temple. I made it before the making of the mountains, and I alone can power it. It is my first temple in this hub of the galaxy. As you can see, it is now clear of most the minor little spells your fools placed in and on it. This child is mine, and as she is in my tower and has prayed to me. I claim her. She fought for and won this tower from the foolish mistakes your old champion made." My tone changed to one of threatening. "Now, be gone and never return to my temple."

My hands started to rise, and Selob ran out of the tower. I watched, and as soon as he was outside, the trees nearly tore him to pieces before he disappeared. I said, "Two things, my god. How can I be yours? Though I would love to be, I am not neutral. And why did he run out? He is a demigod and could remove himself directly from the room."

In my head, I heard, "Child, you have so much to learn. I will help. You are close enough to my alignment that I can put up with the goodness you exhibit. I have some champions that are borderline evil and need some good to balance. I will never ask you to do anything evil, as your blood would turn you too quickly. It is a fine edge you walk, child. In addition, this is and will always be my temple. No god, other than I, can enter or leave magically without my permission. You have won it. It is yours to straighten out and live in. Become my high priestess and arch mage." He was gone, and I fell to the ground.

CHAPTER 8

TRAP LEVEL

I must have fallen asleep, as I awoke to the sound of birds flying by and squawking. Geese, noisy creatures. I climbed the stairs to the top floor and checked the time. The sun was just coming up. I slept until morning. I used a wand of Find Secrets and checked everything all the way down to the first floor. Then I started setting my own spells. Protections, illusions, cleansings, cleaning, everything I needed to ensure that no one would take this tower from me and to clean the stench of evil from the place. I consecrated every inch of it to Magicum. Now I could clear out the stuff in the bottom and do a comprehensive job of clearing, cleaning, and consecrating the basements. Still, I could feel a great evil. It was coming from below.

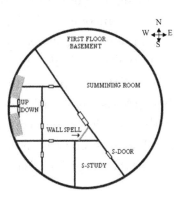

I spent the next two days moving furniture, putting up wall hangings, placing statues, and making my house into a home. Then I started on the basement. I traveled down to the first floor of the basement and rechecked the rooms I had just been in. I found nothing new. I destroyed the stone wall and mended the wall into the secret room. I checked out the last two rooms and found that one went to another set of stairs going down. That door was locked and triple trapped. The other door led to a wine cellar. Shame. That room was not locked, and all the wine had been drank, and the bottles and shelves broken. I took the stairs down.

The stairs ended in a passageway heading southeast and following the curve of the wall above. This level was different. There were foot-wide bright green orbs on four-foot-tall pedestals every ten feet that glowed. The place was all white and perfectly clean. I did a couple of spells and identified it as Laststoneite. That could only mean one thing. Something extremely important was down there. I already figured out that the mage who had the tower last did not use most of it. Probably afraid of traps. Couldn't blame him. If I were not half-demon and half-dragon and tough as nails, I would have died on the third floor. The mage did not make it down this far, which reminded me to refresh all my power-up spells.

There were bones and armor down there. The monsters did not come this way, but early adventurers did. I checked out some of the bones and rusted armor. I did not recognize any of the symbols. These items were ancient, and there was nothing usable. Someone or something had picked the bodies clean of anything worth a copper. Normally, when you come across a body that no one else has found, there are at least a few gold pieces. On these bodies, there was nothing. I checked out the first orb, and it was major artifact level and had something to do with travel. It was not dangerous, so I left it alone.

The first door was on my right. I started to check it for traps, but the trap magically disabled itself as soon as the magical tower pin came within a few feet. I clearly heard a click and whirl. I opened the door, and there was a blank wall. I checked the blank wall for secrets and found none.

Next were two doors, one on each side of the passage. I opened the one on the right first. It opened into a strangely shaped room. The ceiling was only twenty feet tall, making it the shortest room in the tower. In the center back of the room stood a statue and more orbs with broken rock picks and smashed two-handed sledgehammers on the floor. Somebody had tried to destroy the statue and could not harm the Laststoneite, so they defaced it dramatically. It was difficult to tell what the statue was about. I walked into the room and heard several clicks, and arrows shot past me as I ducked and rolled. I saw the arrows come out of a section of the wall in the back and annihilated those areas. It looked like Laststoneite, but I was wearing the tower pin and should not have had any problems with traps. Both walls turned to dust, leaving blank sections of real wall and another orb. The only things in the room now were the statue, orbs, and a short kneeling platform. The statue was covered in some sort of sticky, black, poisonous substance. It smelled like demon piss and feces. I did a couple of cleaning spells, and everything came off.

The statue was of Magicum, and there was a glowing rod in his folded arms. The rod was embedded into the Laststoneite of the right hand. I said to myself, "Well, my tower has a shrine to my new god." I did a couple of consecration spells to Magicum and knelt in prayer.

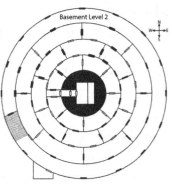

Basement Level 2

"Thank you, Magicum, for giving me a place to worship you. I hope I am pleasing you."

I never was much for dialogue with someone who did not hold up their part of the conversation. I got up and continued my exploration. I paid no attention to the rod. It was in his hands for a reason and belonged to him, so I left it there. The door on the left was a blank wall. In fact, the next twenty-one doors were blank walls. I ended up at the back of the stairs. I was becoming discouraged. I took out my wand of Find Secrets and started back around, looking for other ways in. It figured. There was a secret door right next to the stairs where I started. I had to use four charges on the wand to find one secret door.

I checked for traps on the door and found three. Two were disabled when I came close, but one was not part of the tower. I tried to disable it and failed. Even with my protections on, my cloak caught fire and went up in smoke. *Darn. That was a good cloak.* I added a few more spells to my protections to make up for the loss of the cloak and tried again. I disabled it this time, and now I had to unlock the door. I took my time, and—click—it opened.

I walked into a room with five doors, counting the one I had just come through, and found orbs, the bones of other adventurers, some rusted armor, and weapons. I checked for magic and found nothing except the orbs. I checked for secrets and found none. I tried every door, and three led to blank walls, but the one south was a good door. I thought to myself, *Every door is trapped by one or two traps. Anyone trying to enter this place without the pin would be fighting traps all the way. The chances of actually making it this far was slim unless you were incredibly good. This place is deadly.*

I proceeded into the next room, and it had five doors, orbs, and dead creatures. This time, there was magic and gold on several of the creatures. I checked out their equipment, and they had far more than they should have had. These were the ones robbing the dead in the other rooms. They had made it this far, and then a trap killed them all. I opened my special space and stripped everything off the creatures that was worth anything.

The cloaks I kept out. I did magic Know All spells to find out what the cloaks did. One was better than the one I just lost. I put it on and placed the others into my space. I closed the space and then checked the doors.

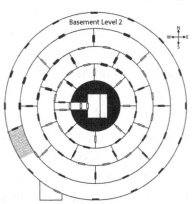

Three of the doors ended in blank walls, but one led into another room. I had to backtrack to the stairs and return to get my bearings. The east-side door to the north was the good one. I opened it and entered a room that had six doors and two orbs. No bodies this time. It was possible that no one had made it this far before. I checked all the doors and found that the south-side door heading east was the good one. There seemed to be only one good door in each room. This was tedious but simple.

I opened that door and entered a room with five doors, and I instantly fell up, tripping a rope trap that snagged me. Gravity was reversed in this room, and I was hanging right-side up about ten feet off the ground. There were several sets of bones on the ceiling. They probably died because they did not have the password for magical travel. I did a simple Shift spell to the last room and fell ten feet because I forgot that gravity was upside down in the other room. Ouch! The other doors were now out of reach. You try disabling traps while upside down and thirty feet away. Good luck! The only thing keeping me alive was the tower pin. I placed a Terrain Fly spell on me so that I would not fall again and so I could reach the doors. I checked each door, and the east-side door in the north was the correct one. I opened the door and carefully entered. I instantly flipped over and flew down to the bottom.

Another room with six doors. I checked each door and looked for secrets. I lost track of what the direction was, so I'll say the door at the far end, small wall was the good door. I went through and entered another room with six doors. I checked all the doors, and both doors on my right were good. What next? Decisions, decisions. I took the closest door and entered a room with five doors and something lurking in the far corner.

It slowly stood up and screamed at me. It looked like a very large ape. It had arm muscles bigger than me. It started lumbering forward, so I shut the door. It took only a moment for the creature to bang on the door, and it sounded and looked to me like the Laststoneite might not hold. Apparently it did not have the intelligence to open the door, and I could not touch its mind through the Laststoneite. What to do, what to do. *I know!* I waited for the creature to quiet down and then opened the door and placed a Force Confinement around it. It had returned to its corner, and now it was up and banging on the bars of the confinement. I did a Speak with Animal spell. Didn't help. I did a Comprehend Language. That didn't help. I had never seen this type of creature, and it wasn't in the library at the university. Thinking, I said, "I wonder." I did a Deportation spell with the password, and the creature vanished. It was an outsider. I said to myself, "I hope in my travels I don't run into that creature's plane of existence. That thing could have snapped a stone giant in two."

I checked the doors, and they were all dead ends. I went back into the other room and opened the door to the next room.

There were five doors in this room, and two were dead ends, one I just came through, and two led to other places. Seemed like every room had two things in general, dead ends and orbs. I listened this time before opening the door. Nothing. I opened the door on my left. Blank room with six doors. I walked in and started sinking. I flew up and had a difficult time getting loose. If I didn't have flight on me already or know the password, I would have never gotten free. The floor started to move, so I departed that room quickly while slamming the door on my way out. The floor slammed the door also, and it opened. I hit it with fire, acid, and cold in rapid succession. It went back in and closed the door. "What was *that*?"

It took a moment for my heart to calm down, and before it did, my contingency went off. As the emergency spell is a travel spell and I forgot to use the password, it did nothing except remind me to use the password. I applied my emergency spell to teleport to the university in case of panic and reopened that door. Nothing happened. I flew gently over the floor and checked each door. All were dead ends. I wondered how many died trying to find that out.

I left that room and headed into the next room, realizing I was going to soon be lost if I didn't do something. I tried to mark the rooms, but Laststoneite could not be written on. I flew back to the first rooms and picked up twenty small finger bones. I placed one in front of each good door, not the ones leading to monsters. I checked out the next room of five doors. Only the one on my far left was a good door, so I opened it and walked in. This room had two other good doors. I had been taking the right side, so I stuck with that. It led to a room with five doors and another creature.

This time, I was prepared and placed a Fire Barrier between him and the doors. I checked each door, and there was another good door at the far end. *Darn. I was hoping this was another dead end.* Now I had to get rid of the creature. It looked familiar, so I shifted through my memory while studying it. *Let's see. Looks like a dog, mouth has no teeth, makes a circle with his lips when screaming, nice coat of fur, thin coat for hot climates—oh nasty, a Shift Screamer.* That's why it was screaming. Its major weapon was its deadly scream. In fact, it had no other weapon. I placed a silent spell on the room center and dropped the force wall. It screamed, and nothing came out. It looked surprised and then tilted its head as I sat down next to it. I let it sniff me, and then I gently petted it. The poor thing had probably been summoned there. Nice magical trap. I didn't hear anything, and the tower pin did not stop it.

I looked all around for the trap and found it. A little sigil set in the top of the doorframe. Open the door, and off it goes. I cut it off with my knife and broke it on the floor. I went back over and comforted the dog until its time was up and it disappeared, returning to its home. This room had another door that was good, so I went over to it and opened it. There was nothing in that room, and all the doors led to blank walls. I checked for secrets and did not find any. I went back out to the room with the doors I had not finished yet.

The other door led to a room with four doors. Two besides the one I came in were good doors leading to someplace. I had been going to my right, so I continued doing the same. The next five rooms only had one direction I could go, but the traps were becoming more deadly. They deactivated due to the tower pin but in several instances I could tell by the sound and the feeling that I had just gone through something insanely nasty. In one spot, the hairs stood up on my body, and in another, I felt dread so strong I almost turned around to leave.

In the final room, there were only two blank doors and one

secret door. I would have never found it except I was using the wand. By my calculations and the size of the room, I was four layers deep in the maze. I checked the secret door and opened it. This room was very small compared to the others, but it still had an orb. It was only fifteen feet long by ten feet wide. There was a door directly across from me, so I checked it out. It led to a blank wall. I checked for secrets and found another door. I checked it out and opened it. Another small room, but this one was different. The room was ten feet by ten feet, and there were spikes sticking out about two feet on each side. This was the first room with no orbs. There were gaps at the edges, making it look like the walls, floor, or ceiling could move inward. I prepared a Force Barrier and an Orb of Protection spell just in case. All I needed to do was trigger them. I walked in, and nothing happened except my tower pin glowed. I walked through to the door on the other side.

The door was not locked. I opened it, and there was another ten-by-ten-foot room. This one had no walls, floor, or ceiling—nothing except a floating door on the other side. I still had Terrain Flight on me, so I floated over. It was really unnerving floating in space like that. I checked the other door, and it was locked. The pin glowed, and the door unlocked. I opened it and floated into a space about fifteen feet by forty feet, full of gold, jewels, gems, art, and hundreds of other things piled thirty feet high. I checked for magic, and there was none. I figured I had found the vault and this was the end, but just in case, I used the wand and

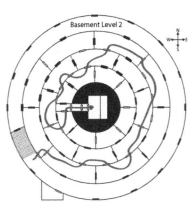

Basement Level 2

MAKING OF A GODDESS   93

checked for secrets. I found another door. I had to move a bunch of stuff out of the way, but after I did there, was a panel that slid into the wall. I walked into a ten-by-forty-foot room filled with items. I prepared myself and checked for magic. It was full of magic, and everything was artifact level. There was a lever on the wall marked in a language that I did not know, and all the spells I have could not decipher it. I left it alone.

I checked for evil, and this is where the great evil was. I magically called out, "King Charles," but nothing happened. I prayed to Magicum, but nothing happened. I tried to teleport, but nothing happened. I walked out of the room and shut the door. I studied the treasure room for an hour and then teleported out. I was on the steps of the university, so I removed the tower pin. I was not ready to explain things about the tower, and people did not need to see the tower key.

CHAPTER 9

UNIVERSITY POLITICS

I walked in and toward the room with the bell. As I did, two mages met me. They both bowed lower than any had bowed before. One said, "The Grand Council would like to talk to you, Great Mage."

I asked, "Did they say what this is about? I have no time for politics."

He looked shocked. "I am only a messenger, Princess Samantha."

Crud! They found out that I have royal blood. Heck, I just found out. Who told them? I asked, "Are they in session?"

"Princess Samantha, they will be very shortly. As we speak, mages and apprentices are running throughout the university to gather the council."

I said, "Very well. Lead on." They took me to the council chambers, a place I was very familiar with for reasons both good and bad." The council chamber was made so that there was a little center area where the student stood, and raised six feet up were the rows of chairs for the masters surrounding the poor child. It was like a small stadium and made the student feel smaller and the masters look like gods. It used to intimidate me greatly. Not so anymore. As I walked in, most of the council was in the center waiting for me. I was greeted enthusiastically—shaking my hand, patting me on the back, saying nice things. In short, treating me completely different from any time in the past. Something was wrong, and it wasn't just my blood.

The council climbed the small stairs into the seating area and sat down. I saw Formack in the first row. "Hello, Master Formack. Master Ohm says hello. How is our queen?"

He smiled. "She is doing much better now that King Charles has affirmed her of your royal status and vouched for you."

"Oh, so it was King Charles that set me up. I'll have to have a talk with him. I was just going to see him until this council sidetracked me. I need his advice on a small matter."

The head of the council banged the gavel several times. "Let's get this started. Princess Samantha Altera Woodcutter, we have been informed that you are in the possession of the Tower of Sight. Is this correct?"

So, that was it. The Tower of Sight. I wondered if they knew something I did not. "Grand Master Kelon, I am the proud sole owner of the Temple of Magicum called the Tower of Sight. Why?"

He looked at me as if I were a child. "You cannot own the Tower of Sight. It belongs to the clerics of Magicum and therefore the University of Magicum. You will turn over everything pertaining to the tower immediately."

I looked at him with puzzlement. "Grand Master, are you saying that all artifacts found by a mage that attended this university automatically belong to the university, or that the university has the right to say where they belong even if the mage no longer attends the university or does not hold any positions there in?"

Master Ohm looked over at the grand master. "I told you it wouldn't be that easy. You cannot bully your way or use your position to obtain this one's property."

The council started talking amongst themselves, and the grand master had to bring order back by banging with his gavel. It was a magical gavel and made a big boom. "Order! Order!" When things got quiet, he turned to me and said, "Do you know what you have, child?"

"Yes. Do you?"

He huffed up and said, "Don't be impertinent, child."

"Call me child again, and I will leave. I am not subject to the council. Your position places you over students, not graduates. I will ask again. Do you have any idea what I have?"

He smiled. "Far more than you can guess. It is said that the tower was made several thousand years ago by clerics of Magicum. He blessed it himself. And that it was defiled by demons."

I smiled back. "Let me straighten you out. According to Magicum, our grand god of magic, the tower was made by Magicum and not by clerics. It was made before the mountains it rests in. How it got there I am not sure. Magicum made it and blessed it as his first temple in this hub of the galaxy. True, it was defiled by demons, devils, and other creatures, but I have taken care of that issue. Most of it is now consecrated to Magicum, as per my wishes and his request. I have talked with Magicum about the tower and who should run it. It is and will always be mine. I am becoming a high priestess to Magicum as well as his arch mage. Why not? I already know most divine and arcane spells and have used many of them."

They started yelling and shouting around the chamber, some saying I was lying and others saying I couldn't lie in that place. In truth, King Charles placed spells on the room to keep people honest, but I knew ways around them. However, right then, I did not need to lie.

I did a spell that raised my voice. "Excuse me." Everyone grabbed their ears, and some fainted. I lowered my voice. "Excuse me, but I am a busy person. I do not have time for this foolishness. If you have questions, I will be happy to answer them. If you want something from me, we can talk about that. However, if all that's going to happen is my standing here while you argue over my honor, then I have better things to do. Some of you have been prejudiced against me since before I was born. You showed it in your teachings and actions. If you do not like me, that's too bad. I don't care. There are enough good people in this room to more than make up for your foolishness. If you cannot look at my actions and see that I am good, then I feel sorry for you. The Great God Magicum took me on as his with the understanding that I am somewhat goodly aligned. He does not care. He needs me, and I need him. I do not need you telling me that I cannot be one of his clerics. He said to me about the tower, 'You have won it. It is yours to straighten out and live in. Become my high priestess and arch mage.' He needs me to keep his temple blessed; therefore, I am going to have to do divine spells. I have no real choice. I am an arch mage, and I have the power to do spells at twelfth circle, both arcane and divine. I do not need you yelling at me that I cannot do what my god has ordered me to do."

It was deathly quiet. None of them could do ninth circle in one discipline, and I just claimed twelfth in two disciplines. That would make me a grand arch mage and pope capable of taking the head place at the council table. Grand Master Kelon asked in a demanding and unbelieving tone, "Can you prove your statement of level?"

King Charles instantly appeared. "She could, but I would

prefer that my university remain intact." He placed a hand on my shoulder and said, "Calm." Instantly, I felt calm. He continued while moving toward the council table. "I have a contingency on my school. If it is in danger, I am instantly notified. The danger was not coming from Samantha. She was willing to be nice, but someone was going to physically attack her to test her statement." He looked at the master on the far end of the table. "And in her anger, she would have leveled this university to destroy the fool. I am here, and I will take over the council for a moment, if you don't mind, Grand Master?"

The head of the council could not leave his seat quickly enough. Everyone shifted down one chair, and another chair was brought up for the council member bumped off the end.

Charles said, "It has been a long time since I sat here. It's not very comfortable." He touched his forehead, and the Star Fire, the ultimate truth stone, flared brightly, ensuring everyone knew that lying would be deadly. Even the gods did not lie in front of a fully powered Star Fire. "Now, Princess Samantha, please tell us in your own words what has happened so far with the tower." In my mind, I heard, "Leave out the items you gave me earlier please."

I stood there and told them all about the tower, except the password and the tower pin key, which I had removed and placed in my pocket before going there. I played down the treasure and played up the furniture from King Charles. I told no one about any of the artifacts. I only said that there was one last room I needed to discuss with King Charles.

They were astounded. I had met two gods, removed traps, and done spells they could never do, and they could not dispute anything said while that Star Fire was flaring. Master Ohm asked, "Magicum was in you, or acting through you, when he confronted the god of slaughter?"

"He was in me, part of me. I was completely taken over, and I allowed it. And it was Selob, the demigod of torment who is a servant of the god of slaughter."

One master said, "As if you could have stopped it."

I smiled. "Correct. I had no choice in that, and I have little choice in what I am doing now. The tower temple is Magicum's, and I am the custodian appointed by Magicum and willing to do his bidding."

King Charles asked, "Are you willing, after you have it straightened out and fully consecrated it, to have others visit and some clerics stay at the temple?" In my mind, I heard him say, "Think on that, as they will hold you to it."

I stood there thinking as fast as I could. I said, "I do not know. I would have to say it depends on the one visiting or the cleric wishing to stay."

The sound of voices started to increase, and Charles stood up. It went back to deadly quiet. He sat down and said, "I think they need an explanation of that last statement."

I looked at him with concern and said, "You know my blood. I walk a blade of fire. I am currently good aligned, and I wish to stay that way. I can ill afford to be surrounded by anyone evil or close to evil, and many of you have proven to me that I cannot trust you. I will not allow you into my home."

The talk increased, and Charles stood up again. He sat down when it became quiet and addressed the council. "Considering the circumstances and realizing that she has made a choice to be good and wants to remain that way, and that someone of her power would not be good for this university or this world if she turned evil, I have to agree with her." He turned to me. "I would hope that you are setting protections?"

I smiled at him. "Of course. If I did not, Master Ohm would have me in his office, chewing me out for hours, saying, 'Didn't you learn anything while you were here?'"

Some laughed and said, "Been there."

Charles asked, "When will the tower be ready for living and study? I would like a tour."

I said, "Point of fact, I need to talk with you about some things, so a tour could happen with you right now. For everyone else, give me a week please. As Formack has probably told you, there is need for war mages in Farnorth. I would be happy to house good-aligned mages and clerics in my tower until the issue is over. On that note, I need a tower staff. People I can trust."

Formack said, "The queen wants to talk to you about housing some soldiers. She will provide you with a tower staff if you agree. After I talk with her about your situation, she will ensure they are all trustworthy and good aligned."

I smiled. "That would be most helpful, Master Formack. Please tell the queen that I have no problems having her people watch me and reporting to her. They can watch the other guests who will be there and maybe save me some issues."

Formack blushed. "Hard putting anything over on you, isn't it?"

"It is fun that you try, but I can feel the energy of the Star Fire, and it talks to me."

Charles said in my mind, "That is not supposed to happen. We will definitely have a talk. I will meet you in the foyer of your tower."

I said to everyone, "I must return. I have much to do if I am going to be ready in one week."

Charles stood up and said, "Council adjourned."

Most said goodbye and shook hands and gave hugs. Some apologized for thinking I was lying, and one apologized for thinking about attacking me to obtain proof. There were a few noted holdouts. They were mostly people known for being evil oriented. I teleported out of the university and into my foyer. Charles was there seconds after I arrived.

Charles asked, "Did you note the holdouts?"

"Yes, sir, I saw and will be watching my back."

"Good for you. Now hold still while I check something." He placed his hands on my face and did two spells. "Just as I thought. You have grown to near demigod level. Be careful. The gods will be watching you very closely now. No wonder Magicum wants you as a champion. Gods love having control over demigods. So, what was so important?"

I looked at him in shock but continued with a tour, showing him the preparations for some long-forgotten war. I showed him the lances. He took eighty of them, leaving me with twenty to use in guarding during the upcoming war. As soon as he teleported them away, they returned. We checked, and the armor had returned also. He looked perplexed and did some spells I had never seen before, but I knew those spells now. I am a very fast learner. He said, "These artifacts are set to this tower. Magicum did not want them to go anyplace else. This tower powers them." He did a few more spells. "The darn tower flies!"

"Flies?"

Charles shook his head, saying, "Magicum's lost Flying Fortress. That god had it all along and forgot about it. I bet he is up there rolling around in his temple with laughter. He knows I was looking for this. Well, I don't need it now. That issue is over with. You, my dear, have two things you had no clue you had: the lost Flying Fortress of Sight and immortality."

CHAPTER 10

GODHOOD

I had to ask, "Immortality?"

"Yes, Samantha, you have grown. Since the demigod Selob was on this world and in this temple, Magicum had the chance to come to his temple and chase him out. He could have done it personally, but that would have overbalanced good, and evil would have had its way on this world. So, he used you. You must have prayed to him, and that opened a channel. Now, the only way to use you with any chance of harming Selob would be to increase you to a level capable of holding one of his aspects. You housed a full god in your body for a few minutes. To do this, Magicum had to do several things: temporarily stop you from dying, raise your life essence to a level high enough to withstand his vestige and live to tell about it, and grant you vessel privileges."

"Vessel privileges?"

Charles laughed. "Personally, I would be totally upset that a god took me over in that way."

I smiled. "I love Magicum. If I were to pick a god, he would be my pick."

Charles said, "Good fit then. Besides, you already picked. That one act of prayer and allowing him entrance was enough. Vessel privileges are simple. You are now a high priestess of Magicum. You can contact him and talk with him without being diminished through the act. Normally, contacting a god, except through prayer, costs part of your essence. This is not true for a high priestess. You have an open channel. Do yourself a favor and don't use it unless you absolutely need to. Pray. He will listen. He likes good, sincere, loving prayers. Don't pray just for the sake of praying. He is busy and will eventually stop listening. All men are like that."

I said, "I've noticed."

Charles smiled. "Men don't understand women, and women don't understand men, and it will always be that way until people start to realize there is nothing to understand. Everyone is different and therefore, as a group, impossible to figure out. Someday you may fall in love. If that happens, spend a lifetime trying to understand just that one person."

I said, "Sounds difficult. I was going to contact you for a good reason."

Charles became all business. "And what would that be?"

"I have found an entire room of artifacts, and something in there is major evil. It's what is radiating the evil in this place."

He put out a hand, saying, "Let me see."

I took his hand and teleported him to the treasure room. He said, "How nice. All in one month, you become a high priestess of Magicum, an immortal, and on your way to demigod hood. You obtain the Flying Fortress of Sight, and now you are also very wealthy. I'd marry you if I wasn't already filthy rich."

The laugh in his voice said he was joking, but it was a shock to me. "I don't think I'll tell anyone about the treasure. Besides, I have far more than this hidden away. The artifacts are in that room." I pointed to the secret door and showed him how to enter. He looked amused. After entering, he noticed the lever and sign I could not read.

Charles said, "This writing is in the language of Musillatics. It is a musical language. The sign reads 'Pull lever to raise wall.'" He did a couple of simple spells and walked over to an object resembling a small globe. "How interesting. This is the Great Ball of Unbalance. I thought this was destroyed a long time ago. Magicum must have hidden it here."

I asked while looking closer, "The Great Ball of Unbalance?"

Charles put up a hand and said, "Stand way back please."

I moved to the door.

Charles went into a lecturing tone. "The Great Ball of Unbalance was a less than practical joke by the Over Gods some thousand or so years ago. Things were in perfect balance on the World of Crystals, and the gods made the mistake of bragging about how well things were going. One god, I believe it was Dimidims of the Halflings, had the audacity to say that even the Over Gods could not mess this world up. Things were perfect and had been for over a hundred years. As soon as she said it, this ball showed up near her feet."

"I have never heard of the World of Crystals. Is it nice there?"

Charles picked up the ball, and I saw a fight going on in him. It took only a moment before his hands seemed to take control of the ball and it absorbed into his body. "I wouldn't know if it was nice or not. As soon as Dimidims picked up the ball, the entire world became unbalanced and destroyed itself. Nearly destroyed Dimidims."

There was a worried look on my face. "Why did it not destroy us when you picked it up?"

King Charles saw my look and said, "Because I am stronger and more powerful and because I am powered by the artifacts that the Over Gods left behind. When I find one, I remove it. It becomes part of me and increases my abilities, but most important, it is removed from the possibility of it falling into the wrong hands. At first, the Over Gods did not like me becoming so powerful. Now they point me to some of their old artifacts so that I can take them out of use. They are dangerous and should not be allowed to remain where evil or good can get their hands on them. My absorbing them does not harm the Over God, and therefore they are using me to get rid of artifacts no longer needed."

"I most heartily agree."

His entire body turned and focused on me. "This temple is powerful. In the wrong hands, it could be a devastating weapon. Eventually, you will find out all its powers. Don't use it improperly. Magicum would be most unpleasant if you do."

"I will remember. I have no intentions of using it for anything other than a home."

Charles smiled. "Good. That is a great way to look at it. A very nice place to live. Safe, secure, good place to study. However, you are going to let others in. Keep this area off-limits. The controls are over there." He pointed to several panels in the corner. "With those controls, you could fly this tower anywhere on this planet. I believe you could even move it to another planet if needed. I may borrow it from you sometime. With your permission of course."

I said, "Of course."

He looked upset and walked over to another item—a long thin rod shaped like the arm of a mad monster. "What do we have here?" He picked it up, and it tried to crawl up his arm. With a touch, he stopped it immediately. "Know what this is, Samantha?"

I walked over and examined it without touching. "No idea. May I do some spells?"

"Of course."

I completed a Myth spell and knew what he held. "That is the Arm of Destruction. If it is allowed to form on your arm completely, you would never be able to remove it short of cutting off your arm to the neck. It is evil and will cause you to destroy anything and everything of goodly nature within sight until someone kills you. Then it reverts back to a small figurine of an armored arm. The next one who touches it becomes the next destroyer. It is a cursed item."

"Very good. You have a lot of evil artifacts here. Some did not start out evil, but after being locked in the same room with the ball, they became evil. Their gods would not be pleased. Do you know the story of my gaining power?"

I looked puzzled at the change of subject. "Yes, sir. Everyone knows. It's required reading."

"Good. Take hold."

I touched his hand, and I and all my artifacts were instantly in a room with several creatures that looked barely humanoid. Charles whispered, "These are Leaches. They like artifacts. Let me do the talking."

We walked out of their office with ten times the artifacts we entered with, except the new ones were not powered up and therefore not functional. We teleported directly to a temple on the same system. An old man met us at the door with many acolytes that immediately took the artifacts inside. He looked at Charles. "Playing your game again, Charles?" He looked at me, saying, "Some people never learn."

Charles went to the man and hugged him. "Princes Samantha, this is Commeatus the Traveler."

I went to the ground, immediately prostrating myself. Charles said to Commeatus, "She's not used to gods yet."

Smiling, Commeatus said, "At least your ward shows some respect. Get up, girl! For goodness' sake. You can't do business with the gods if you're always eating dirt. Get up and face me."

I stood up and looked him right in the eye but turned away after just a short time.

Commeatus said, "This one has a god. Magicum will be upset with this arrangement if he is not included at the beginning."

Charles said, "Then we will call him. Many of these artifacts are his. Samantha, pray to Magicum and tell him where we are."

Magicum appeared on the steps with us. "I suppose this is your idea, Charles?"

I returned to the ground. Magicum said, "Stand, child, and stay standing. It is proper that you fell to the ground for me, but it is not for anyone else. One knee for the others if you want to show respect, or a very low curtsy, but do not prostrate yourself for another god. That is reserved for me and is only required at the first meeting of the day." He looked me up and down, waved his hand, and I was in a tight-fitting gown of purest blue, with gold lace trim and symbols of Magicum on the front and back. A major change from my trap-finding equipment. "Your equipment is back in my tower. This is what I prefer my priestess to wear when with other gods."

"As you wish, my god."

Magicum turned to Commeatus. "You are correct, my friend. I do wish to be present. I can feel many of my toys in your room of trading. This will be fun, but this time let's call in each god separately. No sense bringing undue notice on the proceedings." He tapped Charles's forehead for emphasis, and the Star Fire glared. Both gods laughed. Charles was not laughing.

Charles said, "Afraid of party crashers?"

Both Magicum and Commeatus exclaimed, "Yes!"

We moved into the temple and into a room where the artifacts were taken, sorted, and set into places around tables. Magicum said, "Thank you, Charles, for removing the Ball of Unbalance. I could not go into that room for fear of triggering it."

Commeatus nearly turned white. "The Ball of Unbalance. What in the hidden hells were you doing with that?"

Magicum said, "After the devastation and while it was still charging, I took it and placed it in the safest place I could think of. The problem is, that made it impossible for me to use my own temple for more than a few minutes at a time. Therefore, I forgot all about the temple and the ball. Charles took care of the problem."

Commeatus turned to Charles. "We know what the Over Gods have been using you for, and personally, I agree with them. It's time some of the most dangerous items were removed. But watch your back. Others do not like the idea that you may show up some day and take the Over God artifacts that they covet."

Charles said, "Tell them that I have no intention of taking any of their prize possessions unless they allow them into the hands of someone that misuses them. When that happens, they don't deserve them anymore. Especially if I have to do cleanup after their followers cause a big mess."

Magicum said, "You know, Charles, you're the new kid on the block, so to speak, and some of the gods do not like your attitude. Some feel you treat them like they are below you. You no longer go to one knee, and you do not prostrate yourself to anyone. You try to treat us like we are your friends. Most are not."

Charles sadly said, "True. I tried to act like they are my friends to make them more comfortable around me and with what I am doing. It was not working. I tried to go to one knee and prostrate myself at the start, but they took advantage of my acting like they are above me. Some came to me insisting that I do this or that. My gods had to order me to stop showing respect and start telling them no. That made me a lot of enemies. I am now trying to just be myself. I act the way I am. If the gods don't like it, then so be it. I can't seem to please them no matter what I do."

Commeatus said to Magicum, "Finally, he's learning. It took long enough." He turned to me and said, "When Charles first came to me, he was full of hope, had a voice and used it, and said whatever came to mind whether it caused me issues or not. Lately, he has changed to a reserved god that is irritatingly closed to us. Learn from Charles's lesson and be yourself always."

Magicum added, "Samantha, remember I said I would never ask you to do something evil?"

"Yes, my lord god."

"I said that because I do not want you to change. I will take you just the way you are. If I tried to change your nature, your drive, your essence, you would not be you, and I would no longer want you as my disciple. Always, always be yourself. If you do something I don't like, I will let you know. But don't be afraid to do it if that is what you think is needed."

Commeatus added, "Two bits of advice, Samantha. First, if you can take care of a problem, do so. Pray to Magicum and tell him what you plan to do so he is not in the dark and then do it. Don't expect Magicum to fix all your problems. He has worshippers on 183,000 planets and has no time for minor issues that you may consider emergencies. Second, don't blame him for all your troubles. Some of my followers tend to blame me for silly issues, as if I would take the time to personally punish them for something. It irritates me, and I stop listening to them. That's when others can come in and mess with them. Don't be foolish and blame your god for what happens on your world. When the Clear Water Valley went up in fire, all the gods were cursed by many. The fools had no idea what it took to ensure that they were taken care of in the Sordeath, nor what would have happened if we did not channel all that energy into Shadow Mountain. Charles knew. He could have stopped what we were doing, but he chose not to. He knew better. He was one of the few. Of course, when they found out what we, with Charles's help, had waiting for them, we were all praised. It is difficult to put up with fair-weather followers."

Charles added, "If something is happening that is affecting you badly, then pray to Magicum and let him know what you plan on doing about it. He will let you know if it is going to mess with his plans. There are three don'ts." All three said together, "Don't mess with time, don't mess with the fabric of life, and don't mess with the weather."

They all laughed. Charles added, "Actually, there are thirteen don'ts, but you have been taught them. Another position I have taken that seems to work is don't ask for anything from any god unless you know the complete cost ahead of time."

Commeatus said, "Oh yes. On that matter, Magicum is paying for the use of my temple, so don't worry about the cost."

Magicum laughed. "I know what you want, Commeatus, you old weasel. Very well, it is done."

We moved over to a table, and two artifacts, a neckless and a ring, jumped out at me and tried to attach themselves. Magicum grabbed both and said, "Stop that. If I determine she needs you, then she will have you—not until. Samantha, this is my table, and these are the rules. Charles set them a long time ago, and we have kept with them every time Charles brings something else in for trade. First, everything in this room belongs to you, no matter what another god may say. They would take it all back for free if they could. Second, you get first pick of the things you feel you may need. Third, you trade what you don't want for increases in your abilities. For this session, Charles has called you his ward, so he will guide you and protect you."

Charles said, "I would rather you do, my lord Magicum. You are far better than I at this."

Both gods looked incredulously at Charles. Charles said, "What? I said I was going back to being myself. I am tired of trying to be someone else. That means showing more respect. At least to the ones who show they deserve it."

Commeatus said, "That's more like the Charles I know. Had to add that last in there. Always qualifying what you say."

Magicum cleared his throat, and both Charles and Commeatus straightened up and became quiet. Both had smirks on their faces. "As I was about to say. This is my table. All the items on or around it belong to you but were made artifact by me. I power them. I see it in your eyes, Samantha. You are about to give them to me. Are you not?"

"Yes, my lord god."

"That is good, child, but I am trying to teach you something, so I do not accept. What will happen is this. Someone from the table in question will touch you, and you will instantly know what each item is. All you have to do is state what you think you will need to keep and what you will trade them for the rest. Charles is very good at this; however, I want to see what you do." He touched me, and instantly I knew what each artifact did.

Many I did not need because I could do that already. Many I could possibly use sometime in the future, but I was not sure. Some were just wonderful and could always be used. I asked Charles, "What did you base your choices on before?"

"I knew what I was going to be doing, as I had it mostly planned out, and I picked items that would help me with those tasks."

I turned to Magicum and asked, "You wouldn't happen to know what I will be doing in the near future, would you?"

"Of course I do. You will be instrumental in fighting the Horde and removing it from this world. How you are going to do that is still up in the air. After that, you are going to upset a bunch of foolish professors at my university. I am so looking forward to that. Then I am sending you to another world to work on an issue I have there. Don't worry; it's nothing you can't handle. It's on the list of things that Charles needs to fix, but at this rate, he will never get to it."

Charles sadly added, "It's a very long list."

Commeatus said, "If I had a list of things to do as long as yours, I'd quit and go fishing. At first, I did not think it was a good idea, but after I saw the published list, I knew your talents were highly needed."

Charles said, "You have been a good friend, my lord. Your help is always welcome and appreciated."

Pointing, I said, "I think I need this one item. You may have all the rest, my lord god, for increases to my abilities across the board."

He handed me the little item, and the rest disappeared. I felt his touch as my abilities raised. Magicum said, "I know not why you have chosen a very old artifact pepper grinder, but you have your reasons, and I want the surprise, so I won't ask. What you have done is good.

"I would make one suggestion. Ask the god what he or she thinks will be beneficial and look to me for approval. That will do two things. It will establish that you think the gods know best, and it will show that you look to me for the truth. That will put many at ease, and they will be more generous with their gifts. The next table is Commeatus's."

I walked over to that table, and an acolyte touched me. I again instantly knew what each item was for. "My lord Commeatus, please forgive me for my ignorance. What do you suggest are items I will need to fight the Horde?"

"No, child!"

I turned and went to one knee before my god.

Magicum said, "Rise." He put one hand beneath my chin and raised my head. "Never, ever let them know what you plan to do. What if the god is working with the Horde? You never know the agenda of a god. Always keep your agenda hidden. Only you and I should know what you plan."

I said, "Let me try again." I turned to the traveler. "My lord Commeatus, please forgive me for my ignorance. What do you suggest are items I will need to stay alive when attacked by those I may not be able to protect myself from?"

Magicum said, "Ah, very good. No god would guess you have a war agenda. Protection is something they all will help with. And the wrong gods may inadvertently think of plans they are making and grant you protections against what is most in their minds."

Commeatus said, "Don't count on it. They know where you are. That demigod you chased out told everyone. They are probably making plans to take it from you." He reached over and picked up two items, a staff and a ring. "This ring will protect you better than you can yourself. Wear it always. Charles used it during his first meeting with the gods and was nice enough to return it when he no longer needed it. This staff will give you the ability to ..." He stopped as I put the ring on. "You have the Great Staff of War! Magicum!"

Magicum looked at me and said to Commeatus, "Don't look at me. I had no idea. Charles!"

Charles said, "I never gave it to her. In front of my two gods, I returned it to Potentis, the god of strength, after using it a long time ago. It is too powerful for use on this world. He promised Natura it would never be used again."

All were looking at me. I said, "I found it in one of the dragon treasures during my revenge period. It's a nice staff. How did you know I have it?"

Commeatus said, "That ring is mine, and you leak. As soon as you put it on, your mind melded with mine for only a second. You were thinking, *I think my Staff of War can do anything that staff can do.*"

I must have blushed. Charles asked, "Can you bring the staff here?"

I raised a hand, and the staff was in it.

Magicum put out a hand, and I placed the staff in it reluctantly. There were instantly eighty large creatures with weapons surrounding us, and one huge creature. The huge, overly muscled one with six massive arms asked in a deep voice, "Is this part of this trade? I would hate to think someone was taking without permission."

Magicum waved a hand dispassionately, and they all disappeared, except the one talking. The huge one was surprised and a little worried. Magicum said, "Tell your queen that we keep with the treaty. Also, remind her that she should not upset three major gods all at once. It is not good for her continued existence."

Commeatus said, "I will pay your queen a little visit later. Tell her I am upset that her people broke into my temple without cause. No one has taken anything from anyone against their will. Now, be gone!" Commeatus waved a hand, and the creature vanished.

Charles said to me, "This is the plane of trade, and the queen ensures that there is no funny business during trade. You make a transaction, and you stick to the contract. If no contract is made, then you keep your items, minus costs of course. In this case, they thought that Magicum was taking your staff from you against your will."

I smiled. "They thought they could stop him?"

"They would try."

I said, "Fools. If my god wants something I have, he needs but state so, and it is his."

Magicum said, "Thank you, Samantha, but I was only looking to ensure it is what you think it is. There will not be a trade for this staff. However, you may not use this staff during the war or any other time. You should think about trading it to the Leaches just to teach Potentis a lesson about keeping his word and to get it out of circulation."

Charles said, "No need. I just told Natura. Potentis made the promises to her, not me. She is very upset. She should be here soon."

Commeatus said, "Put that staff away but be prepared to bring it back out. Meanwhile, take the Staff of Travel. If you lose the other, then this one will be helpful. I would prefer you use nearly any other item than the Staff of War."

I blushed again.

Magicum asked very gently. "Child, what is wrong?"

"Um, I think I have something a little more dangerous than the Staff of War. Now don't blame me. I found it in one of the dragon treasures. I am not sure what it does, but it's as powerful as the Ball of Unbalance, or more so."

Charles went into a new aspect I had not seen, something between fatherly and clerical concern. Gently he said, "Samantha, what does this item look like?" I started to raise my hand to try to bring it back from wherever it disappeared, but Charles quickly stopped me. "No, just describe it."

"It is about eighteen feet long, ten feet wide, and four feet deep. It is solid black. So black that you can't look at it for long without feeling like you're falling in. Yet, there is writing, runes of some sort etched deep into the stone. And it has thousands of layers in this etched black stone with thousands of different runes."

Something akin to a solid, brightly lit, flickering, multiple-colored mist entered the room, and all three went to the floor. It floated there above the ground as Charles and Magicum pulled me down. Charles whispered, "An Over God."

It slowly came to me and touched my head. It saw all I knew in an instant. It turned to Charles, saying, "Remove it." Then it disappeared.

Everyone stood up, but all were staring at my neck. I put a hand on it, and there was a collar. I pulled, and it did not come off. I put out my hand, and a mirror was instantly in it. I took a look. Around my neck was a choker-style necklace of Laststoneite in pure white, with the biggest blue diamond in the center I had ever seen. I asked, "What just happened?"

Magicum said, "I am not fully sure. Charles?"

Charles turned to me with tears in his eyes. "You have looked into the Stone of Creation. Not your fault, as you did not know." He looked up and yelled to no one, "It should not have been here!" He turned back to me. "It contains the entire list of spells that the Over Gods use. It is a major artifact even for the Over Gods. You have seen their spells and are considered a danger. Though you do not know it now, as you grow, those spells will surface, and you will become powerful, very powerful."

Magicum said, "For looking at a stone artifact for so short a time!"

Charles asked, "One second by a major magic user would be long enough to learn more than needed to warrant the Necklace of Limitations. Samantha, how long did you look at the stone?"

I blushed again, and Magicum said, "Oh no."

Charles asked again, "How long?"

I said, "Well, it was something new, and I had some time, so I kind of studied it. For about three years until it disappeared. I was just finishing the 687th layer. I don't know where it is at this time, but I can feel it is still around."

Charles reached out to me and touched my head, saying to Magicum, "It is hiding inside her. She absorbed it and all its knowledge. Hold still, Samantha. This is not going to feel good." Charles put his hands on my face and tore the massive stone from my body while he absorbed the entire thing. I screamed in pain until I could scream no more. When he had it all, he fell down glowing and changing into creatures no one had ever seen before. His hands glowed brighter, and he concentrated. The changing stopped, and he collapsed to the ground saying, "Thank the gods for the Hand of Control."

Magicum asked, "Are you all right, Samantha?"

"Yes, my god. I think so."

"And you, Charles?"

"I will never be all right after that." He was upset. "I never look for power. I have always tried to shun power, and now I know all the spells the Over Gods know. I know and control the Stone of Creation." He looked at me. "Sorry, Samantha, but leaving that inside you would have caused you to become evil to no end. Even the gods would have feared you. Eventually you will know many of the spells that the Great Over Gods know. Teach them to Magicum. Right now, and hopefully for several hundred years, nothing has changed."

"Nothing, nothing! I am collared, and everyone can see!"

Charles put a hand on the collar, and it disappeared. "I have placed it inside you. No one can see it. Besides, that was not a blue diamond. The stone in that collar is worth more than a million flawless blue diamonds that size."

I said, "Thank you. What is a Necklace of Limitations?"

Charles said, "An artifact of great power. Feel privileged. The Over Gods have touched you and found you worthy, or they would have ripped the stone from you, and you would be destroyed. That necklace has two powers. First, you cannot use the higher-level creation spells that the Over Gods use. You are limited to go no higher than greater god-level spells plus enhancements. You can become a Great God; however, you cannot go beyond that level. Second, you can take that ring off, as no one, not even the gods, can command you. The Over Gods do not want certain gods controlling someone that has your hidden knowledge. Your mind is fully shielded from all but the Over Gods and myself. I have the power of control over all artifacts and therefore the power to see past that necklace."

I took the ring off and handed it back to Commeatus. I went to my knees and begged. "Magicum, my god. I need you now more than ever."

"Rise, my child. I will not abandon you. Besides, in a few hundred years, when your mind is ready, I will learn new spells. Something that hasn't happened in thousands of centuries."

I stood up and stopped crying. His enthusiasm was catchy, and soon we were all happy again. I said, "Well, at least that is over. Let's get back to the present."

Magicum said, "It is not over." He pointed. Another floating, flickering, mist Over God was coming our way. Darn. We all went to our knees and heard Natura laugh. Magicum got up quickly, and so did the rest of us, except Charles.

Magicum said, "Not funny, Natura!"

Natura, the grand goddess of nature in all her leafy slender with a small, pure white, furred creature in her arms that she was petting and changing in some way, materialized with a smile on her face. "Sorry, I couldn't resist. The three of you look good prostrated before me." Before anyone could say anything, she turned to Charles. "Rise, Charles. Aren't you going to introduce me to your new friend?"

Charles stood up and said, "Natura, this is Princess Samantha Altera Woodcutter. Princess Samantha, this is the great and wonderful Goddess Natura."

I curtsied so low my hair piled on the floor and my forehead touched my foot.

Natura said, "Rise, Magicum's champion. Thank you for the respect. You seem to have drawn the notice of the Over Gods. My sympathy. Charles, did you take care of the issues?"

Charles said, "I have removed the artifact from her, my goddess."

"Then why do I feel an artifact still within her?"

Charles said, "The Over God left her with another. The Necklace of Limitations."

"Oh, I remember that toy. Several gods have worn it in the past." She looked at me and added, "Don't worry, child. They tend to take that one back."

I said, "That is reassuring. Thank you."

Natura replied, "Not a problem. What is a problem is the Staff of War. I know she has it, and I am very upset with Potentis. I would have her trade that one to the Leaches."

Potentis, in the form of a big, well-muscled, extremely hansom man, instantly showed up. "I would not do that unless you want a war in Caelum."

Commeatus said to Natura and Potentis, "I do not remember inviting either of you to my temple at this time." He turned to Potentis. "I thought you made it very clear that the Staff of War was far too powerful for mortals to use and that you would not allow it to leave your temple again. Please explain, and don't think of telling me that it's none of my business."

Natura added, "Charles, please turn the Star Fire up to its fullest."

"As you wish, my goddess."

The Star Fire glowed brightly, and Potentis looked nervous. "Well, it's like this. There was a follower that promised not to use it for anything except research. I loaned it to him so he could see what a proper staff was made of and how. He used the power of the staff to summon a dragon that ate him. The dragon took the staff back to his lair. It was a very powerful dragon but had no ability to use magic, so I left it there thinking it safe." He turned to me. "I was wrong. A little girl destroyed him in his own lair."

Natura said something to Charles mind-to-mind. Charles smiled and said, "Samantha, what would you trade for that staff?"

I asked, "What do you think I need?"

Charles thought for a few seconds, and I could almost see the outline of a chalice in his eyes. He smiled and said, "Done." I felt myself become fast, very fast. I had to concentrate to slow down enough to talk properly. I moved to turn to Charles and turned around six times before I was finally pointed his direction. This was going to take getting used to.

I asked, "What did I just receive?"

Natura answered, "Something the gods cannot grant you. Charles used an Over God spell. You now have what would be equal to a permanent Greater Speed. You know the Speed spell?"

"Yes, Goddess. I also know the Greater Speed spell. It grants you speed so fast that you can do two spells, three if you have a quickened ready, in the time it would normally take to do one."

Charles said, "You now have the speed to do just that, and no one can take it away from you. It is part of you. I made it a natural ability."

I said, "Nice." I held out my hand, and the Staff of War was in it. I handed it to Charles even though Potentis put his hand out.

Charles took it and said a few words. Instantly, a large stone was in the room about ten feet away. Charles walked over to the stone and pushed the staff into it. The stone melted out of his way until the staff was in the center and fully covered. Charles did something else, and pain shot throughout his face. The stone turned to white. He had changed it to Laststoneite. Then the stone disappeared.

Natura said, "Potentis, I had Charles send it to your temple in Caelum. I don't think anyone will be using it for war or anything else, with it buried inside a ten-ton block of Laststoneite."

Potentis was upset. "And when it is needed, I will not be able to access it. You know why I made it. You know it will be needed."

Charles said, "As I changed the size and shape of the Laststoneite Necklace of Limitations, a grand artifact of the Over Gods, I can also remove the staff if I deem it needed." Everyone was staring at him as if he was something dangerous and unknown. Even Natura was shocked. Charles said, "What! You know I am powerful and can do some strange things. So I can change the size and shape of Laststoneite, so what?"

Natura laughed and said, "Charles, you have no idea how many gods would like to make changes to some of the areas in their temples—extensions, a door moved, a new wing added on. A lot of little things and some very large things. That list we made of all the jobs you need to do has just tripled."

Charles looked alarmed. "Oh, for goodness' sake, don't tell anyone!"

A note floated down and landed at Natura's feet. Everyone stared at it for a few seconds. Natura picked it up and opened it.

Dearest Natura:

I am in great need of a change in my wine cellar. It is far too small. An add-on with new shelves I can make; however, I will need a door and connection to my old wine cellar, which is made of Laststoneite. I will pay handsomely. Tell Charles we can celebrate his accomplishment with a bottle of that Treestorm wine he has hidden away.

Thank you,
Ultio

Charles said, "I suppose that is only the beginning?"

Another note floated down, then several, then enough to cover Natura completely. They came in all shapes and colors. Commeatus yelled with amusement in his voice, "Enough! You will send your requests to Natura's temple, not mine." He raised his hand, and all the notes went up in flame.

Natura was looking at Charles with an accusing look. Charles said, "What!"

Natura said to the air while looking at Charles, "Since you are all listening, let it be known that working in Laststoneite is very painful for my champion, and therefore the payment to Charles will be equally as painful for the requestor." She turned to Charles. "That should limit it to only the needed."

Potentis said, "My temple is far too small. I have grown over the years and need to add a large section in the back to house my most ardent followers. Natura, you know that section of property next to your temple in Caelum that you've been trying to haggle out of me for several centuries? I will give Charles that land for his turning my addition into Laststoneite and ensuring openings in the current Laststoneite and melding the two together."

Natura said, "I will think on that. It would be nice to have Charles build a temple next to mine. He has followers that I take care of for him. He grants them to me and Silvestris."

Charles said, "I am not so sure that I want a temple, maybe a home, but being next to the gods makes me nervous. If you haven't noticed, Samantha is thinking of shifting out of here while she thinks no one is paying attention. She is not used to being around gods and is feeling way outside her comfort zone. I think it's time to get back on track. Commeatus, she has excepted the Staff of Travel and has given you the rest, so please raise her abilities."

Commeatus never moved, but I felt my abilities go up. It felt good but strange. It was like I was more, what I was wearing was lighter, my mind was clearer, I could deduce more about what was already known, and I felt very healthy. Strange feelings. We did the same with Natura and Silvestris. Then, one by one, we did the same with the other gods. It took a total of twenty-one days.

At the end, Charles said, "Welcome to godhood, Samantha." I fainted.

CHAPTER 11

SHARING

I awoke back in my temple. There was magical writing in the air.

Samantha:

I have walked through your tower and talked with Magicum about the items. We agree that you should continue with the plan. For protection from evil dragons, allow the queen to have and use a few of the lances. Two of each type should be good, possibly more later.

I know you don't feel anything different, but take it from me: you are a minor god. Don't take chances, as you can still be killed. Strange thing is residual magic from the black stone made it so you don't affect the balance at this time. The Over Gods will likely change that later.

My wonderful goddess Natura felt you needed clothing to match your new position. She left several thousand formal and semiformal dresses in your new magical closet, all magically made to always fit you perfectly. She included twenty different styles for a high priestess of Magicum. She has great taste, so good luck choosing.

Your friend,
Charles

The message disappeared while I read it. I got up and magically made the bed. I used the cleaning room, and the hot water felt very good. I checked out the closet, and it took me an hour to pick a proper dress. After dressing in something semiformal and more a shopping dress than one for court, I went up to the top floor to check the time of day. "Good. Early evening and just getting dark. People are still up and awake." I did my hair and made myself as beautiful as possible. That meant that I was now far lovelier than most gods. Then I put on the bracelet I'd received from the god Proba, the god of elves. The bracelet made my looks diminish to something viewable by humans and removed the lust factor but did not diminish my charisma. I would be seen and admired as the most beautiful girl they had ever seen, but I would not be lusted after. I nearly cried when he handed it to me.

I walked down to the third floor and picked out three lances. Then I walked down to the first floor and out onto the front lawn. The trees were talking with one another and stopped when I walked out. I said hello, and we talked for a few minutes.

When done with the trees, I went over to a clear area outside my grounds and near the guards. I put down the lances and checked the sky. I picked out a shock lance and pointed it toward the sky. I activated it, and a nice, full, very long lightning bolt shot out. Something was different with this lightning bolt. I activated it again and moved the tip so that it crossed the sky a little. The lightning bolt moved with my movement. This lance was a nice strafing weapon, a flying creature destroyer, a dragon slayer. Give a couple of these to the guards, and they would have no more problems with dragons unless the dragon was immune to shock like I was. With two or three of these in the hands of experienced guardsmen, even with protections, that red dragon would have been brought down on the first attack. I put the shock lance down and picked up a fire lance. I pointed it, and a line of great fire shot out a thousand feet into the air. I put that down, picked up a frost lance, and pointed, and glowing ice shot out and dissipated at about a thousand feet.

I picked up the other two lances and started back into the castle with everyone watching me. One guard said, "Nice lance. May I have a try?"

I walked over to him. "Sure." I handed him the shock lance. "Point it to the sky, and say, 'Fire me.'"

He pointed it toward the top of one mountain section and said, "Fire me!" far louder than needed. Lightning shot out and cut across that section of sky. He handed it back, saying, "Very nice weapon."

Just to spread the word, I said, "I found a hundred of these artifacts in my tower. It's nice, I guess, but a little weak and a little short." I raised my hand and did a silent, stuffed, broadened, many-fingered lightning at my highest level. The sky lit up and stayed that way for six seconds. "That would have been better, but beggars can't be choosers." I walked back into the tower, and the guards and trees got out of my way.

I walked directly back to the third floor and put the lances back. I knew the general would be calling on me very soon. I went over to the magic window, and sure enough, the general was outside, and he was with the queen. The guards were all trying to talk at once. I concentrated and could clearly hear what they were saying. I patted and stroked the window seal, saying, "Nice tower, very nice."

It purred. The tower purred to me. I asked, "Can you talk?"

The purring stopped, but I didn't hear any words. Well, it never hurts to ask. I returned my attention back to the conversation outside.

The guards were quieted, and the general asked one to continue. "General sir, she came out and pointed a lance into the sky. She said a word or two, and the lance fired a lightning strike into the sky. It was the biggest and longest lightning strike I have ever seen or heard of. Then she did it again while moving the lance, and the lightning strike curved to take in the entire area. She did the same with a fire lance and an ice lance."

Formack had joined the conversation. "Hold—you say it curved?"

"Yes, my lord wizard. It curved. It followed the line where she was pointing the lance. She was holding it like a staff. She is not a lancer. She looked like she was about to go inside, so I asked her if I could try. She handed me the weapon and told me to point and say, 'Fire me,' so I did. The lance shot out lightning and curved with my movement."

The queen exclaimed, "A nonmagic user can use it!"

"Yes, Majesty."

"That explains the five times the sky lit up. Explain to me why it became daytime for several seconds. Roosters started crowing, for goodness' sake."

The guard said, "My queen. I handed her the weapon back,

and she complained about the hundred of these artifacts she found."

The general stopped him. "Did you say it's an artifact and she has a hundred of them?"

The guard continued, "Yes, my lord general. She was upset that they were so weak. Then she raised a hand, and without a word or gesture, lightning struck the sky in a thousand places. It was stronger than the worst storm I have ever witnessed. Majesty, it is my belief that her one spell, if unleashed on this city, could have done more damage than the red dragon in all his attacks."

The queen said, "Then it is a good thing she is on our side and is of goodly nature, as verified by our cleric and King Charles the Honest." When she mentioned King Charles the Honest, the men and trees relaxed a bit. *So, the trees do speak the standard language. How interesting. I wonder what else they didn't tell me.*

The general said, "Majesty, if we could get a few of those lances and train on them, we could mount a grand defense against the Horde."

One guard added, "And possibly protect ourselves from the sorceress."

The queen quickly turned on him, saying, "We will not need protection against Princess Samantha Altera Woodcutter. She is the kindest, nicest person I think I have ever met. She destroyed that red dragon, put out the fires, saved my life, has or is clearing out the tower, and has pledged herself to our cause. Do not ever let me hear another word against her. Is that understood!"

"Yes, Majesty," came from every lip.

I telepathically sent a message to Formack. "That was a nice thing for the queen to say. Besides, I am immune to lightning, fire, and ice."

He smiled and said out loud, "Listening in, you little minks?"

I answered, "My name was mentioned just outside my tower, and I was watching for the general to come out after I used the lance."

Formack asked, "Why don't you come on down and talk to us in person?"

"I am on the third floor. I will meet you on the first floor. I have disabled all the traps to this point, so it's safe."

Formack said, "I am on my way." He turned to the queen. "Majesty, Princess Samantha has invited us to the tower, where she is watching us at this time. She says it is safe as long as we don't pass the third floor. As you can see, the trees have moved out of our way."

The queen asked, "How many can I bring?"

I answered, "The queen, the general, the cleric Jonathan, you, and two guards."

Formack answered, "I will let her know. We will be over in a few seconds. My queen, she expects us to bring a couple of guards, the general, and the cleric."

The queen said, "Make it happen, General."

The general picked out two captains who had come out to see what was going on and had been intelligent enough to wear full armor and all their weapons. The party moved toward my front door, so I used a Shift spell to take me to the foyer. As they entered the grounds, the captains were sent ahead. The trees did nothing, so the cleric and general followed, and then the queen and Formack. I opened the front doors and said, "Hello, everyone. Welcome." I waved a hand, and they followed me to the third floor. On the way up, I thanked the queen for providing me with such a nice place to live and work.

The queen said, "You're welcome, Samantha. The tower is completely clear? Formack says he no longer feels evil coming from the tower—though he calls it a temple."

"Yes, my queen. I have cleansed all evil from the tower temple and cleared all traps not associated with the original tower. I have set my own protections, which are more powerful than the previous owner's, and I have consecrated every inch of the tower to Magicum, my god. In addition, I have redecorated. I didn't like the early torture chamber. This is much better, don't you think?"

The queen smiled. "Yes, I do." She looked around and saw all the pictures and hangings of good people doing good deeds and places that were fun and nice. She paused in front of a tapestry, looking at a forest picnic seen with a nice family laughing, eating, and playing. The tapestry was very magical, and you could smell the wildflowers and trees as you watched the youngest boy jumping over a log, and you could hear all the children playing. "You seem to be surrounding yourself with goodness."

"I am."

The queen said, "I am pleased. This is a nice place. It feels like a warm and comfortable home."

I smiled. "Thank you."

The queen continued with worry. "I am told that you are very powerful. The sky lit up like full day for several seconds, and that impressed my guards."

"I was trying to get the general's attention." I looked over at him. "It seems to have worked."

She laughed. "I think you achieved the attention of everyone for a hundred leagues."

I quickly did a hand gesture, and it did not go unnoticed. I turned to the cleric. "You were starting to do a Find Magic spell. I dispelled it for a reason. Are you prepared to see Greater God–level power?"

With a worried look, he said, "No."

"I did not think so. I have within me an item placed there by the Over Gods to limit my abilities. They don't want me growing too fast or becoming too strong. If you wish to see it, you need to prepare yourself so you don't pass out, fall down the stairs, and possibly break your neck."

"I am prepared now."

"Then do your spell."

The cleric concentrated and did a Find Magic spell. He continued to concentrate for several seconds before he stopped and said, "I sense the artifact, and it is powerful, but you are nearly as powerful as it, and that is what I wanted to know."

The queen asked, "And what did you determine, Jonathan?"

Formack said most humbly, "You are in the presence of the high priestess of Magicum, and she is as powerful as a god in her own right. Am I correct, Jonathan?"

"You are correct. This temple and she are one. It belongs to her, and she to it. It will go where she commands."

I said, "You see much with a simple Find Magic spell. However, I know better. Solbelli helping you out?"

Jonathan said, "My god is interested in what you will do with this weapon. It is a flying fortress and nearly as powerful as the staff you sold."

I answered, "You do not have to tell Solbelli, as he is listening. Solbelli, oh great and powerful god of war, my god, Magicum, has forbidden me from moving this fortress at this time and until the war is over completely. At which time he will give me new orders. I do not know why he wishes it so, but I will do as told. Even if the war goes against us, I will not move this tower unless I am ordered to do so by my god. Although, it was made perfectly clear that I and this tower can mess with the enemy all we want, as long as the Tower of Sight does not move from this place."

Out of nowhere, a voice said, "Good enough."

Jonathan fell to his knees, and so did the queen. I said, "He is gone, so you can stand now."

Formack said, "You seem to know Solbelli to a point."

"I have been gone for about a month, correct?"

Formack said, "True. We were worried."

I put my hand on Formack's shoulder. "I am sorry, my friend. It is true that I am almost considered a god, but I have no followers, and I plan on keeping it that way. You know about the balance between good and evil on this world, my friend?"

"Of course."

I looked directly into his eyes. "The Horde has a very evil, powerful, greater demigod dragon called Rormantle on their side. They were cheating. Solbelli and many others didn't like the unbalance, so they asked Magicum to limit me to just less than godhood so I could be the balance. I allow that at this time. However, Charles let them know that the Over Gods have not placed the balance limitation on me yet. I am a demigoddess, and it took Charles to place spells so that I would affect the balance and negate Rormantle and the unbalance. Without me, you have no chance in this war. With me, well—with me you have every chance. However, most is up to you. I cannot run a war against a very powerful army and fight a major demigod at the same time."

Queen Iseaia said, "I never wanted to put all this on your shoulders, but I am most grateful for your help."

We reached the third floor. I opened the doors and let them into my workroom. Formack whistled and said, "Nice."

I smiled. "You like? I had to change things around quite a bit. It was originally designed to house eight wizards working at the same time. Now, one or two can do most of the work easily. Note the rows and rows of wands, rods, and staves."

Formack asked, "May I?" as he motioned toward a row of wands.

"Go ahead."

I watched as Formack and Jonathan rummaged through everything. Jonathan exclaimed, "My queen, these are wands of healing and renewal! Mostly minor renewal but some major."

Formack handed Jonathan a rod and said, "Here, the tag says it's a Rod of Rebirth. My queen, most of this equipment, the wands, rods, and staves, and all the potions are exactly what we talked about spending as much as possible on for the war. There is more here than we can afford even with Samantha's generous donation."

I said, "Come with me." They followed me to the door and out to my storage room. I opened it up and waved for them to enter. They saw the lances, but they also saw a hundred times more wands, rods, staves, and potions stored away for use. I said, "It seems that the original owners were preparing for a major war."

After eyeing all the treasures, the queen asked, "Are these the lances you used outside?"

"Yes, Majesty."

She said, "We could mount these on the great wall and stop the Horde long before they reach us."

I said, "Read the tag."

She picked up one tag and read it. "One league!"

I said, "Sadly, these were designed for use at the tower or by dragon riders. They cannot go far from the tower without a rider or they return. I pointed them out to King Charles, and he tried to remove most of them and failed. They will protect this city very well as long as you keep them within one league."

The queen said, "They will protect us from evil dragons. That is a big advantage."

I shook my head. "Take it from me, my queen, dragons

learn quickly. They would be good for a first and maybe second attempt, but then the dragons would find a way to remove them. Fly low and quickly while using their supernatural fear, pull up and snatch the user who cannot move because of the fear, hand the lance back to the rider, and he can then use it against us until someone brings him down. As long as they stay within one league, they can use them as well as us. Though, without the Dragon Rider Armor, they cannot go more than one league."

Formack said, "We can sit around and figure out all the protections later. These will be of great use." He turned to the queen. "What we really need is the help of the dragons. If we could mount several of these on the backs of dragons, we could do much more. They could also protect our supply lines and grant greatly improved surveillance. The only way to fight dragons is with dragons."

The queen said, "Won't happen. They have refused to help."

I said, "Invite them to dinner. A grand banquet."

The queen smiled. "Why would they come to eat when they won't come to talk?"

"Because I will supply elephants."

Jonathan said, "Elephants?"

I turned to him. "Take it from me, a half dragon. Elephant is a dragon's favorite food. Elephants are nearly gone from this world, but I happen to know where I can gather up some nice fat ones on a world that has an overabundance. My queen, invite them to a banquet and ensure fresh elephant is on the menu. They will come. I would suggest that you limit the amount that attend, as I will only be able to bring in six or seven elephants."

The queen said, "Let's just say that gets them to come and talk. What then?"

I said, "Leave that to me. I have a great plan provided by King Charles himself."

She asked, "Can you have the elephants here in a week?"

"I can have them here tomorrow if you can protect them so they don't get snatched up."

She smiled. "Wait five days and then bring them in. How many of these lances and this other equipment can we take?"

I looked very serious in thought. "None, or very little."

The queen was not happy. "May I ask why?"

"My queen, if you move this stuff out, how well will it be protected? I can promise you it is highly protected in this place. Even their demigod cannot enter."

She became very serious. "I cannot protect it from a demigod, but what happens if you are taken and we cannot get in?"

"Exactly. Come with me please." I took them to the second and first floors and showed them the barracks, library, storage, and kitchen areas, which were now fully stocked with the best foods, thanks to Charles. I showed them the showers, sinks, privies, and offices. "If you provide me with some tower staff, including good cooks, then I grant you the right, until this war is over or I receive new orders, to house good men and women in this tower." I took them to the first floor of the basement and showed them all that empty space. "We can set up a lot of people in this area also. Warning, these must be people we know are good, and they need to be watched continuously. If they try to go down lower than this level or up to higher levels than the second floor, they will die instantly. Those areas are extremely dangerous. I will come down and eat with the troops. The staff does not need to go up past the second floor. I will grant several captains the ability to go to the third floor. That should fix my issue with a lack of tower staff and give you a great place to house several hundred men. That will leave room for others to come in and use the regular barracks. I will not grant foreigners the right to enter this tower unless I pass them personally."

The queen was smiling. "I was going to ask you if we could house some of the men in here. Thank you."

"You're welcome, my queen."

Formack asked, "Do you have room for the queen?"

Both the queen and I looked shocked. She said, "Formack! We talked about this."

Formack said, "I am worried, my queen. We set many protections, but we cannot protect you from a demigod. This is new and worrying information."

I said, "I can find room in my area on the fourth floor if needed. When the time comes, it would be a great place to direct the war. However, the queen needs to be seen out and about so that her people do not become afraid. Tomorrow, if you will allow, I will check the protections you have placed and add my own. She will be highly protected when I am finished. Most gods will have to ask permission to enter. I will also check out the great wall and see what we can do to protect it just a little better."

Formack relaxed. "That would be very much appreciated. Thank you."

"Not a problem. Now, there is one more thing I want to show you. But this stays between us and only us. Can your captains keep a secret? I am talking totally secret. They tell no one and don't talk about it outside this group or outside the tower. Creatures may be scrying on you. They cannot do so in this tower, but outside they can."

The general said, "No. I trust no man with that type of information until I know exactly what it is. Captains, stay here and guard that door." He pointed to the front door.

"Yes, sir."

The general said, "I trust this group if Jonathan will promise not to pray about whatever it is."

Everyone was looking at Jonathan. "I will give my word that I will not pray out loud. Is that good enough?"

I said, "No. Prayers can be intercepted. I found that out the hard way. And the Evil Gods would love to tell Rormantle and will be watching."

Jonathan said, "Then I will stay down here and keep the guards company."

I said, "Very well. Thank you for your honesty. Let's go up higher."

We traveled up to the fourth floor, and they saw my bedroom. We had to travel through it to get to the top. We took the spiral staircase up past the room that had the demigod that tried to fool me. I had changed this room into a map room. I showed them the windows and how to use them, and then I took them to the top. "This dome works the same as the windows. Watch." I concentrated on the main gate, and everyone could easily see and hear what was going on down there. The queen walked over to the northern end and looked out, concentrating on the wall. It came into view, and we could clearly see the men manning the wall. One was sitting down. The general said, "Watchman! Stand that watch in an orderly manner!" I thought I could move fast with my new abilities, but that man moved so fast it was hard to see. He was instantly standing a perfect watch with "Yes, sir, general sir," clearly heard.

The queen smiled and said, "Samantha, we need this room. I need watchers in this room constantly. This is the tallest place in the city. My goodness, we can see and talk with the watchers and be far more proactive during the war. What is the reason for the secrecy?"

I said, "You have to travel through my bedroom to get here! When I am asleep, I am vulnerable."

Both looked astonished, and the general started laughing.

I was not, and the queen noticed. "Child, you may be a near god, but you have things to learn. This we can work around. We can place a wall between you and the stairs that is heavy, and you won't have to worry about your virginity." I started to say something about not being a virgin and speaking about being alive, but she placed a hand on my lips. "I will personally guarantee that you are safe from the men."

Going along with them thinking I was a child, I said, "Very well, but I will create the wall and set additional protections tonight—protections that ensure evil gets fired the second it tries to come in."

She smiled and turned to the general. "Have eight men picked to stand watches up here—two or three at a time. Make them married men and have one wife or mother-in-law stand watch on the door to Samantha's private rooms."

The general said, "I will have Formack and Jonathan test and question the men I allow past the second floor and for standing watch up here. I will not have someone we cannot fully trust. And that includes the women who watch the men. We have a lot of work to do, so let's get to it. Samantha, can we start using the rooms on the second floor and below?"

"Yes, sir."

The general started walking down the stairs. "Great. I want all the planning, maps, everything moved to this tower, where the enemy cannot watch our planning. I am going to set up my office on the second floor in the old captain's rooms. All the captains and important men will be moved into this tower when and if they pass, and I want to know who does not pass and why! Let's move it. We have a lot of work to do, and I want it done by this time tomorrow."

He continued to talk as he descended, fully expecting Formack to follow him. I put out my hand and opened my palm.

A small, unadorned rock was in it. I handed it to the queen. She took it, and I said, "I am really not a good person."

The queen's eyes opened wide. "That was a lie, and I know it." She looked at the stone. "A truth stone?"

I answered, "A minor artifact. It can be fooled by a higher artifact. Have people check for magic of artifact level on everyone before using it."

She smiled and said, "Thank you."

I smiled back. "Don't thank me. I am loaning it to you to check out those people who are going to be entering my tower. I need them clean of other agendas. I will set the trees to destroy only those who are evil. That should allow you plenty of flexibility on choosing. I am worried about their families. If the enemy cannot get to us directly, they may use their loved ones to force them to do things against their will."

The queen said, "We will watch for that, but they are sneaky, and we can't watch for everything."

"No one can; however, vigilance is needed. Have you blocked all secret ways into the castle?"

The queen looked shocked. "How did you know there are secret ways into the castle?"

I pointed over to three men standing about a hundred yards away from the back castle wall. "Different men have been standing around looking like they belong there every time I've checked that direction. I am sure your brother knows every possible way in and out. The enemy will think the war is over if you are captured. Of course, it will not be for me. I am ordered to do my best to stop the Horde, and that includes killing you if the enemy is using you to compromise the effort. I thought I'd point that out."

The queen looked very serious. "Apparently, the god that gave you those orders does not know our kind. I will kill myself, or the general, or Formack will do it. No one person is more important than our entire kingdom. We do not compromise on anything that has to do with our freedom. And we won't let the Horde just walk through. You'll come to understand that when you have been in on some of our planning. You are correct, and I will have all tunnels destroyed. Now that we are alone, how are you going to get the dragons to help?"

I motioned for her to descend as I said, "I have dragon pepper. Be ready for a scene."

Her eyes went wide. She started down the stairs, saying, "A scene! A scene! Be ready for war in my own castle is what she is asking."

I smiled and watched through the window as she left and the trees returned to watch. I stored all the dragon armor in the treasure room, and then I went up and made the wall to seal off my bedroom and bathroom. I left no door because I could teleport in. There was a door to the bathroom, which went into the watch room. I sealed that up with another wall. Now, only Magicum and Charles could enter into my bedroom. Hopefully, neither would try.

POST LOG

I sat in my tower the next day, contemplating my life—where it had been, where it was, and where it was going. I looked back on the many things that had happened to build my being: the death of my family, being received into the university, excelling in every study and overtaking every student, being used to teach, being kicked out of every town and city I entered until now, the anger and frustration about the way I was treated by humans until now, the experience I gained taking revenge, the power given me when I became the owner of the Tower of Sight and all the artifacts I traded for increased abilities, the kindness of the people of Landtrap, and the kindness of many of the Good Gods. But especially the friendship of King Charles the Honest. In my opinion, he should have been called King Charles the Kind for two reasons: first, because he could lie better than anyone I knew without telling a lie or deceiving, so honest was out; and second because he was too kind to do so.

Now I was the owner of the Temple of Sight, grand mage, high priestess of Magicum, and a demigod of all things. I thought a demigod had to have followers, but Charles set me straight on that. I was not sure I wanted to be a demigod, and I knew I didn't want followers. I had gone from not having anyone or anyplace to having many friends and a home of my own. I had grown and changed. The hatred and frustration was gone, and I felt wonderful.

Still, the future was uncertain. I had a war to fight, a powerful Great Demigod with thousands of years of experience to battle, gods that didn't like me having the Tower of Sight, gods that didn't like me being so powerful, and gods that didn't like me at all. I had spells flooding into my head from the Over Gods. They sat in my head waiting for me to make the mistake of using them. Many of them would burn me to vapor if I let them. No, the future was not certain at all.

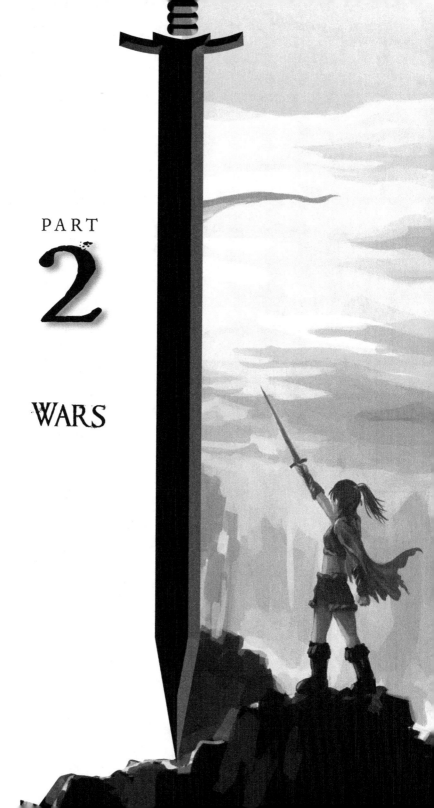

PART

2

WARS

PROLOGUE

Preparations, preparations, preparations! It seems that all I do nowadays is prepare for something. Prepare for war, prepare for battle with a demigod, prepare for this and prepare for that. Now I am preparing for dinner. Probably the most important dinner in my entire life, and I can't figure out what to wear. It used to be easy. I had four outfits—battle mage, rogue, traveling, and shopping. Now I have a hundred different outfits for everything you can possibly think of. I used to think the gift of two thousand dresses was a blessing from the goddess Natura, but now I wonder. If I look hard enough in this magical closet, I am sure I will find outfits just for using the privies.

This one—no, that one would be better. I can't make up my mind. "Magicum! Help me. I am going crazy trying to determine what dress to wear."

Instantly I saw myself in the mirror, and one by one, all two thousand dresses were tried on me. It was a flash and took only a few seconds, but I landed on one dress with hair ribbons and heard him say, "You will wear that one, child, and don't bother me again for such foolishness. Ask Natura next time. She did this to you—and no! You cannot toss them all out. Natura would be on my doorstep in an instant. You accepted the gift, and now you have to use it. Stop complaining."

I curtsied and said, "Yes, Daddy." He chuckled and was gone.

The dress Magicum picked was a little childish and frilly. I am sure he chose this one as punishment, but now I was stuck with it. Dinner was going to be interesting.

CHAPTER 1

DINNER AND DRAGONS

The week went by quickly. When the queen was ready, I brought in six large elephants. Four were sent down to the kitchen and cooked on big iron poles. Two bull elephants were placed in large cages. They promptly tore the cages apart and ran loose into the field outside the main gate. That stopped traffic and caused a panic. I teleported out there, changed into my platinum dragon persona, and herded the beasts to the far northern end, where they fought for a little while and then took to staying at opposite ends of the northern section, uprooting trees and eating the branches.

Dinner was scheduled for the next day, and several dragons showed up on the top of the mountains and hills, watching the area. Two were always in flight and took turns scaring the two bull elephants until they were mad with fear and started standing their ground with tusks raised for a fight. They actually stood back-to-back. Smart beasts.

The smell of barbequed elephant was strong in the air. All

the spices, except dragon pepper of course, that dragons love were being used, and I could tell that the dragons were getting hungry. Their roars increased in strength and length—each warning the others to stay away because the food was for the kings and queens. Apparently, most of the good- and natural-aligned dragons sent back affirmative replies. The elephants were doing far more than I'd hoped in bringing in the dragons, and the queen was worried.

The queen was pacing in her chambers, saying, "What if this does not work? We are going to have the entire dragon council at dinner tonight. Do you have any idea what that means?"

Formack had heard it many times that day. "Yes, Majesty, but you're going to tell me again anyway."

The queen said, "Don't be rude. It means that this is a win or lose situation. If we cannot win them over, then the council will vote to not allow any dragons to help in this war. I won't even get the one or two strays to help protect caravans. They will all stay away. Why did I agree to this! That child is so good at persuasion. Just a word or two, and people jump to do her bidding. Including me!"

Formack said, "Now, don't blame Samantha. Without her help, we would still be trying to gain enough money to fund the battle. As it is, we are more ready to fight than we have ever been in the history of this country. Besides, you jumped on this chance. Let's face it. If we can obtain the dragon council's help, we may even be able to win this war."

The queen calmed down a little. "True that. Samantha has given us hope. With or without the dragon council's, help we are ready to make a grand effort in keeping the Horde back and away from the rest of the continent. Kayland, Ginham,

Treestorm, and almost every other country south of us is sending help. Their words, 'Better to make a stand and destroy your land than let the Horde through and have them rampage through our lands.'"

Formack grimaced. "Even the rose witch is sending a small army of Drow."

The queen said, "The rose queen and dark elves. I am more worried about Ginham. Once in our lands, how are we going to get them out?"

Jonathan answered, "They won't stay. Samantha told one of my acolytes that the king of Kayland has ordered his army to stick around until all others leave."

The queen looked exasperated. "Why didn't she tell us? I've been worrying about this for days."

Jonathan said, "She probably doesn't think it important. Besides, she can probably kick them out herself."

The general said, "Something has changed in Samantha. Have you noticed that, though still extremely lovely, she no longer causes my men to lust? It's almost like she is their little sister. I feel the same way around her. I find myself giving her fatherly advice."

Formack said, "I asked her about that, as I was doing the same thing. She is wearing a bracelet given to her by a god. The bracelet cuts out the lust generation factor. She went into such technical detail that I lost the conversation somewhere in the middle, but I got the idea that the bracelet causes men and women to simply not see her as a sexual prospect. She took it off to show me the difference. Be glad she is wearing it. I could not think straight for hours."

The queen said, "I hope she is wearing it tonight!"

Formack said, "She almost never takes it off. Even a Correct Seeing spell does not penetrate the bracelet's effects."

The queen looked one more time into the full-length mirror. "It's time. How do I look?" All three said, "Wonderful."

The general said, "Change the boots."

"What?"

"The boots! Aren't they dragon hide? Red or not, I would not wear them in front of the dragon council."

The queen quickly changed her boots and then headed into the throne room. People were gathering from all over. The generals from three human armies were all talking in one group, bragging about female exploits, which was a safe thing to talk about without giving away military tactics. Their captains were gathered around them for support. The Treestorm Elves were in one corner talking, Dark Elves were in another, and Southern Elves were in another. Each as far away from the others as possible. A group of dwarves were in the center, keeping an eye on the elves and feeling surrounded. At least none were fighting; however, the evening was early. Good thing Samantha asked us to keep it to three of each group.

The queen asked, "General, where are the dragons?"

"Majesty, I am told they are on their way. Oh look, there is Samantha. My goodness, that is a beautiful gown. I wish I had a daughter that lovely."

The queen looked. "Yes, she looks wonderful in that color. I am going to have to talk to her about not outdoing the queen."

I said to myself, "The elves are doing exactly what I expected, and so are the dwarves. I was not expecting the human generals to be close together." I looked around and saw the queen and general. I waved, and they waved back, but the queen looked a little sour for some reason. I let it go, as I needed to talk with some of the elves to stop the war that was about to break out in the throne room. I headed to the Dark Elves first.

As I walked up, they parted enough to allow me a place to stand and talk. "Hello, I am Princess Samantha."

One older female elf said, "I am General Dramera Dreamchanger." She pointed out the other two. "This is my right hand, Captain Marksman Trollkiller, and my left hand, Captain Mindeater Maddness. We are pleased to meet you. What is your place in this mess?"

I smiled. "Part of my place is to help straighten out the mess. I see that the three different groups of elves do not mix. Is there a reason for this?"

Dramera said, "I see you are not conversant with elfin history or philosophy. Let me school you. Thousands of years ago, we were a part of the Forest Elves. However, because we did not see eye to eye on several important issues, and because the ones who saw differently from us out numbered us by far, we were driven out of our homes and forced to live underground or in hidden places. We were hunted by our brothers and nearly killed out."

"That's horrible!"

She smiled. "We think so also. It is difficult for us to stay in this room with other elves, knowing they would kill us if possible. Normally, they are the enemy."

I said, "I can see why it would be difficult. Tell me, would they enlighten me with the same history if I asked?"

She looked concerned. "Probably not. They think us evil because of our god and will tell you that is the reason we were cast out."

I looked at her with a smile. "True, but you had the same god as they when you were cast out. You only picked the god you worship now because she helped you in your time of need after the casting out. She accepted you into her realm."

Dramera said, "You know more than you let on, Princess. It is true that many of us had the same god as they, but some of us had already started praying to Spirdra, the queen of the underground, and that was a turning point. We do not see the same as the other elves. Our eyes are open to the truth, not closed because of lies and innuendos."

I said, "Wonderful. I like an open mind. I look forward to watching you in battle. I am told that you are great warriors."

She smiled. "We will do our part, and then we will flee this land of too much light to return to our home beneath the surface. I know why you are talking to us, Mage. We will not start anything with the other elves or the silly little dwarves. The rose queen has made it very clear. We stay to ourselves and fight to the death the Horde and only the Horde."

I allowed my eyes to change to their demon form. She nearly pulled back in surprise. She knew that type of eyes. "I am glad to hear that. But if someone else starts something, let me handle it please. I will be asking the same of the others. It will be fun to see which of the three groups is wise enough to maintain composure when others become fools."

She was very serious when she said, "Do not worry, Princess Demon. We will not start or try to finish anything. We will maintain our own and keep it that way."

I said, "I am not as worried about you as much as I am about the others goading you. Especially the dwarves once they get a little liquor going to their heads."

"Ah, yes. That would be a problem. It will be interesting to see how you handle it."

I put out my hand and said, "Wish me luck."

She took my hand and said, "You will need it."

I visited the other two elfin groups and played the same game. They were not worried about the Dark Elves, just the "silly" dwarves. I went to the dwarves next. They did not open a way for me to talk. "I shoved one over, saying, "Don't be rude." I turned to the one who seemed to be in charge and asked, "You in charge of these other two?"

He looked at me as if sizing me up. "You're a strong lass. Yes, child, I am in charge. What does an elf lover like you want?"

I looked back at him the same way he was looking at me, "Call me an elf lover again, stumpy, and you and I can go outside and see if your hammer is as good as my magic."

He laughed a booming laugh. "And what should we call such a skinny little girl?"

The dwarven mage at his right whispered, "Oh, I don't know, Captain, sir. How about dragon demon princess, grand mage, or high priestess of Magicum."

Now the old dwarf looked a little nervous. "I am Helmon Hammerthumb, captain of the dwarven forces. What is it you want, Grand Mage?"

I learned a long time ago that with dwarves you need to be straightforward. They don't play the political games that others do. "I am worried that you consider our allies your enemies and someone to tease into fighting. A fight between allies would be exactly what the true enemy wants."

He chewed on that for a second and said, "We will not start anything. Though we may finish it if they start."

I said, "No, you will not. If you goad them, I will finish it, and if they goad you, I will finish it. Either way, you will not be pleased. You were not sent here by your grand king to be foolish enough to fall for the goading of elves, were you?"

Proudly, he proclaimed, "You do not know dwarves, Mage. We do not fall for the foolishness of elves."

I looked at him long and hard. "I do know dwarves, and elves goad because dwarves always fall for it."

He blushed. "Well, now, I don't think—very well, we will keep the peace. Do not worry about our side, Mage."

I added a little polish to the conversation before turning to talk with the generals. "Good. I can't wait to see dwarves in battle. I am told it is a magnificent and frightening sight."

He smiled. "Well, just you wait and see, child. The enemy will flee before us."

I smiled and turned toward the generals. They were only a few short feet away, and they made an opening for me. They had been watching.

The general from Ginham said, "Don't worry, Mage. The humans will not start anything. We have a battle coming and can ill afford foolish bigotry."

I said, "Good. Then do us all a favor and talk with your nonhuman allies." A little louder, I said, "Knowing what abilities your allies have will be very valuable during the war. If you see the enemy chasing around your left flank, will you know your allies can stop them or will you know they need help?"

The general from Kayland said, "You do us an injustice, Princess Samantha. We know about each other already. Ginham has five hundred men; two hundred are trained lancers, one hundred are heavy mounted Calvary, and the rest are foot soldiers. All are trained and capable men."

The general from Ginham said, "Kayland has five hundred foot soldiers. All trained in the lance. No bowmen, as they knew that the elves would be here with archers. Princess, during this dinner, we were trying to lighten things up and enjoy ourselves."

I covered my mouth, giggling. "I am so sorry, gentlemen. I worry so much about my first war that I get irritated when I don't see others worrying as much as I do. I should have known better. You are right. This is a dinner to enjoy."

The general from Kayland said, "Good. We were told there would be dragons?"

My eyes closed for a second as if I were looking at something far away. I said, "Six are gorging on two bull elephants down in the valley at this time. The others are going to be upset they missed the fun. The six will be done shortly, and after cleaning themselves, they will be here for dinner."

They all moved to the balcony facing south, but my tower was in the way. I smiled and turned to the queen, who was just walking up to me. "Hello, my queen."

"Hello, Samantha. Thank you for talking with the elves and dwarves."

I smiled. "You were doing the same thing."

She said, "It's proper for the queen to mingle during the beginning of the party. Besides, they were getting a little too chummy with themselves and not with others. It is easy to see why their nations do not get along. There isn't an ounce of trust between them."

I said, "I don't know. The generals of the human armies are getting along."

Jonathan said, "I was listening in on some of their earlier conversation, and they exchanged a lot of information about each other. They were talking about how to take out the elves and dwarves and, if needed, the demon mage."

The queen added, "They stopped when their mage told them, in total disgust I should add, that he would side with you if they tried anything of the sort. Notice that the mages from each group are talking. All of them are from the university, and they all seem to be friends, except the dwarven mage. Even the Dark Elf is talking with the others. Another good thing King Charles did for us. He brought the mages together."

I said, "Speaking of mages, I had better say hello."

She smiled. "Please do, but one thing first. You are half-platinum dragon, granddaughter of King Split Tail and Queen Long Tongue, and your parents were in exile by the dragon council."

I said, "I haven't forgotten."

Formack asked, "Do you know what that entails?"

I said sadly, "Yes. I cannot speak to, acknowledge the presence of, or look at another dragon. Not even my own grandparents. However, I can protect myself and what is mine from other dragons."

Formack said, "Is that going to make things difficult on you?"

I smiled. "It is going to make things difficult on them. Wait and see. However, I will play their game and keep with my exile."

The queen said, "As long as it does not interfere with the plan."

"The only change I see is you are going to have to be a go-between. If they want to ask me something, you will have to ask it, and I will tell you the answer, but I have to pretend I did not hear them."

The queen said, "Games! I hate games. Very well, I will play the part, but I will be irritated about it."

I said, "Good. They will see that and keep the questions to a minimum."

A page ran in and up to the queen. "They are arriving, Majesty. They have four escorts each, plus four in the air at all times. We don't know how many hidden."

The queen looked at the general, and he said, "I'm on it, Majesty." He gave quick orders, and a captain ran off to carry them out. He turned to the queen. "We will have the same number in lancers ready for service if anything happens." He turned to movement at the entrance. "They are here."

The queen and everyone except me turned to look. I pretended to be searching the ceiling for something and headed to the mages. Most of the dragon entourage stayed out in the foyer, but one for each lined the wall coming into the large room. They were in human form and stunningly regal and beautiful. The platinum king and queen entered first, then gold, silver, bronze, and brass. The announcer did a great job of pronouncing their names. He should have; I worked with him for hours. They seemed pleased and continued into the room. Their gowns were exquisite, all gold, silver, and jewels. They were wearing crowns but not the ugly, big things some kings wear. Theirs were small and seemed delicate. The queen went to meet them.

King Split Tail saw her coming and said, "Queen Iseaia Danberry, so nice to see you truly had elephants for our pleasure. They were just the way I like them, fresh and warm with a lot of adrenalin running through their veins. Still, the smell of fresh-cooked elephant in the air is welcoming. I was saying to my wife just the other year, 'It has been a long time since I had elephant,' far too long."

Grandmother said, "Dear, let the queen say hello before you jump into a full-length story. Hello, Queen Iseaia. Thank you for the invitation."

My queen said, "My pleasure, Queen Long Tongue, and welcome to our little country." She motioned to them, saying, "All of you are most welcome. It is seldom that I get a chance to have a celebration like today. It is nice to have good friends to celebrate with."

The gold king said, "We are curious as to what you are celebrating. You are about to go into a major war you cannot possibly win. I see nothing to celebrate."

My queen said, "Oh, we don't let a war stop us from celebrating. My goodness, there is always a threat of war, or imminent war, or something. There are two reasons for the festivities. First is that tower you saw outside."

My grandfather said, "Magicum's Tower of Sight. Everyone knows it is here. It is general knowledge. Two of our greatest dragons were wasted trying to clear it of evil."

Queen Iseaia said, "Do you sense evil coming from it now?"

King Split Tail walked over to the balcony and did a quick check. "No. My goodness, there is no evil anywhere near it. How did this happen?"

I saw a look of sneaky pleasure cross my queen's face, and I cringed as she said, "Your granddaughter cleared it of all evil and consecrated it to Magicum."

King Split Tail looked proud. "My granddaughter, you say? I don't remember any granddaughters taking up the warship of Magicum."

Completely against the plan, Queen Iseaia said, "One did, and she now lives in that tower. The second thing that happened, and another good reason to celebrate, is the tower has magical lances that can help greatly in this war. Weapons of grand power. Your granddaughter loaned them to us."

The brass king said, "The lances of fire, ice, and shock. The lances the dragon riders used to carry into battle when someone attacked the tower."

King Split Tail said, "I must have a very good granddaughter for her to have helped you so very much, but those lances cannot leave the tower vicinity. They will not help you protect the wall from the Horde."

Queen Iseaia said with enthusiasm, "True, but it is a grand help and worth celebrating. Enough of war and such. We are here to enjoy ourselves. Mingle, have fun. Dinner will be served shortly."

King Split Tail asked, "Where is this granddaughter of mine? I would like to meet her."

Queen Iseaia's entire appearance changed to one of sadness. "Oh, she is over talking to the mages and clerics in the far corner. You cannot meet her, as she is in exile. But I have it from King Charles that she is the daughter of Princess Nim."

The platinum queen placed a hand over King Split Tail's mouth to keep him from roaring. When he calmed enough, she let go, and he said quietly, "Nim! That demon-loving wayward brat of mine! I exiled her over six hundred years ago. Charles told me they had a baby. I thought he was kidding. I should have known better. Do you have any idea what you have on your hands? What you have living next door to you?"

My queen became very serious and whispered just loud enough for all the dragons to hear. "Yes, I do. I have a child who is the kindest, nicest, good-at-heart person I have ever met. A child that came into my land and saved us from an evil red dragon, helped put out many fires, saved many lives, including mine, cleared the Temple of Magicum, and gave us hope, funding, and weapons so we may have a chance in this war. I have a savior next door that every man and woman in the country would fight for and die for. My own general was war buddies with her father and claims him good. Please be careful what you say about her parents. All here love your granddaughter and would take great offense."

Grandmother said, "Oh my." She hit Grandfather's arm and said, "Fool!"

Several of the other dragons started to mingle around the room. Every one of them took an opportunity to check me out. One said, "For a platinum dragon, she is very lovely but lacks in sexuality." The general explained the bracelet to her, and that made its rounds until every dragon knew.

Grandmother walked straight up to me and said, "Granddaughter, I would have a word with you." I ignored her, to the surprise of the clerics and mages I was talking to. I was showing them a new spell, one that was both arcane and divine and removed warts and birthmarks, and they were happy to learn.

One said, "I am sorry, Samantha, but there is a dragon in human form looking over your left shoulder, asking you a question."

I said, "Really. You don't say. Tell him or her that I am in exile and by dragon law cannot acknowledge his or her presence."

Grandmother left and went over to Grandfather.

The cleric said, "I don't think I have to relay your response. She just stormed off to her husband and hit him hard on the arm. They growled at each other."

Another cleric asked, "What did you do to be exiled?"

I said, "Six hundred years ago, my mother married outside her race, and that got her exiled. Being her daughter, the exile carries over to me. Foolish, isn't it?"

One of the clerics said, "If we humans exiled every human that married outside his race, there would be a mass exodus from Kayland. How did that spell go again?"

I continued to busy myself with the clerics and mages until dinner was called. The announcer addressed the assemblage, and people started sitting where their name marker was. Queen Iseaia, Formack, all the dragons, and I were at the front of the big U-shaped table. The rest were spread out to the sides and other tables. Breads and salads were brought in first. As I was waiting for my salad, the conversation started between Grandfather and Queen Iseaia.

Grandfather said, "This is a wonderful party, Queen Iseaia. The before-dinner snacks were tasty if not a little small for my taste. The idea of having a couple of elephants waiting for us to quench our hunger before dinner was a very good one. I wish others would have the manners to do the same. However, I am surprised that you have not mentioned needing our help for the upcoming war."

Grandmother said, "Men. All they think about is food, drink, and fighting. The elephants for this party must have cost you a small fortune. If you don't mind me asking, where did you get them and how much did they cost?"

Queen Iseaia said, "Just a second. Samantha, where did you get the elephants and how much did they cost?"

I said, "My queen, I have a friend who has a few thousand of them on a small world he keeps as a personal paradise. He is worried that they are overpopulated in the area and was glad to have me take six off his hands. He would love for me to remove some more. The only cost involved was making the gateway to his world big enough to herd elephants through."

Queen Iseaia turned to Grandmother and said, "I know she cannot pay attention to you, but do I need to repeat what she says? If so, then I will leave her out of the conversation completely."

Grandmother said, "No, I heard her. I suppose that removes any chance of us getting some for home. Oh well."

My salad came, and it was just the way I liked it—raw bits of meat and bone mixed with some lettuce and tomato. The servant asked, "Pepper, Princess?"

I thought, *Here it comes.* I was totally unsure of the consequences I was about to cause. I said with a smile, "No thank you. I have my own." I took out the artifact pepper grinder and set it on the table.

You could not smell the pepper while it was in the grinder. I waited until everyone had their salad and started eating. I picked up the pepper grinder and started grinding. All dragon eyes instantly turned to my plate. Dragon pepper has a grand smell, at least for dragons. Humans can smell it, but it smells like normal pepper to them.

Grandfather quickly reached out and tried to grab my pepper grinder while growling loudly. The others were getting up out of their seats and acting upset and about to attack. The general raised a hand, and forty men with powerful lances marched into the room. The dragons looked around in surprise while Queen Iseaia said, "What is this treachery? What are you doing?"

Grandfather roared out, "Sit down!" and the others sat back down. He glared at me and demanded, "Where did you get that dragon pepper, child?"

I paid him no attention at all. I finished putting pepper on my salad and then held out the pepper grinder, and it disappeared into the air as I sent it home.

Grandfather glared at my salad and then at me and growled. Queen Iseaia asked, "What is the problem, King Split Tail?" She raised a hand, and the lancers marched out.

Grandfather was so fuming he could not talk, so Grandmother said, "The child is using dragon pepper on her salad. It is the rarest spice in the know planes and worth a king's ransom."

I must give my queen credit, as she played her part very well. "Really. Dragon pepper, you say. My goodness, I wonder where she got it."

I took a bite, and Grandfather's mouth drooled onto his plate. I chewed with a blissful smile on my face. Dragon pepper has the grandest taste. I said, "My queen, this is truly a wonderful salad. I would offer you some, but dragon pepper is rather hard on humans unless cut a few thousand times, and this is pure dragon pepper." I took another bite.

Queen Iseaia asked, "Samantha, how much pepper is in that grinder?"

When I was finished with my bite, I said, "A little over six ounces. It's almost full."

Queen Iseaia tried to change the subject. "Well, I think that's enough surprises for the night. I have never visited the Dragon Lands. What is it like there?" The dragon royalty were watching me eat my salad and said nothing. The queen cleared her throat loudly and repeated her question. "What is it like in the Dragon Lands?"

Grandmother turned to my queen and said, "I am sorry, Queen Iseaia, but we seem to have a small disaster on our hands. You see, the only known dragon pepper in all the planes sits in the hands of a child we cannot even talk to. Dragon pepper is important to our survival, and that six ounces means a lot to us. Please wait, and I will get back to you about our country." She stood up and said, "I call an emergency meeting of the dragon council, to be held immediately."

The bronze king stood up and said, "I second it."

Grandfather stood up and said in an exasperated tone, "All in favor, say aye." They all said aye. "All opposed, say nay." No one said a thing. Grandfather said, "Then this emergency council is now in session." He sat back down.

Grandmother stood up. "I propose that the exile be lifted from Samantha immediately."

The brass queen said, "I second it."

Grandfather said, "We cannot lift an exile unless both sides agree to the consequences. I propose we lift the communication portion long enough to determine if we can come to an agreement."

The silver king said, "I'll second that."

Grandfather said, "All in favor, say eye." It was unanimous. Grandfather said, "Samantha, you can talk to us now."

I purposefully paid him no attention and took another bite. He started getting upset. Queen Iseaia said, "Samantha."

I swallowed, "Yes, my queen."

"The dragon council has called an emergency meeting

and has granted you the right to communicate until they can determine if the exile can be lifted."

For the first time, I looked directly into my grandfather's eyes and then into my grandmother's. I got up and went outside. Grandmother followed. We did not need to speak. We knew. As soon as we were outside, she changed to her dragon form, and so did I. I curled up into her arms, and we held each other in tears for a good long while. All the dragons were watching. The males were getting impatient, while the women were wondering why we broke it off so soon.

Grandmother said, "Child, we have a dinner to attend, and you have a lot to answer for. Let's go back in."

I uncurled and magically dried my tears. We walked back in and took our seats.

Grandfather said, "We are in council to determine if Samantha is worthy to rejoin our family and have the exile we placed on her mother lifted. Samantha, do you wish to have the exile lifted?"

I knew the law and had to say, "No."

Queen Iseaia looked shocked, and so did everyone else, except the dragons; they knew the laws and knew where this would place me. Grandfather asked, "Your reasons?"

I looked up into his big eyes and said, "If I allow the exile to be lifted, I would be directly under your control as a half-platinum dragon and directly under the control of the council. I am half-demon, and I would be shunned and belittled if I went home with you. I have given my life to Magicum, and by his words, I am to run his temple. I have a home here, and I intend to stay."

Grandfather said, "We can lift the exile and leave you a free agent not under anyone's control. Will you agree to that?"

"Yes."

Grandfather stood and said, "All those in favor of lifting the exile, knowing that Samantha will be a free agent, say aye." It was unanimous, and there were cheers throughout the assemblage.

Grandmother said, "Unless there is something else, I move to adjourn this emergency meeting."

The silver king said, "Second."

Grandfather said, "I adjourn this meeting." Then he turned to me, saying, "About that dragon pepper."

"What about it?"

The brass king said, "I will give you my entire treasure for that grinder and the pepper inside. Or just the pepper inside. I don't need the grinder."

I said, "Being that I don't know how much treasure you have, that's not a very smart deal for me to make. You need my dragon pepper for reproduction purposes. I was told that one and a half ounces will help to ensure a good birth. Am I correct?"

Grandfather said in quick, sharp tones, "That has never been told to anyone outside of the dragons proper. How did you find out?"

Grandmother said, "She is Nim's daughter. How do you think she found out?"

Grandfather turned back to me, trying to be nice. "Sweetheart?"

"Yes, Grandfather?"

"What do you want for those six ounces?"

I said, "I have thought about that, and I will make this deal. For every dragon that comes to help with this war, I will give one and a half ounces of dragon pepper. If two dragons come together, I will give them each one and a half ounces. That is enough dragon pepper to ensure the healthy hatching of two babies."

The brass king stood and pledged, "I will give you two

dragons for every one and a half ounces. Six ounces in that grinder, that's eight dragons to help in your war anywhere you need them."

The silver king stood and said, "I will grant you three dragons."

I held up my hand and said, "I have proposed a deal. I will give each dragon capable of and willing to help in this war their portion of dragon pepper. One and one half ounces."

Grandfather said, "I am willing to help in this war."

Grandmother said, "I do not like being held for ransom by dragon pepper, but I am willing to help in this war for that price." The two silvers and all the others stood at about the same time and claimed the same.

I motioned for them to sit down. I held out my hand and said, "Grandfather, how good is your knowledge of dragon pepper?"

Grandfather said, "All ancient dragons are experts when it comes to dragon pepper."

The grinder was in my hand instantly. I opened it and pulled out one seed. I handed it to him. "How old is this pepper?"

He took it and examined it closely and then crushed it in his hand and tasted a tiny portion of it. He passed the rest on to the next dragon, saying, "That, young lady, is fresh dried dragon pepper. That is impossible. There are no plants anywhere on any plane. We have searched for a thousand years."

I held my hand out again, and in it was a five-pound bag of dragon pepper. I opened it and handed him another seed. "How fresh is the seed from this five-pound bag?"

His eyes went wide. He took the seed and examined it. He proclaimed, "Fresh dragon pepper. Thank any god you want. Magicum is your god, child? I will praise him forever. How is this possible?"

I turned to Grandmother. "When this war is over, I will be

far more generous with what is mine. I will not hold you ransom, but I need dragons for this war. Our supply lines are vulnerable, and so is the wall."

She smiled. "I understand. I will not hold this against you. What can you spare?"

"I have a hundred pounds of harvested dragon pepper seeds, thanks to my great and wonderful god, Magicum, and King Charles."

Grandfather started to spin up. "That human boy child said there was no dragon pepper in the Druid Suppository! I questioned him personally!"

I said, "He was telling the truth, Grandfather. He cannot lie. I found the spice, and I quickly took it to the druid repository so it would not die from the curse. Charles has given me the keys and permission to enter the Druid Suppository for the purpose of harvesting dragon pepper and replanting. He is teaching me farming. It's fun; however, I am limited to that one small area, if for no other reason than to protect the dragon pepper and make it multiply. Charles and I are the only ones allowed in, and it will stay that way. I have been there recently, and we now have twenty plants doing very well."

Grandmother never took her eyes off me as she said, "King Split Tail. What happens if Charles and Samantha are no longer alive? What happens to the entire dragon population?"

Grandfather said, "We will have a hundred dragons here tomorrow, and five of the best will be for protection." He looked at the other dragons and said, "Agreed!"

It was argued over for hours. Most wanted me back in the dragon lands right away. They did not want to take any chances. I put a stop to that. "I have a home, and I am staying."

The silver dragon king said, "If Samantha shares the dragon pepper with the enemy dragons, they will switch sides." That started another round of arguments about who should and should not receive dragon pepper that lasted throughout the night. Meanwhile, Grandfather sent a message, and by morning, our hills were filled with dragons. Five impressive dragons, one from each metal, followed me everywhere.

Several days later, a black dragon came to the border asking to talk. She was nearly killed just trying to get the word out that she only wanted to ask a question. Gold dragons and black dragons are mortal enemies, and it was difficult to hold the gold back. However, the platinum dragons protected the female black when they saw that she did not attack and gave signs of surrender.

One enormous gold dragon, hissing with rage, asked, "What is it you want, little black?"

The black dragon was torn up and needed healing, so a cleric did a few spells, and she was healthy again. "I have come representing the dragons of the Horde. We wish to know why the good-aligned dragons have chosen to die in this war. We have a demigod backing us, and your death is assured."

The gold dragon answered, "We have a demigod helping our side and the Tower of Sight, Magicum's temple, with his lances. You may get lucky and take down this wall, but you will never pass the tower. The reason for our help is simple. The high priestess of Magicum has a renewable source of dragon pepper that she is sharing with us. We will ensure that she is not harmed, as that would destroy the dragon pepper."

The black dragon hissed and said, "You lie! There is no more dragon pepper! Even the gods cannot find any."

I had been watching from the tower when the posted watch informed the general that the dragons had caught a black dragon. It was time to interfere. I took off the bracelet and changed into my most seductive form, a demon dragon of extraordinary platinum beauty. My five dragon guards and I teleported to the wall and down to the black dragon. When I suddenly showed up, the other dragons stepped back and bowed. I had shown them this aspect of me so they would know who it was if needed.

I said, "Rise, my friends." I looked down at the black dragon and said, "You have come with questions in your heart, child. First, your demigod is nothing. He has made the mistake of planning a war that will take him through my home, and I am more than his equal when at home. He will not pass this point. Second, the dragons surrounding you and in this area have all been given allotments of dragon pepper in exchange for their protection and support." I held up a hand, and in it was a seed. I handed it to the black dragon.

She took it, crushed it, and licked it off her paw. Her eyes widened. "Fresh dragon pepper." Her eyes narrowed, and she hissed. "I suppose only the platinum dragons will benefit from this, and maybe some gold."

My demon side flashed red with anger, and the little black dragon cringed back. I held out my hand and instantly held a small bag of pepper, exactly one and a half ounces. "I do not differentiate between one type of dragon and another when it comes to reproduction. As you can see, I am half-platinum, and that helps me to be good, but I am half-demon, and that lets me see and understand your side. It is my belief that all dragons have a right to this seed." Her eyes never left my hand and the bag, but her words let me know she was listening.

She hissed, "What do you want for that bag?"

I said, "The same thing I want from all dragons at this time. This war is threatening my ability to harvest the limited amount of seed I have. It is hidden on another plane that others cannot enter. A plane even the gods cannot reach, and therefore it is protected from the curse. Given time, I could supply all dragons with seed. In fact, I plan on eventually giving all seed to the dragon gods Drajuris and Draquae to distribute to their clerics. They can then ensure all are taken care of in an even manner. Good, evil, natural, all will be treated equally. The problem at this point is the war. My home is in the city on the other side of this wall, and this war threatens my ability to ensure the continued production of dragon pepper."

She said, "For that bag, I will promise to remove myself from the war and to take your words to the other dragons."

I smiled. "Done! But be warned. Hide what I am giving you and take only one seed to the others, unless you want them killing you for it." I handed her the bag, and she immediately took off.

The great gold dragon asked, "Was that wise, Godling?"

I looked up into the eyes of the gold dragon and said with a smile, "Ask your king. It was his suggestion. Personally, I am not sure."

CHAPTER 2

HALF THE BATTLE

Word spread through the Horde dragons, and they nearly all took god oaths not to participate in any war or group attacking the Farnorth area. I even received a note from their demigod congratulating me on forcing him to change his plans. He promised, whatever that was worth, that he would not attack Farnorth. He sent the queen's brother's head along with the note. The queen was not pleased.

The king of Ginham was not pleased either. The Horde shifted its army to the eastern seaside passage, and that would give them direct entrance into Ginham only a few leagues from the capital city. Keeping enough men back to ensure this was not a ruse. The mixed army moved out of Landtrap and to the sea, with two thousand fresh troops from Ginham meeting them at the eastern passage.

Though the king of Ginham was upset that the war was shifting to his border, he was very glad that seventy dragons shifted with it. That enthusiasm changed when he started to feel the cost of feeding them.

He was sitting on his throne when he received the latest

report on the cost of the war. "Eight thousand gold for cows to feed dragons! Are you insane? What are these cows made of? Platinum?"

There were several clerks reporting, and the lead clerk said, "But, sire, each dragon eats a cow a day, and we have seventy-three dragons helping in this war. That price feeds them for an entire month. We have to herd the cattle from the Dead Lands, and it is lucky that Kayland is giving us the cattle at less than half the normal cost and moving the cattle to our border free of charge. Without their help, and I am sure it is costing Kayland dearly to do this, the cost would be double or more. Eight thousand is nothing compared to the price we are paying the fleet to maintain a full blockade up the Horde coast. That is costing us five thousand a day, and we are losing supply ships to the pirates."

The king slumped on his throne. "Shift some of the dragons to protect the supply lines, including the ships. How are my treasure reserves holding up?"

The clerk took a step backward. "Sire, the treasure is already half what it was when this started. As you know, a war tax was instituted last week, but it will be a month before we see any of that money. I am expecting us to be broke in about three weeks."

The king was becoming mad and could easily order the head of the clerk. He had worked long and hard to bring his kingdom up to a standard equal with Kayland and put some reserves away for future repairs to roads and cities. Now it was being eaten away, and the kingdom was going to be war torn. To be honest, he didn't care when it was Landtrap that was paying and their lands that would be destroyed. He cared now.

The witch queen of Rosewood cared also. This war was close to her land, and she was there to ensure the king knew her concerns. In a voice like ice daggers dragging against your spine, the queen said, "King Ordorneath! I will help with this cost, but I can only do so much. The other nations need to support you also."

He looked at the queen. "How much will you help, Queen Cursegranter? And can you get the other nations to help? They didn't look on me favorably after they found out I was the one supporting the pirates—the same accursed pirates that are taking advantage of my situation now."

She stared at him with an evil eye and said, "I will give you five hundred thousand in gold, but I can do no more, so never ask! As far as the others, you have made your life as it is. Now go apologize and beg if you have to."

He stood in anger. "I will never beg!"

Power erupted around both, so I stepped in. "If you two can't get along, then you have already lost, so calm down." I looked at the witch and added, "Turn an evil eye on me, and I will pluck it out and eat it."

She looked away, and when she turned back, her expression was much better. "Why are you here, child?"

I said, "I am here to help. I can go to the other nations and ask for increased support. I can also help with many other issues. Clerk!"

"Yes, Princess Samantha."

"How much is the king spending on consumable magic, especially war-supporting magic like potions, wands, and staves?"

He conferred with his other clerks and then turned back to me. "Nothing, Princess. We have asked, and the generals have made a list of demands, but the king has not had the funds to address this issue."

I said, "In truth, the king hasn't addressed the issue because he doesn't care about the causalities—only about the cost of the war." King Ordorneath started to say something but decided not to push his luck against two powerful women at one time.

The witch queen was looking pleased. "I am glad to see that another can see through your foolishness, King Ordorneath. You cannot run this war with lace gloves. You need to get your hands in the brew and get them stained with your sweat and blood. You should be leading your army, or at least supporting your general. Foolish, young king. Your great-grandfather was far more a king than you."

I addressed the witch queen. "I see things differently. True, his great-grandfather was a grand warrior, but his kingdom suffered with his need for a fight. King Ordorneath has done well by his people, even if it was for personal, greedy reasons. He is not a trained warrior. He is a simple wizard king." I looked at him with my own evil eye and added, "And the laws of power state he should not be both. However, you have a great general, and you should let him run this war. Support him in any way possible and leave him alone to do the planning and fighting. We will support you in this." I looked at the clerk. "Where is this list of demands?"

"I have it right here. I must say that some of the items I do not understand. I have crossed them off the list."

The witch queen nearly lost it. "Wars are not for clerks to run!"

King Ordorneath blushed. "They are only trying to keep the general from going overboard in his requests."

I turned to the king and said, "Queen Cursegranter is correct. Though you have been a good king during peace, you are a fool when it comes to war. I will give you two choices. Give over to the general in all his requests, and we will help and support you and ensure your country does not fall. We will help financially and physically. Or, we will let you and your clerks run the war, and we will lose faith and take our help, people, and dragons back to our lands and shore up our borders, leaving you on your own."

He sat up straighter. "If you do that, the Horde will run right through us, leaving nothing. Kayland would not be happy. Can you afford for Kayland to be upset with you?"

I said as unconcerned as possible, "Yes. Can you?"

Queen Cursegranter added, "I could care less what Kayland thinks as long as they stay out of my country. The Horde will not. If they come into my country, I will hold you responsible. I know you are planning to run if they break through the border defenses. If they don't catch you, I will find you."

I said, "If you give all power to the general, I can assure you there will be no need to run."

He slumped again and said to his clerks, "Turn the treasure and all taxes over to the general. Grant the general emergency powers during the war that allow him to be the hand of the king. Everything that has to do with the war is to be decided by the general, and I will stay out of it. Write it so, and I will seal it."

His clerks wrote it up, and I watched as he sealed it. He gave it over to me reluctantly. "This gives the general power to overthrow me."

I assured him, "This gives the general power to win this war. Your people will thank you for recognizing that the general is better at war than you. They love you, and so does the general. He will not overthrow you."

Queen Cursegranter said, "This means I do not have to visit you anymore. I will be visiting the general."

That perked the king up considerably. "And will you be pestering, I mean, visiting the general also, Princess Samantha?"

"As soon as I secure the rest of your treasure. I wouldn't want it disappearing or becoming unavailable." That wiped the smile off his face. I raised a hand and was gone, and so was everything of value in his castle.

I showed up in the small sea border town of Blackcove. Not much there to see. There was one stable, a tannery, and a small port for small ships and fishing boats outside the town walls. Inside, there was a small castle, a temple to Solbelli, eighty or so homes, four shops, one blacksmith, and one inn, which was full and overstuffed.

I walked up to the gate and announced myself to the surprise of the gate guards and the cheers of some of Farnorth's men who were lounging around.

"The princess!" Men bowed, and many ran up and asked, "Are you here to help? We need your help. This show is being run horribly, and we have no supplies."

I held up the scroll and said, "I have a proclamation from the king giving the general full powers, and I have brought the funds to back it up. I need escorts to enhance my dragon guard."

Fifty men fell in immediately, and they were not all mine. I was pleased to see twenty or so were Drow. I said to the captain, "It is nice to see you are getting along with our friends from Rosewood."

Queen Cursegranter showed up as planned and walked up next to me. "I am also glad to see they are getting along with your people."

The captain bowed to the queen and said, "We are much the same—your people and ours. We have a lot of things in common."

A sergeant said quietly, "I trust the Drow far more than I trust the Ginham men."

A Drow cleric said, "And we trust Farnorth more than we trust Kayland or Ginham, but we are working with all—as our queen requires."

All the Drow, except the cleric, were in full knee on the ground, bowing to their queen. She said, "Rise, my people, and follow."

The queen and I talked to our people to ascertain exactly what had been going on and what needed to happen. By the time we reached the castle, we were both extremely upset but realized it was not the general's fault.

General Bigman was widely known as one of the best generals that the nations had to date. Nearly as good as King Charles, though General Bigman could not boast taking out ten thousand demons without losing a single man, like people claimed King Charles did. Charles told me once that it was only two thousand demons. I was still shocked. We walked into the castle after going through several checkpoints. We could have easily passed them, but we decided to keep it slow so that we could pass the word at each point about the king's proclamation and the needed help. It would spread like wildfire and raise the morale of the army considerably. We reached the throne room, and the general was talking to, of all people, Master Ortherntus, the caravan master of the group that I met when I first entered Landtrap. That cantankerous old man was telling the general that if he didn't get paid in gold, and soon, his caravans would stop bringing in the requested supplies.

"Look, General Bigman, I am not trying to make a profit off your problem. I am trying to pay my drivers and the hired men that protect my caravan. They have families and do not understand not getting paid. The mercenaries will have my hide if I can't pay them. And now you ask me for twice as much as I have already delivered, and you haven't paid me for the first two shipments yet. I cannot do this."

Queen Cursegranter is not a patient person. She walked right up to the two and said to Master Ortherntus, "How much does the general owe you?"

"He is in debt to me eighteen thousand gold. Who are you?"

She was not big, but the queen could have an imposing presence if needed. She did that then, and both men backed up just a little. The general's hand went to his sword, and the caravan master's hand went to his money belt. "I am Queen Cursegranter of the Rosewood and leader of the Drow. You are Master Ortherntus. You have stayed out of my lands, and for that I thank you. Princess Samantha, can you pay this fool?"

I walked up, and Master Ortherntus's eyes went wide in surprise. The last time he saw me, I destroyed a red dragon and saved his caravan.

Master Ortherntus said, "Samantha, you are a sight for sore eyes. I am so glad to see you. Perhaps you can talk some sense into this man and the queen." He had moved so that I was between him and the witch queen.

I held out a hand, and a small bag was in it. I rattled it just a little. I opened it and placed one gem in his hand. "It's nice to see you again also. I am sure you can appraise this gem, Master Ortherntus. And don't try to cheat me. I know its worth."

He took the stone and rubbed it against his vest, took out a small eyepiece and placed it in his eye, and then looked at the stone. He turned it over several times and then took the eyepiece out and placed it in his pocket. "In the right place, I can get two thousand for this blood stone. No more but not less either. It is a good stone and in demand."

I thought, *Two thousand. That's better than I thought.* To the caravan master, I said, "Then here is twenty thousand in blood stones." I dropped the bag in his hand. "I will trade any one of them for gold if you need to pay off some debts before you can cash them in."

He quickly said, "No, no, my good friend. This will be easier to carry and protect. Thank you." He turned to the general. "You seem to have some new backers. This payment will allow me to obtain the supplies you're requesting."

I said, "General, did you order all you need?"

He looked skeptical at the two women who just saved his supplies, wondering what now. "Thank you, Princess Samantha and Queen Cursegranter. I am surprised and pleased. To answer your question, no, we need ten times that amount yesterday, but I cannot afford what we need."

I turned to Master Ortherntus. "Sir, how much can you obtain and how quickly can you bring it to the general?"

"If I can be reassured of payment, and with a little up-front money, I can pull together the resources and obtain ten times what he has on this paper. It will be difficult, and I will need to hire more protection."

I turned to one of the dragon guard and asked, "Caravan protection?"

The gold dragon said, "I will send two youngsters with him to protect. Add enough to the supplies to feed them so they don't eat the horses."

I smiled. "Thank you." He walked over to the window and roared. Two young dragons showed up immediately. They talked, and both looked at Master Ortherntus, then flew away.

I said, "As you can see, sir, you will have your protection. How much to obtain the supplies?"

"Another twenty thousand should do it, and that includes the food for the dragons. It will be another one hundred and fifty thousand when I return. Can you afford that?"

The general was about to yell, but I said, "Here is the twenty." I raised a hand, and a small chest appeared, open and spilling platinum. "The rest will be waiting for your return."

Master Orthernus bowed to me and said while motioning

for his men to grab the chest, "I will return with those supplies quickly, and they will be the best available."

As he was walking out, I yelled to him, "They had better be very good for that price!"

He turned and bowed far more gracefully than I would have thought possible as he continued to leave. I turned to the general and handed him the proclamation. He opened it, and the tension left his shoulders and face.

He asked, "How did you get this?"

The queen said, "You have a good king. He just needed a little persuasion that you would do a better job running the war."

I looked at the queen and added with a smile, "It didn't hurt that we made him think we would be on his doorstep until he decided that you needed us more than he did." She smiled, and we both turned to the general and waited.

He looked at us for a minute and said, "Women! Sometimes you have to love them." He yelled, "I want copies made of this proclamation, and I want criers to tell the rest of the nation the king has transferred all powers to me for the duration of this war. Ensure they know that the king is still the king and he will have all powers back as quickly as possible." He turned back to us. "Did you spend all the treasure? There are a lot of things I have asked for and not received." I handed him the message that he sent to the king with his original requests. He asked, "Why are some of my most important items lined out? Are they on the way?"

The queen said with distaste, "They are lined out because the clerks were handling your requests, and they did not think you really needed them. No, they are not on the way."

The general turned red with anger and said to his clerk, "I want all those clerks transferred to me, and I want them stationed in the front. They can take orders from my captains. Maybe that way they can see firsthand why I need what I ask for."

The lead clerk said, "I have good men in those positions, General, and I am not replacing them with fools. I will send them for training under my men. Will that suffice?"

"Make it so." He turned back to us. "One of the best ways to do well in any situation is to surround yourself with knowledgeable people who will rein you in if you are about to do something silly."

The queen said, "You have all the funding and resources you need to ensure success. If you need what is on that list, then get it. I must return home. Samantha has agreed to help you as much as possible." My dragon guard all growled, so she added, "Without endangering herself. She is needed by others, so use her for important issues but keep her safe. Goodbye, General. Goodbye, Samantha. It was interesting meeting you." She departed.

I said goodbye, but she had already left.

The general said, "The witch queen is helping us? I am impressed and worried."

I said, "Don't be worried, General Bigman. She is helping because she wants you to stop the Horde and not allow them to pass through Ginham and into her lands. There is no need of worry. She is a nice person, not good but not evil either. Just very protective about her land. Charles once told me, 'She is a good person to know as long as you remember not to mess with her property.'"

He asked, "What can I expect from you in this war?"

I said, "I will help in any manner I can that does not place me in danger. I am presently taking care of the demigod issue. However, it will take me a few days to prepare for that battle. Meanwhile, I can support you in many ways. For instance, I can go to the kings and queens and see if they can give you more men or other support, I can go to the university and get you many more wizards, and I can go to the temples and get you clerical support."

Something manifested near the window, and the demigod in question was standing there looking at me. I smiled. "I was wondering when you would show up. You are Rormantle, are you not?"

He answered, and his voice echoed so that he seemed more than he truly was. It did not fool me or the general. "I am the great and deadly Rormantle. You are interfering in my plans far too much. I cannot afford for you to give any more help to these fools. Therefore, I need to destroy you before you gain whatever it is you need to battle me." He raised a hand, and the general, my escort, and all others were paralyzed. I was not, and he did not look pleased about that. "You are not a god. You have not lived for thousands of years like I have. You have not fought your way up through the ranks to your position as I have. You do not have the experience that I have. You will lose this battle, and I will take all that you own and eat your skinny soul. I challenge you to the death."

I clapped. "Oh, that was good. I am almost impressed. We should not fight here. You challenged, so I get to pick the place." I raised a hand, and we were both on a plane of total emptiness, in a large oval stadium with two metal, twenty-foot stands, one on each end. Eight gods of greater good were on one side, and eight gods of greater evil were on the other. The bleachers were full, and creatures were making bets. The two of us were in coarse wraps. All our magic items and clothing had been removed.

He recognized the place instantly and yelled, "What am I getting for odds?"

One of the Evil Gods answered, "One thousand to one."

Rormantle laughed. "They feel I will win that quickly? Oh, child demigoddess, you cannot escape this place. You have brought yourself to your doom."

The Evil God said, "You did not understand me correctly, Rormantle. The odds are for Samantha to win—and win quickly."

Another Evil God said, "I have placed a million gold that she will destroy you within ten seconds."

Another said, "Samantha. If you hold out for eleven seconds, I will destroy the insignificant Horde for you." That started an argument between them that the owners of this place had to quickly stop.

An old man stepped into the arena. "There is only one rule."

Rormantle yelled, "There are no rules! There have never been rules before. I will not allow rules!"

The old man said, "The rule is not for you, fool. It's for her."

"Oh." He quieted down.

The old man turned to me saying, "The one rule is simple. You will not use any magic that will destroy this place."

The crowd started changing bets, and odds started changing. The Evil God said, "No one mentioned that. I want to change my bet."

I looked at him and said, "I wouldn't if I were you." Then I returned my attention to Rormantle.

Rormantle was getting a little worried. He looked like he wanted to run, and in fact that was his normal way to fight. Hit and run, hit and run, hit and run until the one he was attacking made a mistake. Then it was in for the kill. Except, in this place, you could not run. That was why we had picked it. Two entered, and one left. Sometimes neither left if the battle was that close. You were on your own, for no one here would help you. In fact, some of the betting was for both to die. Those odds were normally astronomical. Still, no one interfered, not even the gods. The gods did have to sanction the battle, and that was seldom allowed. But Rormantle was on the world without permission, and his gods were not happy. I knew because King Charles was curious and asked them.

The announcer said, "Take your positions and ready."

I moved slowly to the metal stand nearest me and waited. My eyes never left Rormantle. He tended to cheat when he could, and he was not allowed to cast until told. Rormantle moved to his position and waited. I could see by the glow and strength that power was already strong in him and getting stronger quickly. I instantly powered up, and that shocked him, as I powered up with Over God spells. I had already readied myself for this fight, and that was why I bragged to the general about all the help I could give him but told him I wasn't ready to fight. I knew Rormantle was watching.

King Charles and I had studied Rormantle in the Druid Suppository and developed a plan. Getting him to show up and challenge me was part of that plan. Charles received permission and booked the arena. I prepared my spells just for this battle. You see, when Charles and I studied Rormantle in the Druid Suppository, we took our time. Three hundred years of continuous mock battles and testing new spells.

The announcer said, "Start!"

I did eight seeable spells before he could get off one, and he died, and his soul was destroyed. His scream was long and loud.

The announcer said, "Two point three seconds! A new record!"

One of the Evil Gods yelled, "Foul!"

The old man came into the ring again and turned to the Evil God. "In what way do you consider this a foul?"

The Evil God said, "I counted. She did eight spells in two seconds. That is impossible. Someone was helping her. No god at her level can be that fast."

The old god turned to me and asked, "How is it you could

do eight very high-level spells in only two seconds? Three should have been your best."

I smiled. "I used a spell that slows time surrounding us. It does not affect the gods, but it does effect demigods and below."

The old man said, "That is a fast spell if triggered from a scroll, only because the materials and the spell components are already spent. To do it on the fly is not possible, and you were not allowed scrolls or other magical devices. That spell takes several minutes to cast due to the time required to pay the material cost and create the symbols. It is a very costly spell. The only way you could do it is if you had it prepared beforehand and on a device for triggering. You had no device."

I told him, "I did the entire spell on my hand. All I had to do was say the trigger word. Did you not notice the explosion from my hand as the spell triggered?" I raised my hand, and all that was there was a bloody stump. The crowd went wild in appreciation. "I will grow my hand back when I have the time. I nearly fainted from the pain, but I completed a full heal so it no longer hurts. I did not do eight spells. I did ten. Two were for my own needs to heal me from the spells I cast. I nearly destroyed myself with the sixth spell. All were nonsomatic and nonverbal."

The old god said, "Then you were prepared before entering the arena. The next question, which one of you made the challenge?"

I said, "Ask the gods. They were watching."

The Evil God said, "That fool Rormantle made the challenge. She goaded him into it, and he fell for it. A little girl child beginner demigod took out my favorite, highly experienced demigod. I am impressed. And I just made a good bit of gold. Not that I need it, but it was fun."

One of the Good Gods, I think it was Brevis the gnome god,

said, "Malificus, we made a bet on the Sanctuarium Plane. We have won without foul."

Malificus, the Evil God of tyranny said, "We will keep with the bet. The girl child may stay on the Prime Material Plane as a high priestess to Magicum until the current war is over. After that, she must leave, or there will be repercussions. It has been agreed by us all and the bet made and signed in blood. It will be interesting to see if she can maintain her alignment to good. Her attachment to her alignment is very shaky, and we did not agree to leave her alone. If she changes to evil, she still remains on the Prime Material Plane for the entire war, which we will drag out and without complaint from either side."

Brevis thought on that for only a second and then turned his eyes on me. "True, that aspect was never mentioned. However, it was agreed to not force her into anything. You cannot turn her evil against her will, and she has a strong will."

Malificus said, "I do not need to force her in any way. My new champion will come to me eventually. That is not an issue." The Evil Gods all looked at me with grins of triumph and disappeared.

I turned to the Good Gods, and Brevis said to me, "You are a fear. You can do much good and much bad in the galaxy."

I said, "What they did not know is I must be good or die."

All the Good Gods looked shocked. Brevis said, "We cannot kill you. We made a bet and must keep our hands off unless you pray for our help."

I said, "I pray to Magicum and only Magicum. However, King Charles has warned me that if I change to evil, he will kill me himself. It is an agreement I made for his help in training me personally."

Again they looked shocked. One asked gently, "When did this happen? We have watched you closely, and you were visited by Charles several times but not long enough for training."

"Charles took me from Magicum's Temple to the Druid Suppository and trained me there. We were there for three hundred years of constant study and practice. He foresees a time when I will be sorely tempted to become evil. Sorely tempted. He waits to see what I will do."

They said together, "So do we!"

They disappeared, and so did the arena. I was back with the general in Blackcove's castle. They were still paralyzed. I said to myself, "Well, that was half the battle, but that was the easy part. Painful but easy. Taking out the orc king and his evil dragon general will be the difficult part."

CHAPTER 3

MAGICAL SUPPORT
AND PROTECTION

I removed the paralysis and waited. Some people come quickly out of paralysis when released and some take a little longer. My dragon guard, all the Drow, three half dragons, two half demons, and the general were quick, but most of the rest of the humans were not. The dragon guard was not happy, and one stood over me, looking most impressive, and threatened me.

"Princess, you will not do that again. We go with you whatever the circumstances."

I raised a hand, and they were paralyzed again. I said, "I don't like being dictated to. Besides, you would be dead before we reached the place of battle. You are here to keep the little bugs off me. The big bugs I will swat myself." I raised my hand, and they were free. I said, "General, issue number one has been removed from existence. What would you like me to do now?"

He looked at me long and hard, and his hand slowly relaxed on his sword. "I don't like it when the enemy can just come and go as they please in our headquarters. Can you do something about that?"

I smiled. "Give me two days, and nothing harmful will use magic to enter this castle."

"Princess, you can take three, as I may need you for some payments between now and then. I still need the items on that list, and the mages and clerics have a long list of items they will need."

"General, send me the mages and clerics list, and I will personally take care of it. They knew about your lack of prior funding and may have tried to cut the cost. I need to know what they really need. Between my own supplies and the university, we should be able to complete the list. Besides, I will know if they are being foolish with their requests."

The general said, "Consider it done." The clerk was holding up a parchment. A young trainee took it and handed it to me with bows and a look of adoration. The guard growled, and he moved back quickly.

I read the list and said, "They need much more than this, and they know it. I looked over at the Drow mage and cleric. "Where can I find the makers of this list?"

The mage said, "Follow us."

Three hundred men followed us out of the castle and into the town. I stopped the entire group and said, "Don't most of you have something to do? Repair armor, sharpen your weapons, something? I don't need hundreds following me." I said it with a loving smile.

Several laughed, and almost all peeled off and started running throughout the town. But as I walked down the streets, I noticed that ten men, and exactly ten men, were on each corner, all waiting the chance to give assistance. I could not help but think that, for a common soldier, war is 10 percent training, 89 percent waiting, and less than 1 percent fighting and dying.

We entered the temple of Solbelli and were led by an acolyte to a large room where there was some excited yelling going on. Mages and clerics lined the room, and all were talking about what they needed for their assignments.

One cleric said, "We ordered twenty wands of Cure Minor Wounds. They are not something you can use during battle. We need them in the hands of clerics wandering the battle field ensuring that everyone gets healed as time allows. You pull out a wand during a fight to heal someone, and the enemy will cut it in half, losing all the charges instantly."

"I need those wands up front and in the battle. As a war mage, I cannot heal others, and we cannot leave the battlefield even if bleeding to death."

"That's what potions are for. You have an opening, then pull a potion and drink it. We ordered enough potions for everyone to have one each."

I listened for several minutes before opening the door and walking in. "Good evening, distinguished colleagues." The entire place went quiet. "How are we today? Some of you seem a little irritated."

Formack looked at me as if he were drowning and I was the lifeboat. He said, "Samantha! It is wonderful to see you again. We are debating what the best uses are for the magic we have asked for. It seems to be rather heated. How are your plans coming?"

"Hello, Formack, my good friend. I have finished with part one and am starting part two."

Formack's eyes showed great concern. "My princess, wasn't part one removing the demigod that is supporting the enemy? Won't that remove you?"

"The demigod is destroyed." Instant jubilation was followed

by a barrage of questions. I raised my stub of an arm and said, "I need to grow this back, so how about being a little polite and letting me say a few things."

Several higher-level clerics took over and quieted them down, while two other clerics gently looked at my arm. When everyone was quiet and waiting, I continued. "It is nice to see that the clerics and mages are planning together. I have several things to say, and then I am going to the tower to heal myself. Please refrain from saying anything until I am done. First, apparently you have not heard, but the king has given over all power to the general for the length of this war and all treasure. Queen Cursegranter and I have added to the treasure. Second, as my good friend Formack can assure you, I have a lot of magic supplies that I can add to the resources. Tomorrow, Formack can bring several people and take from my stockpiles. The general has given me the responsibility of getting you everything you need. I was listening for several minutes, and it occurred to me that potions are the best for the immediate fight, but all my potions are in glass vials. You will need to transfer them to metal vials if you want to take them into combat. If I were fighting you and saw glass vials on each person, I would do a spell that would shatter all of them at once."

They all looked at one another, as if saying, "Why didn't we think of that?"

I continued. "Find out where we can get our hands on a lot of metal vials. Formack has seen what I have that can be used." I turned to Formack. "Remember, the lances cannot leave the tower area."

Formack said, "I remember, my lady, and I can quickly obtain a copy of the inventory of magic in the tower temple of Magicum."

"Good. Use that inventory. I will make it all available with the understanding that, if not used, I get it back. Please look closely at that list and make a list of anything else you need and where we may be able to obtain it. I will try to pull together the resources you request within reason. Now I must leave. I will be expecting you tomorrow morning." I turned and walked out to a completely different type of yelling, most of it directed at Formack. They wanted to know what was available and when they could have it. I took my guards home with me and went to my workrooms. I started the very painful process of growing back a hand.

Formack showed up the next day with twenty mages teleporting into the courtyard. Each mage brought three people each, mostly clerics and fighters.

A paladin of Magicum took up residence when I wasn't paying attention, so I had him check for evil, and then I allowed Formack and ten of his choice to go through the supplies and take whatever they needed. It took them eight trips, and they still took only about half of what was there. I asked for the list of other necessities, and there was none.

Formack said, "My princess, you have all the expensive magic items we needed. Everything else, including the metal vials, is being supplied by others. Apparently the Drow use metal vials whenever possible and could obtain thousands of empty containers. We have a hundred acolytes cleaning the poison out of them at this time. Then those same acolytes will transfer and mark the vials. We have brought in several from the university who are too young to be in the battle but can do Find Magic spells and recover all the magic items from the field so they can be reused until depleted. Also, they will keep inventory of what we have and what we've used so we can return the rest to you. This was a big debate. Many wanted to retain the items, but the other countries would not allow it, as all that magic gives too much of an advantage. They decided that keeping it in the tower would be best. That way, they know where it is when needed. It seems that Kayland has word that another continent has an emperor that is getting a little jealous over the Sordeath and its food supplies. Kayland is worried, and that makes the rest of us worried. The mages and clerics know you are busy, so they are handling as much of the war preparation as possible themselves. However, they have one question."

I asked, "What would that be?"

Formack said, "They know you are a god—though minor. They know you are trying to be good and are in fact good at this time. They realize you destroyed the demigod. What they want to know is what the Evil Gods are going to do to even out the imbalance? The Drow tried to tell them that the Law of Balance was not placed upon you yet, that you are being limited by the gods in some way so that you cannot overly interfere. Therefore, you can stay without harming the balance but can only do so much. In truth, few believe the Drow."

I said, "That's a shame, as they are telling you the truth." I told him about the battle and the bets.

He looked thoughtful. "Until the war is over, the Evil Gods will try to turn you to their point of view, and King Charles is poised to destroy you if they succeed. Not a good position to be in, my princess. I am sorry."

I smiled. "Oh, I think I can handle it. On another issue, I've been doing a little scrying. Want to see what that demigod, and now the orc king, has in store for you?"

He looked hesitant. "I think it would be a good idea. They have been very quiet."

I took him to the tower top and showed him my bowl. "This is a minor artifact called the Bowl of Mirrors. Just add water, and the water becomes crystal clear and then black. When it turns black, though that may take several weeks, it is ready for scrying. I have been watching the castle of the Drop for many days, and nothing was noticed until I focused on one general who seemed to come and go a lot. I followed him, and this is what I found."

Formack looked into the depths of the bowl and pulled back. His look was of pure terror. "This is not right! They cannot do this!" He looked again and watched for some time. "This will change our plans. I need to report immediately."

"I have sent a note to the general, but it would be good if you told him personally."

Formack said rather formally, "I am on it." He turned and left.

I looked into the bowl and shuddered a little, as I did every time I saw the army that maniac demigod had created. Along with the tens of thousands of orcs and goblins, he took the dead from our battlefield during the battle between Ginham and Kayland and made them undead. Our own people. Our fathers and brothers would be fighting us. I turned away before my blood could run cold. What was he thinking? I doubted he could control an army like that. Undead are hard to control even for undead. "Fool!" He must have had something for control. I might need to make a little visit to the Drop.

I told the general that I would fix the protections around his headquarters, so, for the next three days, I did just that. When I entered the main room to complete the last of the protections, he said, "Samantha, I received your report, and that stupid mage Formack told everyone. We are completely changing our plans. Do you have any other surprises for us? It would be nice to know now."

I looked up from my current spell casting as soon as I was finished and said, "Only one. Apart from the main Horde army, there is a small group of amphibious undead creatures that number no more than three hundred. They are preparing to remove your blockade. I sent several dragons to feast on the creatures. Their numbers are quickly diminishing. Have you not noticed that the dragons have been taking turns leaving and returning and that they come back well fed?"

The gold dragon guard said, "The water creatures are nearly all gone. We will be back to eating cattle soon, but the water creatures were a good relief from the tedium. An elephant or two would be nice." He said that wishfully.

The general said, "I need to know these things. Please continue to take care of the issues if you can, but I need to be aware of every issue. Three hundred water creatures to remove our blockade means they have ships that number in the hundreds. They were preparing to go around our defenses. I will need to ensure that those ships are destroyed."

The gold dragon said, "If you wish, I will send a flight of dragons to search their coast. We will destroy any ships we see."

The general said, "Not yet. Let them think they are getting away with their plan."

"Very well, General."

I went back to placing my protections while the gold dragon and the general talked.

The silver dragon came over to me and said, "You are very good at one-on-one combat, but you have no idea about war. We have vast experience when it comes to war. We are around you all the time, and that allows us to see many things we could pass on to the general privately. He wants us to report to him anything that we deem he should know. Is this all right with you?"

I stood up from placing my last spell and said in the language of dragons, "Sure. I've never been through a war before. Please let me know what you are going to tell him and why. I may learn something from you in that way."

She smiled. "You could learn much from us, child. For instance, how to properly pronounce draconic." She patted my head, turned, and walked over to the general to report. I started to fume. I learned my draconic directly from my mother, and she was born to it.

Then I remembered what Charles once told me: "Don't worry when someone treats you like a child. Work with it. They do it on purpose, and you can use it to get your way. Let them think you're still young, let them train you, let them be the older brother or sister. It makes them feel good, and it gives you power over them, as they think you are a child, and we both know you are smarter than they can possibly understand. Besides, sometimes we are the child compared to the one with experience. We don't know everything. When you start thinking you know everything, that's when you'll mess up the worst. I hope you live through it so you can regret it. I did, but many don't."

The way he said it made me know that he, at one point, thought he knew it all and did something extremely stupid. It was nice to know that someone other than I could mess up. I messed up all the time, but I knew I was going to mess up sometimes, so I did everything I could to ensure I didn't. That included asking someone I could trust if it was a good idea.

About two weeks later, I was talking with the general during dinner. We had just received a thousand men from Kayland, five hundred from Dailith, three hundred more elves from Treestorm, and a thousand elves and druids from the Rainwards. The rest I understood, but the Rainward was a surprise. Still, support I had asked for, and support we received. When talking with the kings, I found out they wanted this over with for good. Other things were coming up, and they did not need this distraction. I said, "General Bigman, I was wondering if, while we have the resources, it would be a good idea to take over the entire Horde lands and stop them permanently. Many of the kings and queens I talked to want that to happen."

"I have been thinking that myself. If we can remove the current army without too many losses, we could push on into their lands and hit them where it hurts. No one has ever attacked them. Their lands have never seen war. Orcs and goblins breed until there are too many of them to feed, and then they try to spread out. It is a destructive issue that keeps us from being able to grow."

I said, "Then let's work our plans as if we are going to take out their main castle, The Drop."

The general laughed. "I am already ahead of you on that, but I have not advanced my thoughts to the royal liaison for each land. I am waiting for the correct time. If we could have Charles's help? I am told you have a connection with him."

"I do, General, but Charles is currently trying to save an entire sector of this galaxy with hundreds of occupied worlds. He is not available at this time. Not even for emergencies. Even if he were here, he cannot interfere. He can go into his druid trap and study for a thousand years without issue, because it takes no time on this plane. Charles could have easily taken out the demigod, but he did not. I had to do it because he is far too busy with more important issues than to be chasing one tiny Evil. The gods work through champions for a reason. I am one of those champions."

A young dragon flew in through the window and changed instantly to human form. She ran to the general. "Sir, the war has started. They are moving their ships."

CHAPTER 4

HORDE WAR AND TRAITORS

The general stood up. "This is it, ladies and gentlemen. Man your stations."

General Bigman had it all planned out long before it started. The enemy, under cover of darkness, sent orcs and goblins in hundreds of ships to attack us from the rear. At the same time, they sent undead against our border wall. The undead were uncontrolled and could not stop. Then the enemy's mages tried to teleport into the castle. However, without their demigod, the enemy was uncontrolled.

The general waited until the ships were well out to sea and then sent dragons to sink them. One fireball, and any ship is in deep trouble. A good lightning strike at or just below the water line, and your ship is sinking. Sink five hundred ships, and you have two thousand lifeboats. The dragons had a lot of cleanup to ensure none escaped to make it back to land.

The general had set up fire traps throughout the pass, and when the lead undead ran to the wall, a mage set them off. The entire pass was full of fire so hot it melted rock and part of the outer wall to slab. All undead were consumed in the fire.

Good and neutral-aligned dragons met the enemy dragons, and the enemy fled. Just like I paid them to do.

The mages who tried to teleport into the castle were instantly shunted to a small bowl of a valley that was lined with our clerics and mages. They died so fast they had no chance to escape or do their own spells.

The war was over two days after the start. Several times, I tried to talk to the general and warn him, but he was busy with the war, and in his eyes, I was just a little girl. The general pulled all troops together and all representatives and announced that we were moving into the Horde lands.

I said, "General! We need to talk first!"

The general paid no attention as he said, "Ladies and gentlemen, the attack is over, but the war is not! We have no losses. The enemy is wiped out to the creature, and we lost not one man." There were cheers for several minutes before the crowd could be quieted. "We have had this problem for thousands of years and have lost many thousands of men over the fighting. Now we have a massive army, and the enemy does not."

I whispered, "General, we need to talk!"

He whispered, "Later."

Then he said to the crowd, "For thousands of years, they have come to our lands, killing and eating our people, our women, and our children." The crowd burst into anger with yelling and threats toward the enemy. "With your help, we will put a stop to this devastation. I am taking this war all the way to the Drop." The crowd went wild. "I will have a talk with the kingdom representatives this night. There will be no celebrating our victory, no drinking to the joy of no losses, no staying up all night bragging. Get some rest, for tomorrow we move into the Horde lands. Prepare!"

The general moved back into the castle with cheers ringing throughout the entire land. The king showed up and gave the general permission to continue the fight. The representatives all agreed, and I sat there waiting. I knew something they did not, and it was surely going to change their time schedule.

When I was scrying on the Drop, I found out that the gods were interfering, though they were doing so in a roundabout way. The Hoard was planning to use only half their army and then wait for the general to attack them. That would leave the wall open and vulnerable. In addition, two of the people in the room with us were helping the Horde in this. Eagerly pushing the plan forward and smoothing all objections. No, not the Drow. It was the elves and druids from Rainward. I touched the Drow general's arm and asked, "Can we talk?"

She stood up and said, "I am sorry, but I need to have a discussion with a friend. I will be right back." She turned and walked out. I followed. When we were out of the room, she asked, "What is it, my friend?"

I raised a hand, and she, my guard, and I were in my tower. She looked around and said, "It's a little drab in here. You need some color. What did you want?"

"General, when I was snooping around at enemy headquarters, I found out—"

The gold dragon exclaimed, "Snooping at enemy headquarters! Are you a total idiot? When did you do this?"

I said, "While you thought I was sleeping. Now be quiet or be paralyzed. General, sorry for the interruption. Now, while I was at their headquarters, I found out that the army they just tossed against us was fodder. They were nothing. The real army is waiting for us to attack them. They know the general, and they know he will push on into their lands. The undead were the ones that were not needed. The ships had few goblins and fewer orcs. Just enough to make it look real, and they were not the fighters. The evil dragons were paid to flee this one battle. They were not paid to flee another. They want this land and control of what I have, the dragon pepper. In addition, two of the people in that meeting, the elf and druid from Rainward, were there discussing the plans and our plans with the orc king."

"Spirdra, save us! Why haven't you told this to the general?"

"I have tried. Because of this bracelet, he thinks me a child and not worth listening to. I took off my bracelet, and he was mush for three days, not thinking of the war and looking all over for me. I tried again during the attack and just a little while ago. He is not listening to me."

The Drow general exclaimed, "Men! Take me back. He will listen to you or he will wish he had."

The gold dragon said, "If you had told us, we could have told him."

I said, "If I had told you, I would have received only complaints that I put myself in danger!" I raised my hand, and we returned to the castle.

She stormed into the room and pulled her sword. The sing of a massive dark blade leaving a metal scabbard caused instant quiet. She said, "General Bigman, Samantha has been trying to tell you something important for several days now, and you are ignoring her. Considering without her you would not be bragging about this little victory, I ask you why?"

The general had his hand on sword, and many were backing up quickly. My dragon guard surrounded me, making it difficult for me to see. The gold dragon said, "It is important, General, but we did not know of it. She is a sneaky little girl." I kicked him in the shin good and hard and hurt my toe. He did not flinch.

The general relaxed his grip on his sword hilt. "I receive all information about war requirements from her dragon guard. I have had no need to ask her for anything because of that. I figured they had already told me and she was just trying to repeat the information. I am sorry. What is it that is so important?"

The gold dragon said, "Wait." He moved a hand, and several dragons quickly moved out to flank the group. He roared, and several dragons flew in, and he whispered to them, "The druids and Rainward Elves may be helping the enemy. The war was a farce. Prepare for attack. Quietly pass the word to all others. Quickly!" They flew out.

The representatives of the druid and Rainward Elves found themselves with a dragon at each shoulder and claws at throats. The gold said, "Try a spell, and they will rip your throats out before you can begin." He turned to me and then looked at the Drow. He whispered, "With that bracelet on, I doubt any men will pay attention to her. Go ahead, General Dramera Dreamchanger."

The Drow general looked over the assembly and addressed the women only. That irritated the men. "Ladies, due to the beauty of this girl, she has to wear an artifact bracelet to allow her to be around men without driving them crazy. However, the bracelet makes her seem childlike, and that makes the men pay her no attention. As we all know, men are fools, and this proves it. Believe me, and I say this to her dragon guard also, she is not a child to be cuddled. She is a godling and probably more intelligent than all the people in this room put together. To prove my point, let me tell you what she did and found out."

The general said impatiently, "I'm waiting."

General Dramera Dreamchanger said, "I'm not telling you this, fool. I'm telling the women. I could care less if you are waiting."

I smiled. Charles told me that Drow women didn't pull punches when it came to men. He was right.

General Dramera Dreamchanger continued, "Ladies, Samantha decided to check on the enemy and visited the Drop recently to listen in on some of their planning. How she did this I did not ask, as she may need to do it again. To her surprise, our esteemed representatives from the elves and druids of Rainward were there telling the orc king all about our plans and helping them make counterplans. The little battle the men so proudly won was staged for them. The real army is waiting for the men to foolishly run into their hands. They know we are coming, and they are prepared."

A lady from Kayland asked, "These two were the ones at the Drop?"

I said, "Yes."

She quickly stood and pulled her sword. The two were dead before anyone could stop her. She said, "Then I don't want them hearing what we may plan next. Some evil spell could be on them that allows the enemy to hear."

A dragon flew in and ran up to my guard. "The druid and elves from Rainward are gone, my lord. We have sent dragons to find them. Others say they pulled out during the first attack."

The gold said, "Thank you. Continue to check everywhere. I want those traitors found. When you find them, do not attack. Report immediately, and if possible, do so without them seeing you. Does anyone know where they are headed?"

She looked at me nervously and answered, "My lord, it is said they went west toward Landtrap."

As I took off the bracelet, the look on my face must have turned to something scary. I transformed into my demon dragon persona, and people started to flee in fear. I was now thirty feet tall, on fire, and looking like I wanted to rip something apart. I was causing panic, and the general drew his sword as he quickly backed up. In a deep snarl, I said, "I will handle this!" I flew out the grand window, and my guard and fifty dragons followed me.

General Dramera Dreamchanger turned to general Bigman and said, "Fool. Still think she's a child?"

General Bigman quickly took charge and brought order to the group. Pointing to the two dead ambassadors, he told the servants, "Clean up that mess, bring me a new pair of pants, and bring us some food. It's going to be a long night."

King Ordorneath asked nervously, "The war is not over?"

General Bigman said, "Apparently not, sire."

King Ordorneath turned to his personal mage and said, "Home, please. General, call me when you are sure the war is over and it is safe. You still have all authority, but don't upset that Samantha creature. I don't need her upset at me like she is with the elves and druids." The mage touched the king, and they were instantly gone.

A dragon flew in. "General, they must have been watching. A massive army of orcs and goblins mixed with undead just came out of hiding, and they are headed toward the wall."

The general said, "No, we are not ready!" He ran toward the throne room and out of the castle.

CHAPTER 5

ATTACK ON LANDTRAP

I used telepathy and stated in all the dragons' minds, "They have a two-day head start on us. Reach Farnorth as quickly as you can. Do not try to protect Landtrap's borders." The guard and I teleported to the tower and ran to the castle and the queen.

She was at dinner. "Hello, Samantha. Nice outfit. I hear the war is over."

I said, "The war is not over, my queen. It has just begun. The elves and druids of the Rainward are marching this way. They left the coast two days ago. They are hostile."

"Darn it!" She threw down her lap towel and stood up. "Call my general. Set the war guard. Contact the eastern border gate and see if they are still there. Go!"

People started scrambling up from the dinner table and running throughout the castle, yelling, "War! The enemy is approaching! On your guard! Landtrap is under attack!" People started hastily donning armor and preparing for imminent attack.

The queen and I, followed by the general, transferred to my tower. On the top floor, we set up and started checking the borders. The watch said, "We have contacted the eastern gate guard, and they are still there, my queen."

The general said, "Contact them again and all other patrols. Tell them to fall back to the city. Abandon their posts immediately and take all the citizens with them that they can without slowing. Warn the towns and villages. Retreat to the city now."

One of the good things about having a small country is you can pull back behind the city walls quickly, and in case of attack from Ginham, that was the established plan. As soon as we found the traitors, only four leagues from the eastern border, I started using portals to help bring in the people. The queen and I worked on that, while the general set predetermined plans into motion. The plans changed a little because of the style of the enemy. Most were archers and magic users.

Bridges were burned when areas were cleared of people. The enemy could easily see they had lost the element of surprise and stopped for the night. Now was my chance.

I teleported to the Rainward and into the castle of the elves. I had been to all castles trying to gain support for the war, and thanks to bureaucratic stalling, I knew my way around. I found the king and queen sleeping and teleported them to the tower and put them in antishifting chains. Then I did the same thing to the druids, though I had to navigate several nasty traps first. Neither were expecting a direct attack at home, and I was in and out in seconds. I brought them to the top floor, where the general and queen were, and introduced them.

I said, "Queen Iseaia Danberry of Landtrap, this is King Entrub and his wife of the Rainward Elves, and this is King Poresinse and his wife of the Rainward Druids."

Queen Iseaia turned, looked at them, and ordered, "Have them stripped and fully searched. Check for magic, ensure they have none, and fetch my stone. Then I will ask them why they are attacking me." She turned back to watching her people, ignoring the protests of the kings and queens. I helped the queen as best as I could to ensure all were within the walls. Extra lances were given out, and dragons were given lances—a dangerous combination.

The kings and queens were verbally protesting, but no one paid them any attention. One made the mistake of threatening my queen. I walked over and slapped him once. The closest cleric healed him quickly, so he didn't die. After that, they were quiet. The cleric whispered to them, "You are alive only because the queen has questions. You should be praying she doesn't have you killed when she is done. Princess Samantha seems a little upset. Please don't provoke her."

When they were ready, the cleric said, "We are ready, my queen."

Queen Iseaia turned and looked directly at them for only a moment. She held out the stone and angrily asked, "Why am I about to kill several thousand elves and druids that I thought were my friends?"

The elf king answered, "We want the Sordeath. Having dragons working for us will achieve that goal."

My gold dragon guard growled and asked, "What does attacking the Landtrap have to do with dragon pepper?"

The king looked disgusted. "Do you count us as fools? The gods have told us she keeps it here. This tower is the place where she grows the pepper."

I asked, "What god told you this?"

The king said, "Proba, the god of elves. Who else, you idiot?"

I smiled when two of my guards beat the crap out of the king and then had him healed. The brass dragon said, "Do not call our princess names. It upsets us."

I was smiling, and the queen of the druids was wondering why. "Gloating, Princess?"

I said, "In a way, yes. Not for the reason you think." I turned to my queen and said, "They have been duped. I am sure that Proba would not lie to his own followers."

Queen Iseaia asked, "How sure are you? You have told me they will do almost anything to achieve their goals."

"I suppose I could check. It's dangerous to my sense of humor to go to Caelum, but I could go ask."

The queen's eyebrows rose. "Dangerous to your sense of humor?"

I said most seriously, "I have never done it before, but Charles tells me it is a humbling experience."

My queen asked, "How long will it take?"

An angel stepped into the room and said, "Not long. She has no need to go to Caelum at this time."

I whispered to Formack, "Get the queen and others out of here now!"

Formack and the queen ran for the door. The others were leaving also.

I instantly powered up and slammed the god with every killing spell I knew, and so did my dragon guard. It did very little. She tore into us like a hot knife through pig fat, and if it hadn't been for the clerics doing mass healing spells, we would have been dead very quickly. She did evil things trying to destroy us, including summoning evil creatures that the clerics tried to dispel, but it took several tries, and the creatures did mass damage until they were gone.

I yelled, "Pay no attention to the summoned creatures! Kill the god! Magicum, a god is attacking us!"

The battle continued, and the furniture and maps in the room were destroyed. The tower rocked with the blasts. Two of the dragons died, as did one of the clerics. The Evil God had been trying to make it to the door and escape, but I stood in front of the door and stairs and blocked his path. I was out of spells and in demon dragon form and cutting his flesh to ribbons, but I was near dead also. We had won, but at what cost? The god could come back, even if we destroyed it. Gods were immortal in more ways than one, and I was not prepared for destroying his soul. We tore the god to pieces, and at the moment of his body death, everything froze. I could not move, and neither could the guard. The god was dead but coming back quickly, as parts were healing on their own.

Magicum nonchalantly walked into the room, and the room lit up like noon day. He gently placed a hand on my face and caressed it. "You did well in this battle. Unexpected and unplanned, yet he is dead. Still, as a god, he is hanging on to life with the smallest of threads. At his full power, I could never hold him. But weakened as he is, well, let's just say our goodbyes to Nirallotheral the Fallen."

He walked over and said, "Messed with the balance and lost to a child goddess. How embarrassing." He touched the god, and I had never heard or felt such a scream before. Hopefully I never will again. The god Nirallotheral died. He permanently died. I knew that no resurrection would ever bring him back. Magicum departed with a smile on his face, saying, "Proba and Natura will be displeased when they find out their followers have been following Nirallotheral. I will leave it up to you to tell them. Go to Caelum, daughter, and ask them to straighten this out before Queen Iseaia destroys many of their followers. Be careful. Nirallotheral had some nasty friends." He stopped and thought. "You have to give Nirallotheral the Fallen credit. They don't call him the god of deception for nothing. But trying to deceive my high priestess in my temple." He chuckled. "That was just plain foolish. I wonder who put him up to it." He was gone, and we could all move again.

He raised a hand just before disappearing, and we were all healed, and all the dead were resurrected. My energy and powers were back as if I had not used a single spell that day. However, the room was still trashed, and so were our clothes and armor. You don't fight a god and live to tell about it, but if you do, it's going to cost you anyway. Magical armor and weapons were not cheap, especially the ones my guard had. *Had* was the word, as they were all trashed.

I said to a cleric, "Please bring the queen and others back up here and find out if anyone died trying to keep that god out."

The cleric asked, "Is it safe?"

I said, "It should be safe for the queen to be here with us."

"Not for the queen. Is it safe for me to be walking through this temple alone?"

I looked at him with amusement hidden under a false concern. "Take two others with you to report if something happens. You stay there to fend off the issue and send them to report to me. I will resurrect you later if there is anything left."

His eyes widened, and I heard as he left, "Fool, never ask questions. *Never ask questions!*"

The queen came up, and she was full of questions, but I think the cleric was still mumbling to himself because the first question was, "Samantha, why never ask questions?"

I told her what happened, and she smiled for the first time since I had returned. I turned to the kings and queens. "That was Nirallotheral the Fallen, often known as the god of deception. Magicum, blessed be his name, says that someone probably put Nirallotheral up to fooling you. I can think of several reasons. However, you will not believe me, so I have been ordered to go to Caelum and talk with Natura and Proba. They need to know about this and straighten the mess out. However, I am going to point out your evil intent and my displeasure. I have yet to decide if you should live or not, and my queen may kill you long before I return." I turned to Queen Iseaia and said, "I will be back as quickly as possible."

She said, "If not, there will be a lot of deaths. Go quickly, and I will get reports of what happened from the others."

Just before I departed, the cleric came in and said, "Only one died by the Evil God's hands. The paladin saw through the farce and challenged him. I am told he died quickly."

"Is the body still here?"

"Yes."

"Preserve the body, and I will bring him back. He deserves that much for his loyalty and honor. We will hold the ceremony when I return and this present danger is over."

"As you wish, High Priestess."

I plane-shifted to Caelum and found myself in the center of a large square with a wonderful fountain. There were Caelums everywhere. They looked worried. I stopped one and asked, "What's wrong?"

He said, "Child Goddess, did you not hear the scream? A god just died. Something killed a god."

I said, "Oh that. Sure. We did it with Magicum's help. It was Nirallotheral." The Caelum ran screaming from me. I said to myself, "Uh oh."

A god I did not recognize showed up, and others pointed toward me frantically. He turned my direction and walked over. I went to one knee. He said, "Hello, Samantha. I am Valoris, the god of valor. You are standing in the square in front of my palace. It seems that some of our friends think you—a very little beginner, minor child godling—killed Nirallotheral, an experienced god. We all heard the scream. Please explain."

"Yes, my lord god. I was in Magicum's tower temple preparing for a war that did not make sense. Someone had told the Rainward Elves and Druids that I grow dragon pepper in the tower and that they should go and take it. We are being attacked, though the elfin and druid army has not reached our city yet, they are in our lands and headed our way. When I said I was going to go to Caelum to ask the Great God Proba why, Nirallotheral showed up disguised as an angel."

"Wait! Wait. Are you telling me Nirallotheral tried to fool Magicum's baby godling high priestess in her own temple?"

I was not happy about the "baby" remark, but Charles had warned me about the way you got treated up here. "Yes."

He nearly fell to his knees laughing. He stood back up and said, "Magicum! I want the whole story."

I heard over my head, "I trust you to take it but no other. Allow it, daughter."

Valoris touched my forehead, and the entire scene played back for him. He said, "Oh, this is great. Not only did he try to fool you in your own temple, but he did it with six major dragons guarding you. I will tell this story for many centuries." He sobered up quickly. "Little girl, Nirallotheral had friends. Be very careful." He turned to the crowd, and instantly everyone saw exactly what happened. Many laughed, and many did not.

One came to me and said, "You need to see the goddess Natura first. Come with me please."

We took a step and were in front of a lovely little temple. We walked straight up and passed all the guards and acolytes. I was taken inside, and it was the biggest temple I had ever seen. It went on for thousands of feet. I was led directly in front of the goddess. I went to one knee.

"Rise, Samantha. What does Magicum's little toy want with me? Did Charles not warn you about coming to Caelum, child?"

The Caelum showed her what Valoris showed him. Anger became plain in her beautiful face as she saw what happened, and she sat straighter. She raised a hand, and her eyes went blank for a second. "That fool is going to get many of my followers killed." She looked at me and said, "I bet Magicum sent you so I would see this issue. I will thank him later. Right now I have some clerics to communicate with. And they will not like the communication. Your problem will go away soon."

"Will it?"

She smiled, and her entire tone changed. "How pleasant. You doubt my abilities?"

"I doubt you are going to stop them from anything more than their suicidal attack on Landtrap. After all, you do want your followers to live. They want the Sordeath and will stop at nothing to steal it. Charles will not be happy. And I am worried that they will try to take the dragon pepper. That would mean killing Charles and me."

Another god showed up. "Yes, please explain what you are going to do to stop their attack on the Sordeath. This is the third time."

Another god showed up and said, "This I would like to hear." Several more gods popped in using teleports.

I turned around and started to leave. Natura said, "Where do you think you are going, child?"

I answered, "When more than two or three gods show up, it gets the attention of the Over Gods. I'm leaving before that happens." I could not move. My legs would not work, and I was being turned around and brought back to the center.

Natura said, "You don't accuse a god and then leave before you hear the explanation, child. Magicum needs to teach his toy some manners."

I heard Magicum's voice saying, "I will not show up at a place with eight other gods. Do they never learn?"

I looked around, and even Natura was upset. She was just

about to tell them to get out, but it was too late. An Over God showed up. Predictable! I felt Magicum instantly leave my mind. The others went to one knee, and so did I.

I heard in my head and knew it was in all their heads also. "Natura, you are wrong. This may be Magicum's precious high priestess, but she is our toy, not his. Arise, toy."

I did, and it wasn't by using my legs. I just rose up. He touched my head, and I felt a burning, and then he was gone.

Natura said, "Okay, out. All of you—out!"

I started to leave.

"Not you, child."

I was turned around and brought back again.

She stood up and walked around me, looking closely. She said, "Let's see. What did they do to you this time? Do you feel any different?"

"No."

"Do you have any more knowledge?"

"Not that I am aware of. I have no idea what he did. He put a finger on my head, and it gave a burning sensation. Then he was gone."

"Hum. Puzzle. Magicum! We are alone. You can come out now."

My god appeared, saying, "Fools all. I am going to limit the number of gods physically able to enter my home. I will not have them popping in unannounced. What do you want, Natura?"

"You know your priestess better than any except Charles. What has changed?"

"Good question." He turned to me and said, "Open your mind, daughter."

I, of course, did as I was told.

He looked and said, "The necklace is gone."

Natura said, "You're joking! Do they know what that will

unleash if she turns evil? Of course they do! What are they thinking?"

Magicum said, "They probably don't care. Another thought. I can sense that the abilities are growing, and the Over God spells are arranging. Anyone attacks her again, and she will destroy them instantly."

Natura walked over to her throne and sat down. "I don't like that, Magicum. I don't like it at all. What are you going to do?"

Magicum smiled. "Watch and try to learn what she does."

Natura laughed. "You know what I mean. She is a danger to us all."

Magicum said, "She is not a danger. Charles is watching her. I can feel his tag in her mind, but I can't remove it. I tried, but it is too strong. If she turns evil, you will hear her scream, and it's your pet god that will be the cause."

Natura said, "Ask Silvestris. Charles has not been our pet for some time now. Oh, he plays at it for the fun of it and because he loves us, but he is far beyond being a pet."

Magicum said, "The gods are comfortable with him now. They don't care so much that he has great power. However, they are not comfortable with your followers trying to take over the Sordeath, and the two dragon gods are really upset that you were after the dragon pepper. They were promised the dragon pepper by Samantha. If she is killed and those two don't get the pepper to share, you are going to find all your followers systematically destroyed. Count on it." He touched my arm, and we were in Proba's temple.

"Hello, Proba. Been watching?"

"Hello, Magicum. Who hasn't? My followers knew better and still attempted to gain the dragon pepper. I am tired of this group's stupidity. I have plenty of other elves, so killing a few will not hurt. Though many of the elves in the army are good elves just following orders. I hate to waste them. Especially with the other issues that are coming up. No, better thought. I will turn them back. Kill the king and queen only."

I said, "If I kill the king and queen, they will see it coming from Magicum. Is that what you want, my god?"

Another god showed up. A dragon of grand size and beauty. He turned into a man in one step and came forward. "Hello, gentlemen, and lovely lady. Samantha, I do like it when you change into your platinum self. You are far lovelier than my last bride. Please take off the bracelet more often and change. I will be watching." He turned to the others. "The point is mute. While you have been debating this in committee, both the good and evil dragons from ten worlds were told, and now there is no army. Problem solved. Let it be understood, the dragon pepper is off-limits. If anyone attempts to obtain the dragon pepper without permission, they die. Put that out to your followers. We will destroy all, even if it destroys all dragons. Without that pepper, we will die anyway. My counterpart is telling the Evil Gods the same at this time. Watch what your followers are doing, as we will not believe these phony excuses."

Proba said, "How dare you."

Then Charles showed up. Charles did not look happy. He walked right up to the gods and said, "I am extremely busy trying to fight a space army of pure energy. Please explain to me why an Over God showed up and ordered me to come here. Something about a god war that is about to start if not stopped!"

Magicum said, "Charles, I am sorry, but this is what has happened." Magicum leaned forward, and Charles touched his head and instantly knew the entire issue.

Charles said, "Mother, Father, your presence is requested. Bring along all the gods you want. No Over God will show up."

Natura and Silvestris instantly appeared, and so did twenty other gods.

Charles said, "You know what is going on?"

Many said yes, but a few said, "Not really."

Charles placed the information in their heads and then added, "Samantha found the dragon pepper exactly where the Over Gods placed it. It was not a leftover from the old times. It was not in status from a priest of long past. It was made to seem so, but I felt it instantly, and the Fire Star confirmed. It was a gift from the Over Gods. Samantha is doing exactly what the Over Gods wanted. She is using it to secure the future of the dragons. The Over Gods were waiting for a dragon they could trust to help both good and evil. She is the one they picked. Now the dragon pepper is being argued over. I am warning you this one time. The Over Gods will send me in to correct the situation permanently if anyone tries again to mess with the flow of dragon pepper. You know I have to do as they tell me. Father, Mother, don't make them give me the order to destroy you. Don't let that happen. Please. I beg you. If they tell me, I will have to do it. I will have no choice. It will destroy me also. I truly see you as my parents, and I love you both."

They both hugged Charles and said, "It will not happen. Don't worry."

Charles looked at the dragon god and said, "I am sorry for the issues in the past, but I am working hard to correct many that you yourself created. Think before you act. If you start a war, I will be asked to finish it."

The dragon god raised to his full height and extended his wings. He was very impressive. "You think you can stop me, boy!"

Charles touched the Star Fire, and it flared. Sadly, he said, "In an instant."

The dragon god deflated quickly. He had not been expecting that answer.

Charles turned to me and said, "Need me, please don't call my name. For you, I would answer, and it would kill millions." He looked at Natura sadly. "I am very busy!" His gaze returned to me. "I will let you know when I am not. And you will never affect the balance. That is what that Over God did." He disappeared.

CHAPTER 6

THE QUEEN'S ANGER

I said my goodbyes, shifted back to my world, and teleported to my tower. As I entered, I heard shouts of joy. "The war is over! The war is over!" rang throughout the town and the tower. When I reached the top, I heard my queen lecturing the others.

The gold dragon guard came over and quickly filled me in.

"Princess, it is good to see you. While you were out, we were visited by several angels, one from Natura, one from Proba, both the evil and good dragon councils, and an angel dragon from our own god Drajuris. All made it extremely clear that you and this tower are off-limits. That anyone attacking you will be destroyed, along with their entire heritage. To show how much they meant what they said, thousands of dragons appeared, ate the entire enemy army in a matter of minutes, and then disappeared. We watched it all from this room. Your queen was still upset and asked the angels about reimbursement for her costs. They said that she should take that up with the fools that attacked her, and they left."

I asked, "Did they walk in or teleport in?"

"They all walked in. Some were upset that they could not

simply enter this room. The evil dragon council took much pain just crossing the front doors. A little healing, and they were fine."

I said, "I will fix that issue."

The gold dragon said, "You're going to let them come in?"

"No. I'm going to make it impossible for anyone to come in that I do not invite personally. I thought I did that before, but I must have missed something. I will plug the holes and place warnings. I noticed that my trees are missing."

"Yes, Princess. The Evil God we destroyed killed them on the way in."

The queen saw me, and she left off chewing out the kings and queens of the Rainward. "Samantha! Good to have you back. From the visitors we had, I take it you were successful?"

I smiled. "In one way I was, and in another I was not. Apparently, when a god dies, all other gods know. I have made some enemies even though he attacked us. At least twenty gods understand that other gods may be foolish and try to gain the dragon pepper. We have gods on our side and gods on the other side. Some don't want the dragons to have the pepper, and some do." I stopped. Something had just entered the room. No, two creatures had just entered the room. They were totally invisible and evil. I powered up.

"We are not here to harm, Samantha. We are here to make a point." They materialized. "I am Malificus, and this is Malum."

Both were horrendous looking, and I did a spell to stop all in the room but the gods and me. My dragon guard was about to attack, and they no longer had weapons or armor.

Malificus said, "Good choice, Samantha. You are wiser than I first thought. Killing my pet god is not a good thing, but attacking us would be fatal. You have no worries at this time. Magicum, Natura, Drajuris, and Proba are all watching. We have come to tell you that we were not part of this scheme. We have our own plans to convert you to our side. I actually told Nirallotheral not to interfere at this time. It is a shame he is gone, as I had great plans for him. Still, I have others to take his place. As I told Charles once, when he was in an evil phase, 'You have to watch your friends very closely.' I did not watch Nirallotheral close enough. Now I have others laughing at me. Not because of you but because Nirallotheral failed miserably."

I moved my hand over into the queen's hand and took the Stone of Truth. "Great Malificus, what are you here for if not to destroy me?" I looked at Malum and curtsied a little to show I included him.

Malificus said, "If nothing else, you are polite."

Malum said, "I have warned the others away. I do not want you harmed." He looked at my hand and the stone and added with a smile, "At least not at this time. I need the evil dragons. They are an intricate part of my plans. I am told that you are going to share the dragon pepper with both Drajuris, the god of good dragons, and Draquae, the evil dragon god of chaos. I wish to point out that they do not represent all the dragons. Will you allow the others to die out or will you help them all?"

I said, "Can we meet at Commeatus's temple in the Plane of Sanctuarium? This is an issue that requires all the gods that have dragon followers and a god to represent dragons that have no gods to make this decision. I am neither wise nor intelligent enough to decide the correct displacement of the dragon pepper."

Malificus turned to Malum. "Believe me now! I told you she would understand and see our side."

Malum said, "I see. She is truly open-minded. It is refreshing." He turned to me and said, "I knew your father. I allowed him to leave my worship to join another. I was displeased, but it did not harm any of my plans. Please note that it was not the evil dragons that tried to hunt your mother down. We understand mixed relations and often support it. You will meet someone that you will want to stay with. Think on who will understand. Know this, and you should ask him. Magicum will not care as long as you do not turn too far from his indifferent alignment. You are not being forced to be good all the time. If you need something, call me."

I said, "I will keep that in mind."

Malificus said, "Do not worry about the meeting. Magicum will set it up and inform you. You are correct in that it will take some time and much discussion. We know where the pepper is. Charles has told us. He will not allow us to help harvest, but he is very trusting in you and has told us to trust you also." He laughed. "He sometimes forgets that it is not in our nature to trust. The Good Gods do not understand this about us. It would be helpful during these discussions if you keep it in mind."

I felt them walk out, and one said, "Magicum did not put these protections up. She is becoming very powerful."

The other said, "She knows we can get around them. She is not a fool." They disappeared.

I let the others go, and they all started asking questions. I raised my hand and said, "Before we go any further, I need my dragon guard. Please follow me." I took them to a secret room where I stashed all twenty sets of the artifact dragon armor and weapons. Charles and I found out that the armor was like the lances, tied to the tower and would return to the tower. That was probably why I had all twenty sets. I told them, "Harder than Adamantine, lighter than Mitral, spell resistant, and element proof. This armor will withstand attacks from minor gods. I place these on loan to my guard until I can find replacements for what you have lost. My apologies to your god, but my beloved god, Magicum's, symbol is on each piece."

The gold dragon said, "Drajuris will understand. Is this the dragon armor used by the tower dragon riders?"

"Yes."

"We thought it all gone. This is some of the best armor ever made for dragons. All others, including artifact armor, pale in comparison. Note this symbol in the corners of each piece?"

I said, "Yes. I noticed that, but I can find no reference to it anywhere."

The gold dragon smiled. "That is the earliest symbol of Drajuris. It is said that Magicum and Drajuris used this tower at the beginning of time to help Natura and Silvestris place life on this planet, and during the planner wars to protect this world from outsiders. You do know this tower flies, teleports, and shifts to other planes?"

"I know it flies, but that is all. Magicum told me not to move it at this time."

The gold dragon looked thoughtful. "He must have his reasons. Thank you. These will be most helpful in protecting you. You have twenty complete sets. That is all of them accounted for. One set is worth more than my king's treasure, and that is saying much. Why did you not give these to us before? It would have been most helpful during our last battle."

I said, "I am worried that they will draw unwanted attention to my guard. With the artifact level and the intricacies of the design, they are both beautiful and unmistakable. I do not want planner thieves on top of everything else we have to deal with."

The gold dragon nearly laughed. The others were smiling. "Samantha, no dragon has ever lost Drajuris's Armor of the Tower. When given out, it is connected to us. If we die or it leaves our possession for more than a day, it returns to the tower. We will not lose it."

"Charles and I noted that when we took it to the Druid

Suppository, it returned the next day. However, others do not know that and would never believe you. Some will try. Mark my words."

The silver dragon was in the middle of donning a set of the armor and said with warning in her voice, "Dragons know better, but others do not. Let some dark, hugging thief try and steal from me. I often need a midnight snack."

The brass dragon said, "When word of this gets out, there will be many volunteers for guard duty, just for the chance of wearing the greatest armor ever made."

The bronze dragon added, "And the greatest weapons ever created for a dragon. I have studied this armor and looked longingly for the day I could try it on. When I first became a dragon guard, I searched this tower. Everywhere except the bottom dungeon floor. That is far too protected for me to enter. These have weapons that fit over my claws perfectly. Each weapon aids in dealing increased damage with fire, ice, acid, shock, and sonic burst. The armor is also blessed, lawful, and holy. Five claws, so five different weapons on each paw. There are tiny hooks on the inside of each claw that make grappling near automatic and rending ten times as powerful. Add to that, the wearer can do True Touch and Devastate Evil at will as a supernatural ability. Good luck attacking the guard."

I asked, "Why did Magicum care about adding Devastate Evil? He is a natural god. He is neither good nor evil."

The gold dragon answered, "Because Drajuris made the armor for Magicum, and he is a god of good."

"Oh."

The gold dragon said, "Now you begin to see. We are donning our god's armor, created for his followers, made for the protection of his agenda. He will be most happy, and he will instantly know where we are and if we are in need."

In a panic, I said, "Quick! Take them off. Don't put that armor on."

They all looked up, worried and shocked, and asked, "Why?"

The gold dragon said, "Samantha, do not worry. It will do you no harm if Drajuris knows where we are."

I laughed. "I was just kidding."

The gold dragon grabbed me, and I turned into my platinum persona, and we wrestled and snapped at each other in fun for several minutes. We parted tired and happy when the gold dragon said, "We have kings and queens waiting."

I finished dressing in one command set of the armor, and we returned to the viewing room. The new armor felt good. As we walked in, there were whistles of appreciation. Queen Aseaia asked, "Where did you get armor like that?"

I said, "I have resources you do not know about. Now that my guard is ready for anymore issues, even godly ones, we can continue. I am told that the army attacking us is no longer there?"

King Entrub sadly said, "This is true. We watched as thousands of your dragons, demons, and others showed up and ate my people."

I said, "Sad that is, but I am not the cause. Your attempt to attack this land was seen as an attack on the dragon pepper, and therefore certain gods stepped in and corrected the issue before your gods could do anything about it. I was in the process of talking to Magicum, Natura, and Proba, but Drajuris and other gods believe in making examples of those who attempt to control dragons. Another mistake of yours is the dragon pepper. It is not in this tower or any place you can possibly get into, and you should know it. All planes except one are cursed, and the pepper is in that one plane. With the god curse going on, I could never keep it here. Another mistake you have made is thinking that I control the dragons. I have been nice, and they have been nice in return. I am partly one of them. I am a dragon princess, and therefore they are working with me in this war issue. If I tried to control them? Dragon guard, what would happen if I tried to control the dragon council using dragon pepper?"

The gold dragon said, "My god would ensure your death and find another way to get it out of Charles. Dragons will never be controlled by someone other than dragons, especially not half-demon dragons. I am sorry, but that is the truth."

I said, "It is as expected. I have dragon blood running through my veins, and I know how stubborn I can be. I am sure that pure dragons can be just as stubborn. You are fools and do not deserve the right to rule your lands." I turned to Queen Iseaia and said, "However, they did not attack me. General Bigman may be interested in getting his hands around their necks. What are you going to do with them? I don't want evil people kept in my tower. Besides, I removed all the torturing equipment. If you want them dead, I will gladly do the deed."

She smiled. "Correct, they did not attack your tower. They did not make it that far. They did attack Landtrap. We had to burn bridges, displace people, and prepare for war. I will hold them until their countries reimburse us for the cost. Then I will let them go. Their army has been destroyed. General Bigman will have to be satisfied with that."

I said, "That's very generous of you. There are many that want them dead. Giving them protection until they make restitution will give the gods and others time to calm down." I turned to the kings and queens of the Rainward and said with venom in my voice, "You owe her your life. If I were you, I would stick around for at least a moon. Don't ever forget her generosity."

Queen Iseaia said, "Find nonmagical clothing for them and take them to my throne room. Our little talk is not over."

The gold dragon asked the king of the elves, "How's it feel to be chewed out by a short lived and deserve it?"

King Entrub answered, "Embarrassing, especially since she sent for the Treestorm king to help her explain to us our folly."

The gold and several other dragons said, "Ouch."

CHAPTER 7

BACK TO THE WAR

They left my tower, and the watch was reset and doubled in case some of the Rainward army were missed or others came looking for their missing royalty.

I went down to the bottom and pulled out some more furniture. Charles had left me plenty of extra. It hit me that every time I thought of Charles, I felt nice. I wondered if it was the tag he placed inside my head. We were great friends for those three hundred years of training. I truly enjoyed his company, and he seemed to enjoy mine. I chided myself, *Wishful thinking.*

The gold dragon said, "Wishful thinking, Princess?" I must have blushed, as he said, "None of my business. I understand."

I said, "No, it's not that. For the first time, I was thinking about a man and a possible relationship."

The gold dragon asked with amusement, "And who would be fool enough to fall in love with a half demon?"

The silver dragon hit him hard, and so did the brass dragon. They pushed him to the back and asked, "Who's the lucky guy?"

I said wishfully, "Charles. I think I love him."

The brass dragon said, "Charles is so lonely. Always busy

fixing issues that others created. When he has any breathing space, it would be nice to have someone to come home to."

The silver dragon added, "It would be a lonely life. Charles is almost always gone, but he would not care about your demon side. He is very open-minded. The two of you would make a very good couple."

The gold dragon said, "That's true. It's said that Charles had a demon lover before. He had to kill her when she did something wrong, but he truly regretted it."

Both female dragons looked back at him with looks of, "Shut up!"

The brass dragon said, "Charles has been alive for a long time. It is also said he has only had two females in his entire life, a demon and a god. That's rare in a man his age. Most are far more experienced. Do you have any experience?"

"No."

There was a pause in the conversation. The bronze male asked, "None at all?"

I said, "A man once tried to take me unwillingly. I changed him into a very beautiful girl and sold him to a man as a sex slave. He won't be bothering women anymore."

Both the female dragons giggled, but the males did not. Suddenly, they were very quiet. The silver dragon asked, "Have you told Charles anything yet?"

I started to panic. "For goodness' sake, no!"

The brass dragon said, "Men are so dumb. You nearly have to bite them to get their head turned to the right point. Tell him how you feel and ask him to think about it. The worst that can happen is he gently turns you down."

The bronze dragon said, "Or laughs."

The platinum dragon said, "Enough! The girls should take

up this conversation when the males are not around to ruin things!"

The silver dragon looked at the platinum dragon and said, "You are wise for a male."

The platinum dragon said, "I am trying to stop you before I say something as stupid as the gold and bronze."

The brass dragon said, "Samantha, we will take this up later."

I said, "That sounds like a good idea. We need to return to the general and see where he is in the war."

The gold dragon said, "Let's give him a little present."

The platinum dragon asked, "What do you have in mind?"

"Dragon Riders."

Protests went up quickly, and everyone was talking. The gold dragon said, "Stop!"

The brass dragon said, "I will not allow a human to ride me like a horse!"

The gold dragon said, "Listen, I am not talking about humans. What about a dragon in human form? If we have riders, we can use the lances at a distance. Six dragons with riders could be devastating."

The silver dragon said, "Can't do it. We cannot put Samantha in jeopardy. We would be making her a target."

The platinum dragon said, "Good point, both of you. Let's go find out how things are doing with the war and think about this later."

I said, "Very well. Everyone ready?" We all touched, and I teleported them right into the castle throne room and the enemy.

A fight was going on, and we joined in. There were eight enemy dragons, a couple dozen magic users, and one greater ice demon. The place was crowded. I said, "The ice demon is mine. Destroy the others." It did not last long when five dragons and a demon dragon, all magic users and all protected by artifact armor, popped right in the middle of the fight. We went to full size and devastated them all very quickly. The demon was shocked we were there and more shocked that his ice touch did nothing. However, fire was his foe, and when I saw how well my Fire Claw hurt him, I instantly radiated intense fire and grappled him. He died quickly, trying to escape. All I had to do was hang on.

I was the last to finish my foe. The dragon guard ripped through the other dragons and their mages as if they were nothing, and then several did wide, mass heal spells to save as many of the defenders as possible. When I finally dropped my demon, he was nothing but fire-cleansed bone.

I changed into my human persona and walked up to the general. My guards took point at the windows and doors. Clerics were checking everyone still alive. Others were removing the dead.

I asked, "What happened, General?"

He said, "First, thank you for the help. The war was going extremely well, so I sent most of the protection and all the dragons to chase down and finish the enemy before they could get away. I cannot believe I fell for such a simple tactical move. They were waiting for me to give chase. I was here with minimal protection when eight dragons with riders and that *thing*, made of ice, flew right in the windows about a minute before you showed up. We didn't stand a chance."

I said, "That, General, was a greater ice demon. Mortal enemy of my father's home. How is the war going? Or were they pretending to run?"

The general said, "I won't know until I receive reports."

My gold dragon came over. "Where are the two dragons I placed to protect you, General? I do not see their bodies."

"When the demon showed up, they disappeared."

He looked at the general with distaste and then at me. I said, "Did any of the dragons or the demon say anything before they attacked? Something that sounded like nonsense?"

The general said, "There were a lot of spells going off as they approached."

The gold dragon said, "Labyrinth?"

I nodded. "Yes. They were probably the victims of a heightened Labyrinth spell. It's a specialty of ice demons. They like to Labyrinth their opponents and then set up for a devastating attack when they reappear. The dragons should be back soon."

The general said, "Explain."

I said, "A Labyrinth spell sends the fragile minded to another plane and into an immense four-dimensional labyrinth that is constantly changing. It is harmless, but it takes time for the victim, depending on how frail his mind is, to get out of the labyrinth and return. High-level wizards can return quickly. Fighters, especially those less experienced, take longer. When they return, the enemy is waiting and ready with attack actions. The victim never knows what hit him if he is not really good or well protected."

The general asked, "Why not do it to the magic users?"

I said, "Because magic users tend to do spells that boost them up and ready them for the return. It's not a good idea to give the magic users time to prepare. Besides, magic users may have less strength physically, but it's because their time is used in strengthening their minds. Labyrinth may work but not for long. The best way to use Labyrinth is to remove the front-line fighters and destroy the magic users so when the front line reappears, they have no magical support."

"Oh."

A dragon flew in and saw the damage. He also saw we had it under control, so he reported. "General, the fall back by the enemy was false. They had demons in reserve, but as the demons attacked, Caelum Archons appeared and destroyed them. The enemy has been defeated."

A Caelum Deva showed up, bowed to me, and said, "Evil has taken too much interest in this war. It has brought the attention and ability of good to interfere in return. Natura gives her regards, *child*, and *orders* the general to continue into the Horde lands. Evil and good will not interfere again." It disappeared.

The general said, "Well, that's good news. If evil is staying out of this, we have a good chance of success."

I watched the place where the Caelum had been. "Don't count on it, General. Something is wrong, and I don't know what it is."

The gold dragon asked, "Are you thinking that message was not from Natura?"

I thought for a minute. "No, the reason it said 'child' and emphasized it so bluntly was to show it was from her. No, it was from the goddess Natura all right but for what reason? And why 'orders' the general? She knows the general is not her follower, and neither am I."

The general said, "I don't like this. Why would Natura order us into the Horde lands? There are a lot of her followers in there. Why send us in?"

I said, "Wait here."

I took my dragon guard and teleported back to my tower. I went to the shrine of Magicum in the basement and closed the door. From there, I did several spells to ensure I would not be noticed or watched. Then I teleported to the Druid Sanctuary and summoned the Caelum that took me to Natura before.

He materialized and looked around. He saw me and said, "I cannot talk. We are being watched."

I said, "In the druid trap?"

Nervously, he said, "They will know you are in here."

"I went to my tower, down into my shrine to Magicum, did several high-level Over God spells that entered my mind at my need, and teleported here. I doubt anyone, including the gods, know I am here."

"Oh, thank the gods. Listen, there is much trouble in Sanctuarium at the temple of Commeatus. The issue of the dragon pepper is being discussed, and it is getting heated. Several gods have made threats of war between the gods. It's not the Evil Gods doing it. The Good Gods don't want the issues of too many dragons in one place. When they saw what happened to the elf and druid army and how quickly they were destroyed, it brought back some bad memories and proved that the dragons have not learned. Do not believe me or anyone else that comes to talk with you."

"What does Natura want? Why the cryptic message?"

"First, she wants to warn you. Second, she wants you out of the way so you are out of their minds. Out of sight, out of mind. Staying in your tower would be best. You cannot hide here, as time does not pass correctly."

"I understand."

"Good. Do not pray to anyone. For the love of the gods, don't pray to Malificus or Malum! They would love to take advantage of this situation."

"I understand. You will be going soon. Tell Natura I said I understand and thanks."

"Not going to happen. They would hear and ..." He disappeared.

I paced back and forth, frantically thinking and worrying.

"Would the gods start a war over the distribution of the dragon pepper?

"Would good fight against good?

"He told me not to pray. To stay hidden. As if the gods cannot find me anytime they want. Magicum can find me anywhere except here. I am wearing Bahanut's dragon armor, so he can also find me. I have a couple artifact rings, the necklace, the bracelet, the diadem, and my belt. The gods can easily find me.

"Why come to me with this? Do they think kidnapping me will help them? They must know I would go directly to Charles. This does not make sense. They know Charles would be sent to put a stop to any god war. Charles should be warned. I will contact Charles immediately. Wait! Hum. What if that is what this is all about? What if they want me to contact Charles for some reason? Why would they want Charles to show up? Because Charles is working on an issue, and one or more of the gods are on the other side? Pull him away from the issue, and he loses ground. If I recall, Charles looked directly at Natura when he said he was very busy. I wonder if that was a message between them or a warning. That makes more sense. That hussy is trying to make me contact Charles. Why would Charles come at my call?" My shoulders dropped. "Because he cares about me." Determination hit my face like fire, and I plane-shifted to Sanctuarium.

As soon as I arrived, I teleported directly to the temple of Commeatus and walked up the steps. An acolyte saw me and intercepted me on the steps.

"May I help you?"

"I am late for a meeting with the gods. I have information they may need."

"This way then." He moved into the temple and turned to me. "Samantha, do not lie to me. What are you here for?"

"I need to talk with Magicum in private and, if possible, not noticed."

"Come with me." He turned and started walking. "No one

sees into this temple without our knowledge, not after the last Over God visit. The gods are being blocked at this time. There is a discussion going on that may take some time. I will privately let Magicum know. It is up to him to depart the meeting and see you. I would not wish to be in your position if it is not very important."

We walked to a white room with no chairs, nothing but a room and one door.

I waited for only minutes before Magicum opened the door and quietly entered. He closed the door and said, "This better be good. I'm missing the discussion of the century."

I said, "Look into my mind."

"Not wasting my time. I like that." His hand touched my head, and he watched what had occurred. As his hand moved away, he said, "Figures. Now I know why her representative, Foreknock, is trying so hard to stall. I thought he was trying to gain time for her to join us. No, she wants us out of the way so she can mess with Charles and advance her plan on another system. We wondered why Foreknock blinked out for a few minutes. You summoned him. Nice work. Charles and Natura are having a falling out at this time. She is trying to take an entire hub of this galaxy with hundreds of habitable worlds just for herself. Charles is putting a stop to it. Lucky for her, I have no followers on the main planets. They've forgotten how to use magic on those worlds. My fault, as I pulled on a rift in space and accidently sank an island called Atlantis, and that was the last of most of the magic users. Their god would help, but she is sleeping."

"That's sad."

"It is. The main race has few magic users, and they have stagnated and stayed on one planet. They don't even know the true name of their planet anymore. They call it Earth, and they are ruining the planet. Someday I will send a champion there to start things back up, but for now, it can remain as is.

"I would be happy to help, my god."

He smiled. "I know you would. As for Natura, I will take it from here. Go directly back to the tower, pick up your guard, and then go to the general. Tell him I said he can enter the Horde lands or not, but be very careful. Several gods banned together to trim back what Malificus was doing. Natura must be using that to advance her own agenda. I am not sure who is on her side in this, but you can trust Solbelli, Drajuris, and Valoris. You did well, Samantha. Natura tried to drag you into her plan, and you did not fall for it. I am very proud of you. Do your best to stay out of the gods' plans if possible. Whatever you do, don't call Charles. I will take care of the rest. I don't like it when someone messes with my champions." He opened a door on the other side of the room I would have sworn was not there and walked directly into the discussion, and he wasn't quiet about it. Very loudly, he said, "Thanks for the report on Natura. Return home, Samantha." Total quiet was instantly established in the discussion room.

As I left, I heard Magicum say, "Now, to discuss what Natura thinks she is trying to get away with, Foreknock."

I picked up my guard at the tower and returned to the throne room. The general saw me return and said, "Well?"

"Hi, General. Magicum says that he could care less if we move into the Horde lands, but he warned me to be very careful. The gods and their representatives are very busy at this time and may not be watching to help for a little while. Also, Natura did help remove the demons, but she had assistance from other gods. Apparently, she has an agenda that may interfere with our situation, so do not trust her representatives at this time. Trust in Solbelli, Drajuris, Valoris, and Magicum only. They have an interest to see this war over. Other gods, and he is not sure which, may be helping Natura."

The general sat in thought for some time before saying, "The plan does not change, only how we are going to execute it. Samantha, can you create a portal into another land?"

"I can, but that portal can be used two ways."

"Hard to use it two ways when an army is marching through. How long can you keep it open?"

"Weeks if needed. I would have to stay behind and renew it daily. I am not as powerful as Charles. I cannot make permanent portals. I have the diamonds to make a big portal and keep it open about a month. After that, well, you cannot afford after that."

The general smiled. "One month is all I need. This is what we are going to do."

We debated the general's plans until all the ifs and buts were finally removed and we had something we believed in. It took three days, and I ensured we were not watched. During that time, the general had the army pull back behind the wall, and the gates were removed and replaced with more wall. Now there were no gates. Nothing to bash in. To enter through this pass, you had to go over or underneath the wall. That would be almost impossible with no army left to mount such a monumental task.

I talked with the university about more high-level mages, and they were completely against giving us any more help until I mentioned the fact that there had to be some artifact to control undead and some book that told how to create large amounts of undead quickly, and that those items would fall into the hands of normal nonmagical humans. A hundred mages and twice that in clerics were at the general's doorstep the next day.

Also, during that time, three large caravans came in with supplies and information that six more caravans were on the way. Plans were in place, the supplies were in or on the way, morale was high, and we had an intact army loaded with magic. The general said with confidence, "I'm ready."

The next day, the army was assembled and set. That night, I scried on and studied the Drop. The following morning, I opened a portal directly into the heart of the enemy.

CHAPTER 8

TAKING THE FIGHT
TO THE ENEMY

The portal opened into the courtyard of the castle called the Drop. It was called the Drop for a very good reason. It was mounted like a spider above a gigantic bottomless pit on the top of a mountain. Heat traveled from the planet core up the pit to keep the castle warm. The castle sat in the center, supported by natural stone legs. Normally, there was only one way into the castle. You had to climb up tens of thousands of steep steps to the central leg at the top of the mountain and then travel up and across the leg and through the one and only gate. The gate was eighty feet high, forty feet wide, and thicker than two men lying down. The Drop was considered impregnable. All the legs, except the one going to the gate, were thick at the bottom and so thin at the top it was nearly like a razor. No army could use the legs to cross the pit and assail the walls. No one could fly in due to the updraft from the hot pit. The center leg was only five feet thick at the top, and everything coming and going had to be by hand. Wagons could not pass, if somehow you could get one up the steps, and the steps made it difficult for horses. However, we bypassed all that by placing the portal in the center of the keep. Our army ran right in.

Alarms were sounded as dragons flew through the portal first to keep the enemy dragons from messing with our soldiers. Next came hundreds of soldiers, all tasked with killing anything and everything while running through the castle. They were to remove the fodder and isolate the true threats. Next came elfin archers to man the walls and take over the gates. Last came mages and clerics to help with the real battles going on throughout the castle and to find and remove any evil artifacts.

I wished I could have been there, but the general and my dragon guard insisted I stay with the portal to ensure it remained intact. Bull! The portal wasn't going anywhere, and I only had to check on it once a day. They didn't want me in danger. I helped as much as I could by receiving reports, from Ginham and the pass, to warn the general if we had issues on this side of the portal, and ensuring supplies remained in constant flow. Where they were putting all the stuff, I had no idea—until ten mages returned, flanked by thirty clerics. They had several items they were protecting as they ran through. I stopped one and asked, "What's going on?"

"We found the rod and the book you said may be there. We also found several more artifacts that are extremely evil. We have them all, and we are taking them to the Church of Solbelli for disposal. The castle is ours, and so are the surrounding mountains. The battle goes on, as many of the goblins and orcs are entrenched in caves and tunnels and are difficult to fight on their own ground. They constantly surprise attack and run. We are winning, but it is costly. The orc and goblin kings are dead, and so are the evil dragons, all but the ones that fled. The problem is most of them fled. They have not returned, but the good-aligned dragons are watching just in case. It's the dragons that are making this win possible. From their height, and at night, they see when the goblins and orcs are massing for an attack, and we send mages and clerics to that area to support the troops. The dwarves are best at ferreting the creatures out of their caves and holes. When a dwarf enters, they run and for good reason. It seems the dwarves know how to kill orcs and goblins and do it quickly. One dwarf told me why, but he was longwinded, and it took hours. I am still not sure, through all the bragging, which parts were true. He said they once chased goblins through tunnels all the way to the dark side of the smaller moon. As if! Everyone knows you can only reach the larger moon from here." He turned and left to catch up with the others.

I continued to stop people and get reports so that I knew what was going on.

CHAPTER 9

ANOTHER WAR

I sent messages to Ginham and Kayland for reinforcements, but they turned me down. One note from Kayland said, "We are preparing for another battle. Send our people back as quickly as possible."

I teleported to Kayland and the castle to ask what was going on. I received an audience immediately.

King Larry said, "There are over a thousand ships headed this way from the western continent of Maraget. They want the Sordeath."

This upset me greatly, and I said, "Give me one day to turn them around," and I disappeared. The gods were busy, so it was up to me and my dragon guard. We teleported to the ocean and then flew southwest. As we flew, we passed island after island and picked up more dragons. We also picked up other creatures that could fly, a Roc, several Lammasu, and a gigantic Fillidend. We saw the ships, including a large lead ship with many flags, but paid them little attention as we flew toward the continent of Maraget. The gold dragon knew where the capital was and led us directly there. We created great panic as more than eighty flying beasts darkened the skies. After a short, one-sided battle, my guard and I flew down to the castle and turned into human form. We were greeted by many guards and a single wizard.

He said in a challenging tone, "Who dares come directly to the emperor's castle without proper permission? Who dares?"

I cut him off. "Shut up, fool! I come from Kayland. Where is your emperor? I will have words with him."

"You cannot see the emperor." He made the mistake of raising a hand to say a spell. My gold dragon guard ate him. All the others fancily dressed people standing around started to scream and flee, but I held one back who looked important.

I walked over to his paralyzed body and asked as I released the mental hold, "Where is the emperor?"

"You cannot reach him. He has retired to his inner chambers where even the other gods cannot reach him."

I smiled. "Have you ever been there?"

"Of course. I am the royal clerk."

I placed a hand on his head and took the information from his mind. I tossed him to the side and teleported all my guard and myself to the inner chambers. There, on a pile of pillows, sat a fat man with a long beard. He was eating cherries from a bowl. He did not look happy.

He yelled, "Guards!"

Fifty men ran into the large room and died so quickly the emperor choked on those cherries. I said, "Your men are no match for experienced dragons." I reached down, touched his hand, and teleported him outside and up in the sky. I carried him in one hand while we flew to his fleet and his largest ship.

I ordered, "Destroy one half of this fleet." We had talked about what I was going to do, and this was part of the plan. They destroyed the ships but not the men. They allowed them to climb aboard the other ships. They even helped some by picking them up and gently setting them down on selected ships. Even with help, many died. You cannot attack a ship without being attacked back, and we were in a fight. As dragons and others became wounded, they returned to me, and I healed them. They then returned fresh to the battle. As they were fighting, I had that talk with the emperor.

I raised my claws so that I could see him face-to-face. "Greedy little human. You think yourself a god because you are in charge of so many people. You are not a god, and you never will be. Though your gods may help you, the gods of Kayland and the Sordeath will help them. It would be a battle that would destroy the Sordeath and your entire continent."

He looked at me defiantly. "I need that food to feed my people! We have outgrown our resources and need to expand."

"I see. You feel that you have the right to take from others so your people can have more resources. What about the rights of the ones you kill? What gives you the right to take their lives and land?"

He said as if it was obvious, "They are barbarians. They have no rights. They don't even pray to the correct god."

"What god do you pray to that would tell you to kill the followers of another god?"

"I pray to no god. Everyone in my empire prays to me."

"Fool mortal."

I watched the battle and waited. The lead ship was left alone, and the ones being attacked saw that certain ships were not being touched. They tried to get closer and started abandoning the doomed ships. When all the magic users and fighters were out of magic and their arrows were exhausted, I took off the bracelet, swooped down, and landed in full platinum glory on the brow of the lead ship. The ship was packed with refugees, and they were all in a panic.

I said, "Calm!" as I completed a calming spell. Instantly, they all calmed down and turned to watch me. "I am Samantha. You have never heard of me because I am a minor little nothing god, a toy of Magicum's." I raised my hand, and they saw the emperor squirming there. "I am tired of the greed of this mortal. I do not like when someone pretends to be a god to advance their own greed. Nothing has been said to stop him because you have kept it to your own continent, but now you are headed toward mine." I squeezed, and his head popped off, and blood splattered. "Turn around and keep to yourself, except trade. Do not ever mount a war against my lands. It would make me very angry." I dropped the body and jumped into the sky, nearly sinking the huge ship with my weight and causing people to fall over the side and need rescuing. I roared, and all the other dragons and creatures followed me. Some had full bellies. They did not mind me very well.

When I was sure that the fleet had turned around and headed for home, I thanked the others for their help and then teleported my guard and me back to Kayland and the king.

As I changed to human form, the king said, "Thank you."

"You were watching?"

"Yes—and remind me never to act like a god."

I blushed. "Listening too. Well, someone needed to put a scare into them, and that fool of an emperor was too far gone in his own self-made glory to understand his position. They will try to resurrect him, but I have it on good authority that no god will help him. His land will go into turmoil for a while. Watch him closely. Now, about those reinforcements."

King Larry laughed. "You shall have as many as I can send."

I said, "This war is going to go on for some time. The reinforcements are more like replacements. Send some to me, and I will have the general send back as many as possible."

King Larry said, "Good idea. Rotate the troops. Keep them fresh and well fed. I will talk to the Sordeath about sending increased supplies, and I will increase the amount of cattle for the dragons. I would like a favor."

I smiled. "If possible. What do you want?"

"I would like to start an elephant population in the Dead Lands. We are not using that much of the land, so there is plenty of food, and dragons will pay very well for fresh fat elephant. I hear you have a resource."

The platinum and most of the other dragons looked at me and were drooling. It was almost comical. I said, "Not a problem. I think I can obtain an entire small herd, but it will take some time for the population to become large enough for trimming. It will cost you, but you will surely make it up many times over."

The platinum dragon said, "I can speak for the dragon council. If Kayland is willing to supply the grasslands, the dragons will buy the elephants."

The king said, "I think we can afford to buy our own elephants. I hear it gives good incentive for dragons to grant peace talks. What with dragon pepper becoming available, the population may increase, and I want to be on good terms."

I could not help but think, *This king is well informed and intelligent. Relative of Charles and direct descendant of King David, Charles's father.* I asked, "Seen Charles lately, King Larry?"

He looked at me funny, but the woman on his right side said, "We received a message several days ago. It said something I don't understand. Perhaps you can shed some light."

Curiosity got the best of me, and I asked, "What was the message?"

His daughter answered, "I just spent three hundred of the most wonderful years of my life with a fantastic woman. I don't think she knows, but I am deeply in love. Wish me luck, Charles."

I fainted.

She smiled and said, "Cleric! Well, I think that answers who Charles is so in love with, Father."

King Larry was holding in his laugh. "I think you are correct. Natura is going to be jealous."

POST LOG

It took several years, but the goblins and orcs were cut back to just a few tribes. Malificus tried desperately to turn me to evil, but love kept me true to Charles. The Horde lands were now occupied by a joint Kayland, Ginham, and Treestorm group that was dedicated to making it produce enough food to help supply the other continents. There are a hundred stories I could tell of heroes and villains in those few years, but that's for another time.

I was ordered to move the tower to Caelum. It seemed that Natura, now Mother, had some land right next to her temple that Charles was building a home on. The tower made a nice place to live while waiting for our home to be finished.

Yes, Charles and I married. Silvestris performed the ceremony, and Natura set it all up. Magicum grumbled it was all for show: "Gods do not need to marry!" But the look on his face as he gave me away was priceless. Many gods showed up, including two Over Gods. They blessed the joining and merged me with Charles. Though our bodies are apart, we are one, and we are beyond epic.

Printed in the United States
By Bookmasters